MW00974517

THE SPY

Additional Material
by Norma LeGallee

Based on an original story,
"The Violins of Autumn," by Valerie Sinclair;
reconstructed for the
final draft by Lewis Green

THE SPY

Marc Eden

M. Evans & Company, Inc.
New York

Library of Congress Cataloging-in-Publication Data

Eden, Marc.
    The Spy / by Marc Eden.
      p. cm.
    ISBN 0-87131--703-6 : $19.95
    1. World War, 1939-1945—England—London—Fiction. I. Title.
PS3555.D445S68   1992
813'.54—dc20   92-19226
                                                 CIP

M. Evans and Company, Inc.
216 East 49th Street
New York, New York 10017

Manufactured in the United States of America

9 8 7 6 5 4 3 2 1

Design by Joseph Mills
Typesetting by AeroType, Inc.

"Wyoming Lullaby" (Worton David/Gene Williams) © 1920, reprinted
by permission of EMI Music Publishing Ltd., London WC2H.

"It Had To Be You" (Isham Jones/Gus Kahn) © 1924, reprinted
by permission of Warner Brothers Inc.

"The White Cliffs of Dover" (Nat Burton/Walter Kent) © 1941,
reprinted by permission of Shapiro, Bernstein & Co., Inc. and
Walter Kent Music.

To Gary Stevens —
who set the correct course.

Acknowledgements:
The author thanks Miss Carolyn Rand for her unswerving loyalty in the face of the five years of research. Very special thanks to my agent, Rosalie Siegel, who entered late with both guns blazing; and to Mrs. Dorothy Twomey of Chicago for her invaluable help in the early drafts. A kudo to my lifelong friend, Clyde Ware, of the Directors Guild of America, Inc., for his insight in straightening out the central character; and to the Catalyst Group of California, national signatory, for their courageous supply of hard fact.

PHOTOGRAPHS

Somebody is like nobody else.

Her name is Valerie Sinclair.

She takes pictures.

Bletchley Park and the British Official Secrets Act, without their license, have opened for business on the midway of the deadliest attraction in history.

The proofs are in the hands of The Spy.

"What one man can invent another can discover," said Holmes. — Sir Arthur Conan Doyle
The Adventure of the Dancing Men

I

Click!

The lens caught it on the fast shutter.

The bomb would go off just when the sun was at its highest, before lunchtime, making a loud noise and a very deep hole about a mile up the street from the photographer who was lucky not to get killed and who had begun to wonder if The Spy really was back in town—rather like God in his Heaven, all's right with the world—and if not, why not.

The Spy was on the lam.

Later, wags would place him in Glasgow, in Dublin, the North Pole, the South Pole, and in London in the back room of Bobby Blake's, around the corner from Harrod's and just up the street from the El Flamingo, said to have a dress code and an active bar, frequented, as we now know, by Orson Welles. Once, on a side street in Paris, prior to the outbreak of the war, somebody had called in to *Le Monde* to say that he had been seen near the Tuileries, a bottle of Armagnac under his arm and talking to Josephine Baker, but the newspaper didn't buy it. And there were also a couple of rumors near the end of the war, attributed to Ed Murrow but circulating out of Kansas, that put him in the train station at Inverness, following his alleged appearance in Southwick, where he narrowly avoided British Operatives who thought they had him traced to Blackpool—where people had started wearing sunglasses.

Bloody odd business, that.

One thing was certain. In those dark and long-ago days, in the Summer of June 1944, The Spy was definitely known to be in England; his precise location, firmly fixed.

A witness had surfaced, bearing photographic record.

Her name was Valerie Sinclair.

In Occupied Britain, overrun by American troops, there had been some talk among the soldiers; but none of them, save that Sergeant, ever really knew much about her. Most of the Yanks were already in France, having gone to Normandy. Those who had stayed were either writing letters home or talking about the weather: "Sun's a BITCH," the Sergeant said.

Hot stuff!

Beams of late morning light, poking at her sharp as needles, were pouring through the blinds. It was at the back of the hallway on the second floor, the British Intelligence Office in Weymouth, on the south coast of England. Grasshopper Bay, officially known as HMS Grasshopper, was supposedly out of range of the flying bombs that were falling on London; and it belonged to the Royal Navy. She looked, remembering the American soldiers who had owned the sidewalks.

Beyond, where the bars had emptied, the harbor was full of ships; dark clouds forming a backdrop. She would have liked a snapshot; but for some weeks now, she had been careful not to take any. Just that one print, for good luck, snapped moments ago. Under the circumstances, she thought it best not to mention it. Valerie Sinclair, you see, was a living camera.

Down below, on oil-stained concrete scored with tracks, smoke was rising. Welding rods sparkled with arc-lights. The dockyards banged with metal, thrust with cranes. Dark interiors, concealing high roofs, spilled into the midday sun.

This morning, walking to work, she noticed the colors of the leaves had changed, curling like discarded negatives, left to decay along the curbs. Claimed by sea gulls, protected by fences and guarded by gates, HMS Grasshopper was turning brown. Tar was cooking on Dockyard Row. The smell reminded her of persimmons. Turning from the window, she moved to her desk.

Early figs in summer often have the ripest bodies; and there are girls like that. New under the sun, they must be careful of strange birds. A dark-eyed brunette, just under five-three, this one had ripened near the top of the tree. For the past two years she had been on ice with the Ferry Pilots. Valerie Sinclair had qualified as a candidate for British Naval Intelligence and was waiting.

Completing a page, she popped in a fresh one.

The door opened. A British Intelligence officer entered. Sinclair tapped out the heading and looked up. It was her boss, Lieutenant Carrington. He moved to his desk, sitting down and sorting through his stacks of mail. Carrington could feel the ghost of guilt. It was standing behind him. Nervous, and with something on his mind, he picked up an envelope.

"A bit quiet, now the Invasion's been launched, don't you think?"

"Yes, sir" She was erasing something; it was a smudge on the print. Brushing at it, she stopped as though frozen.

It was one of those sudden interruptions.

An unearthly buzzing, like the approach of a wasp, was coming through the windows. Work in the dockyards ceased. Men stepped out; they looked up into the sun. It was too bright for them to spot it—sputtering over clouds, approaching Weymouth, humming in the sky. In blinking her eyes, just before turning from the window, she had seen it conversionally, as in a mirror. The image, captured upside-down on the negative plate, had snapped within the mechanisms of her mind. Delivered by her Camera Shop—erroneously classified as a photographic memory by MI.5—the bomb, moving through the studio of the sky, had been captured on the print. It was her picture; she had taken it; she was looking at it. There would be a tree, two houses, and—!

Clear as glass!

Overhead, the sound had stopped!

Carrington sat stiffly. His heart pounded...the clock on the wall: the seconds. When the noise stopped, it would fall. It would come, like an earthquake. It was death, seeking weakness and wiping out time. He had seen it before; his nightmares, black: killed in an office, trapped like a rat...humiliated!

Sinclair, knuckles white, gripped the edge of the desk.

The explosion boomed, shaking the floor! Windowpanes rattled, and it echoed through the yard. The V-1 had fallen a mile north of the harbor, blowing up a petrol depot, leveling two houses, and reducing to twigs a three-hundred-year-old oak tree.

Across the bay, hidden by low hills, a spindle of dark smoke was rising. Flying bombs, falling for more than a week, had exploded in the streets of London, turning the city into a place of bad dreams. Firestorms were raging through Whitechapel. Reporters like Edward R. Murrow were huddled under stairwells, arms raised against flying bricks, jabbing microphones up into the night skies ablaze with jutting lights. Throughout the week, along England's south coast, other bombs had dropped within a fifty-mile radius. This last one, errant and landing to the south, was off course.

She stared at him as the sounds reverberated away.

"All right, are you?" Lieutenant Carrington unbuttoned his collar, the inside band was wet. "Well now, that was quite a *show*, wasn't it?

"Yes, sir."

He picked up the calendar. It had fallen off his desk: 20 June, 1944. Too many explosions! He had to get away. A return to sea-duty, that was the ticket. On the preferred list for more than two years now, his superiors at the Southampton office—namely, David Hamilton and Martin Seymour—were steadily moving him up to the top. Small price, actually: All he had to do was keep supplying them with information about Valerie.

Older than most for a Lieutenant, and with younger bucks at his back, he would have to gain what advantage he could from the Navy, while they still needed him.

Carrington glanced at her. As a man, he wanted her. A lover, that sort of thing. He had seen girls like her on cutie calendars, standing in the sun in yellow bathing suits about to put their lips on a bottle of Coca-Cola and...something twitched, officially, in Carrington's pants. Sinclair looked up, her lips wet, and slightly parted. Carrington cleared his throat, feeling naked. Mentally, he grabbed the calendar and put it behind his desk. The girl was a *mother* for God's sake! More, she was a Wren, his secretary. He knew what they would say: there were rules, *policies*. But he masturbated a lot, and he often felt tired in the

4

morning. Unofficially, she was wearing him out. He returned her happy look, smiling thinly. Muzzled in the white blouse, her breasts stared at him like accusers. Not that it would matter, but if he were ever tortured—which he imagined a lot of lately—the most they would get out of him was that he admired her legs.

Tugging at her skirt, she crossed them.

Concentrating on his mail, Carrington reached absently for the ashtray. He tapped out a cigarette, finding assurance in the brand. His hand raked through his hair, which was turning grey, a lock falling to his forehead, framing a worried face.

Behind her, his lighter clicked.

Returned to her typing, her fingers went flying over the keys: cargo shipments…tonnage of guns. It was quite photogenic. She reached over to get a Kleenex. The Lieutenant, cigarette smoking in his ashtray, was reading a letter. Such a dear! She had often wished to take a picture of him. Something really good, in black and white.

He could certainly use a wife….

Valerie finished typing. She straightened up her desk. In moving the picture frame, she saw that it was facing away. Sinclair looked. It was a photo of Basil, her late husband. Drowned at sea, he was listed as missing. Left with a four-year-old son, she had placed the boy with her parents. Lieutenant Carrington had arranged it. She sighed, turning it back to the wall.

It was really not a very good photo….

"Why don't you take a break now?" Carrington said.

There was a lounge on the first floor.

As she walked out of the office, he thought how attractive she looked in her W.R.N.S. uniform. When he heard her footsteps on the stairs, he removed the envelope from his desk. It had arrived without a stamp. The memo—demand, actually—from Lieutenant Commander Loot, down the hall, was outright indecent. Loot, a rival officer pulling rank, had requisitioned his secretary!

Couldn't he get his bloody own?

Well, he would take care of it. Lieutenant Carrington listened, making sure the quarry was gone. He squashed the cigarette and reached for his phone. He punched in the Code. The scrambler kicked in: Southampton.

His party was on the line: "Martin? John here—! No no, squire, it's not about the bloody buzzbomb, it's—"

Go ahead....

"—about Sinclair. She's up for grabs."

There she goes! Catch her!

Like the White Rabbit's watch, women in the service were looked upon as inferior machines: fast-running, but running backwards. Officers of the Empire agreed among themselves that it was true. God saves the Queen! Remember, chaps, a man's duty is to protect the Crown!

At the moment, its name was George.

His Majesty's picture used to hang on the wall of the lounge until it got hit with a wrench last Saturday during a misunderstanding between two boilermakers. They had been fighting over a woman.

Aside from herself, the lounge was empty where she sat.

Sinclair was busy putting on her lipstick.

It was not that she was trying to keep out of the war; she was trying to keep it out of her future. The war had delivered her into a world of new opportunities, and she had grabbed them. As often as not, they were revolving doors, like the ones used to enter public places. At the Royal Hotel, new bird in the manager's school, where she had worked as a receptionist and before her job with the Ferry Pilots, she had watched the proud and powerful coming through the doors, never having to go back through them to do battle in the streets again. Like all young employees, she had been told—and at first had believed—that her pitifully paid job was a chance to rise. Blocked by Management and Rules, Valerie Sinclair had come to see that those who rise, arise from those who have already risen.

It was life at the Top, at the Bottom.

One afternoon Duncan Sandys, Winston Churchill's son-in-law, walked in with half a dozen men to make the prearrangements for Mrs. Churchill's arrival. Valerie's accommodations were so excellent that the grand lady herself, despite suffering from insomnia, had come downstairs to thank her. Women being women, they had a chat. Two days later, Clementine Churchill, reporting to Winston, fan of Lewis Carroll, described the girl's childlike face to her husband.

He had made a note.

When Churchill made notes, he intended to use them.

Military types who frequented the hotel had begun to impress her. She was keen to do her bit, and while the F.A.N.Y.s looked promising, it would not be as a nurse. She had considered the Royal Marines, not that they would take her. She had to decide quickly: word had it that the hotel was changing hands. When Valerie was offered a job with the American Stage Door Canteen, the Brits raised the ante. If she joined the W.R.N.S., she would be excused from the barracks life at the Wrennery, which she detested. Any deal, including housing, was usually what British Intelligence wanted it to be; and she would get her own flat. She held out for and received additional pay, and found herself with a contract that didn't call itself a contract. They would make it easy for her: all she would have to do would be to move up the street.

Sign here.

Immediately, they sent her north to the Ferry Pool until someone figured out what to do with her. That someone was Winston Churchill, the girl's recall to Weymouth predicated upon his pleasure. Thus when the hotel was taken over by the Americans, it was the Royal Navy who caught her when she jumped.

Feet clutching its northern rim, a single sea gull was perched on the drainpipe looking for pickings. Following her with suspicious eyes, he flapped off the roof and sailed overhead. Birds that shit on people, a welder had told her, were supposed to be a sign of good luck. She looked hopefully at the bird.

"Save it," she said.

Flashing her card at the gate, Valerie jaywalked to the Dorothy Cafe, a favorite hangout for naval personnel. It was Tuesday, which meant fish and chips. Her Security Pass said she was twenty-three, but half the guards thought she had faked it. It didn't keep them from whistling at her. As Mrs. Churchill had observed, her face was that of a child, and it turned them on; but mostly it was because she was stacked. She knew what they wanted alright; and she went along with it, enough to whet their whistle. As for the rest, she was rather like her purse.

She kept it to herself.

In the restaurant she sat alone, feeling what young people feel when they are strong and impatient, but have yet to decode their potential. Normally hungry, she picked at the fish, which was beastly. A repeat performer, it had been carried over from last week. By the end of the hour most of it was still on her platter staring up at her.

Back in her office she selected a stick of chewing gum from the pack that she got from a Yank, hitched up her enthusiasm, and returned to work at her desk piled high with its secret files. She felt a rush of energy humming in the reaches of the room—magnetic, as if she could taste it.

Something had entered her thinking....

It was like a projector, the soft whir of a shutter, bringing fresh prints of the day's activities. As she worked, she found herself remembering the years at the vicarage. Where classmates had seen bushes and buildings and the walls of a church, Valerie Sinclair had seen misty living figures, whom she had befriended, and whom she had personally named the *Inhabitants*. She had not told the other children of these ghoulies, bodies standing there between the trees, ever in the evening, as real as Puck. Occasionally, during these reveries, Carrington would look up to ask her some question that related to the endless forms, some thousands of pages ago, to which she responded quick as a wink. He depended on her memory.

A warm wind was blowing through the window, bearing creosote and salt, and she got up to sharpen her pencil. Lieutenant Carrington gathered up his own. "Here, do mine for me while you're at it, will you?"

"Yes, sir."

And she ground them all fine, sharp as needles, like razors. Retouch pencils used in the dark stalls of the Camera Shop, they were like weapons. Carrington tested one and was impressed. "Bloody fine job," he acknowledged, "wonder why I can't get them that way?"

The afternoon passed and the phone rang. Carrington, at the other desk, picked it up. He nodded and spoke something in a low voice. Replacing the receiver, he reached for his hat.

Valerie looked up.

"I shall be visiting ships in the bay most of the afternoon." He was on his way out the door. "You know how to reach me if I am needed, don't you?"

"Yes, of course."

"By the way, should a call come in from a Lieutenant Commander Loot, please ask him to ring me at home, will you?"

"Yes, sir. Will he be calling from MI.5, sir?" She would have to use the scrambler.

"I hope not." Carrington grinned. "No, he will be calling from Demolitions, I would think. You will recognize him by his high-pitched voice. It sounds like a whining shell."

How peculiar, she thought.

Carrington hadn't been gone five minutes, when his telephone rang. She checked her pad: Loot—voice like bullet. She picked up the phone. "Lieutenant Carrington's Office."

"Am I speaking to Wren Sinclair?"

Loot, it wasn't.

"This is Commander Hamilton."

"Yes, sir," she replied, turning quickly to a clean page. She wondered how he knew her name.

"Is Lieutenant Carrington there?"

"No, sir, not at the moment."

"I shall be arriving at Weymouth by train tomorrow at 1500 hours. Can you have Lieutenant Carrington meet me?"

"Yes, sir. I will let him know immediately."

"Do that," said Hamilton. "I shall be wearing a grey suit, with a white carnation in the buttonhole." He sounded important.

"Yes, sir. I will give him that message."

"Good show. I'll see you then."

"Sir?"

Lines clicked, she was holding Carrington's phone.

Had her call been recorded?

The next day, and late in the afternoon, Lieutenant Carrington introduced David Hamilton to Valerie Sinclair. Staring into a pair of steady grey eyes, the girl from Newton Swyre was impressed by the demeanour of the tall, broad-shouldered, thirtyish-looking man in the well-tailored suit. "What do you know about Operation OVERLORD?" he asked her, watching closely as to how she answered.

It was a TOP SECRET exercise.

"Not a thing, sir," she replied.

She blushed when she heard, "Carrington, let me congratulate you on having a very smart and efficient secretary."

She liked him.

Carrington glanced at his watch. Hamilton said: "Well now! Perhaps we shall see you again—shall we?—before we leave." As they walked down the hall, she peered after him.

Was he single?

That evening, on the 21st of June, having returned to Southampton, Commander Hamilton immediately rang up his Adjutant, Lieutenant Martin Seymour. It was Seymour who had trained Valerie Sinclair as a candidate for Naval Intelligence. The Commander suggested dinner at the Officers Club at 23 Greenapple Street, convenient to both, before going to the office where they could work undisturbed. Arriving early, Seymour met him in the entrance.

They entered the busy bar, and found places.

"Two whiskeys, please."

The ice, in the bucket to Seymour's right, was on hand for the Americans. "So then," said Hamilton, "Loot's drawn a course on Wren Sinclair, has he?"

"Well, sir, he certainly thinks he has."

Hamilton fingered his drink. Loot's attempt to purloin Carrington's secretary was on the table before they left the bar. It was academic, really: MI.5 would have first dibs.

"Pack of Ovals, will you?" Hamilton signaled for the orderly. They found their table, ordered, and were soon eating. Glasses clinked in the background, and low conversation hummed. The entire country had tightened its belt, but not here. Seymour, taking advantage of the invitation, skipped over the fish, going straight to the chops. Hamilton, opting for the steak, attended to the meal with efficiency and dispatch: couldn't run a war on just fish and chowder. The orderly came up. The Commander passed on the dessert. Seymour followed.

It was not the time for small talk.

"Carrington reports that Lieutenant Commander Loot, the D.E.M.S. officer in charge, has already filed the requisition for her transfer."

Hamilton put his cup down, and dabbed at his mouth with a napkin. "Suffering a labor shortage, is he?"

"Yes, sir." Hamilton lit Seymour's cigarette. "He as much as told Carrington to make sure that Sinclair cleaned her desk out by the weekend, and to inform him the moment she was ready."

"He did, did he?" The Commander eyed the Gainsborough on the wall. "Yes, well," he said: "Scratch an Englishman and you'll find a German."

Seymour grinned. That was Loot, all right.

"Did he bother to tell the girl?"

"The girl? No, sir. He just told Carrington."

"I see," quipped Hamilton. "Trying to get his hands on our spy, is he?"

"Well, no. It's more than that, of course. His own secretary is perfectly competent. It's just that the *second* Mrs. Loot— she's a friend of Kay Summersby, you know—is still going with the French Major, and has taken up with one of the Eisenhower chaps. Poor Loot has run aground again with his first wife as well."

"Come come, Seymour, have you no sense of decency?"

"Not really."

"Hmmm. I remember…sordid affair. Last year, wasn't it?"

Seymour said that it was.

"Loot's requisition—copy to Bletchley?"

"No, sir." Seymour was still reading the desserts. "I took the liberty of intercepting it this morning—"

"Very good, Seymour."

"We caught it just before it went in."

"Close one, that," noted Hamilton. He was embarrassed to think a 'chaser like Loot could have upset his plans. "See the new orders for Loot are sent over to Parker, will you?" Lieutenant Conrad Parker was Martin Seymour's counterpart. At Bletchley Park, home of the ULTRA secrets, the German-speaking Parker, recruited from the London School of Economics, served as Adjutant to Commodore John Blackstone. One of two at the Top in the Royal Navy, the other being Lord Louis Mountbatten, Blackstone's clout was one notch above an Admiral and just below God: an ultimate rank obviously reserved for Churchill, Lord of the Admiralty before he became Prime Minister. Hamilton, mere mortal wedged between the two Commodores, and choosing the one closer to his advantage, had thrown his allegiance to Mountbatten. Blackstone, the *Keeper of the Files*, theoretically Hamilton's boss, was not unaware of this. Touchy about Mountbatten, who enjoyed more prestige, and determined to keep Hamilton in line, Blackstone had appointed Conrad Parker as *Keeper of the Codes*. Filed under P for PRICK by the Southampton office, Parker, no match for Seymour, was of the old school, an institution not attended by these two enjoying their dinner.

"Loot, sir. New orders?"

It was as good as done. Invergorden, in North Scotland, was too far. Dover, or Hell-Fire Corner, where the barrage of the big guns at Calais had not left a windowpane standing, was too close.

"Special Assignment in Manchester sound about right?"

"Yes, sir!" Ratio of sailors to women: fifty to one.

"You see, old boy, we just can't have the likes of Loot running off with our candidates, and still call ourselves a company."

Seymour picked his teeth.

"Jolly good then!" Hamilton eyed the desserts. "Finished?" Seymour threw the menu on the table. The Commander called for the orderly and settled the bill. "We had best get on to the office."

Pushing his way through the bar, Seymour grabbed some ice.

Holding against the wind, they crossed over.

...With the doors unlocked, the curtains pulled, and the lights on, the Lieutenant came up with her files. Hamilton had loosened his tie, and pulled a chair. "So then, how did our Wren Sinclair stack up as a candidate?"

At the moment, no other question mattered.

The Lieutenant grinned and made a circle with his forefinger and thumb. "Better than expected on the cross-country, sir. Since she has the appearance of a girl men would want to protect, it's unlikely that anyone suspected her of being an agent."

Hamilton made a note, it was why they'd selected her.

In the cross-country, starting out from New Forest in Hampshire, candidates for Intelligence traveled hundreds of miles across Britain: without money, and with the police looking for them, as though they were actual criminals.

"Had she been caught," said Hamilton, "she knew the password. The local authorities, of course, would have taken care of it, but she would have been disqualified."

In a class of six, Sinclair had been the first to arrive at the rendezvous in Cornwall. The police, put on high alert, arrested four of them right off; Sinclair had beaten her remaining competition, a trained male agent, hands down. Cycling furiously ahead of her, he had been run off the road by a speeding car, an antique Lea Francis.

Stolen from two R.A.F. pilots who had picked her up when she stopped to adjust her stocking, she had used the car to get to Bournemouth Central Station, where she had conned a member of the Home Guard out of lunch before catching the Express to Penzance while avoiding the ticket inspector. The runner-up, lucky to be alive, had escaped by diving head-foremost into a ditch.

Hamilton appeared pleased. "I've often thought that this is one of the most useful and rewarding exercises. After all, if candidates cannot cope on their home ground, how can we expect them to fare in occupied territory?"

Seymour agreed.

"Right-o. Well then, her family matters in order, are they?" Her background was already known to them. In any event, Hamilton would go over it personally with her if he decided to send her.

Seymour said, "As you know, sir, her parents have taken charge of her son—name's Brian. I'd say it's relieved her mind. Her husband was killed in action and she is still hoping he was picked up in the North Sea. You remember his destroyer, The *Glowworm*?"

Hamilton nodded. "It took on a cruiser, then rammed the battleship *Hipper* and sank straightaway. Blackstone wrote up the report himself, said it reminded him of the days of Drake and Frobisher."

The Commodore, a banker who was not in favor of female agents, had spent the day doing battle with the Free French until—bending them to his will while at the same time giving them what they wanted—several names from the Dieppe Professionals, survivors of that disaster, had been rigorously pursued. In Bletchley Park, behind steel-trapped doors that contained the brain cells of British Intelligence; specifically, in Blackstone's office, the lights were out and negotiations were over for the day.

"Bring that lamp over here, will you Seymour? That's it. Can't do business in a bloody blackout."

The mission clock was ticking. It was time to work.

The Lieutenant's job, aside from training the agents, was to double-check the double-checking, making sure that the parts fit. Standing at his desk, he showed Hamilton the Clearances, they went over them together.

"Bridley in, is he?"

"Bridley?"

One of the Boffins, or "back-room boys," the civilian arm of counterespionage, Bridley and his signature were necessary links in the chain-of-command spy business, enabling MI.5 to get on with it. Flamboyant deal-maker and a friend to Noel Coward—in war-restrictive England where homosexuality was practically a State crime—James Bridley flowed in and out of the citadels of power as smoothly as silk. Civilian assigned to Blackstone, he had just been borrowed by Seymour. The Lieutenant, who kept him on his personal Blackmail List, said that he hadn't signed yet, but that he would.

"Very good! Well, Seymour, I couldn't be more pleased."

"About her commission, sir?" Special Operations Executive, SOE, was a joint venture between the British and the Free French. Employing *Egalité*—a political military principle of exact equality—the French would supply their own combat officer as Sinclair's partner for the mission, providing the British assured them an officer of equal rank. John Blackstone, in his deal with General LeClerc, would be expected to rubber-stamp it. LeClerc, heading up the Free French, represented De Gaulle. "The Prime Minister will issue the Crown License then—is that right? I'll have to file it by tomorrow, midnight."

"Relax, Seymour." Hamilton had it figured. "We have already waived her examination. Prior to the honor, the Admiralty will bounce her to Third Officer via the War Office."

What part of the War Office? Seymour wondered.

Hamilton said: "Normally, a commission like this would be escrowed until she returned from the mission, presuming she's selected, of course." Churchill himself would code-name the mission. Her uniform was already being issued.

A bold play. "Two rings, is that right, sir?" Female Lieutenant, line officer—it was unprecedented. Commander

Hamilton would certainly get a King's Medal for this one.

"Good show, sir."

The Commander reached for a cigarette. "Seymour, you may consider this mission as good as signed, sealed, and delivered — just as soon as we clear it with His Nibs." Winston Churchill, expected to approve the final commission, would do so quietly.

"Commodore Blackstone, sir? Any special instructions that...?"

"I wouldn't think so, Seymour. I have absolute confidence in your abilities. Still, one never knows when the higher-ups may decide to pull a fast one." Blackstone, he meant. "If it should come to that, you have Grimes' number." Hamilton was considering Grimes, of the Royal Marines, for special security. A petard that might blow away Parker, and divert Blackstone should they muck about in his business at the wrong moment, Mountbatten could help him there: Grimes worked for him. Hamilton wouldn't care for Blackstone to get wind of it.

Blackstone, who was probably tapping his phone...

"I'll take care of Bletchley Park, sir."

"Yes, well, you know where the bodies are buried."

Seymour didn't, but nodded. "Speaking of bodies, sir." It was about Valerie Sinclair's husband, left unattended. "Could the poor devil still be alive? She seems to think—"

"Don't they all, Seymour? No. He wasn't picked up with the known survivors. It would be a miracle if anyone survived for more than a few minutes in that icy water."

Seymour closed the file. He dropped it in the drawer.

"So much for the husband," Hamilton concluded. "Let's get on with the widow."

"Yes, sir." Seymour read: "Two years ago, sir. The Royal Hotel. That report from Duncan—?"

"Ah yes." The Prime Minister, enthralled, had been quick to see the possibilities, routinely channeling it to Blackstone. Hamilton had discovered it through Bridley.

"You pretty well know the rest, sir. We sent her up north... to the Ferry Pool. Her superior was Captain Gilbert. Her husband came from that area."

Hamilton got up. He walked over, and glanced through the blackout curtains. A light rain was falling. The dockyard cranes loomed dreary in the distance.

Seymour waited.

Hamilton returned to the desk. "Pray go ahead, Seymour."

"Yes, sir. Captain Gilbert spoke highly of her. Says it seems to come natural to her to be discreet. He's of the opinion that she is absolutely trustworthy."

"Gilbert?" Hamilton laughed. "Wonder what he's hiding?"

"Well, a little personal item I found: Geoffrey de Haviland was very much attracted to her—"

"Surely, not Sir Geoffrey!"

"Of course not, sir, his son. They hold the same name."

"Yes...so they do."

"She accepted his invitation to dinner. You remember, before he left...the Lord Beaverbrook matter?" Hamilton nodded, he squashed out his cigarette. "When Gilbert told her what a hero young Geoffrey was, she fell all over herself to go out with him, relaxing her code, as it were."

Hamilton grinned. "Impressed by that sort of thing, is she?"

"Yes, sir. Though a number of pilots tried to date her, it appears that none of them had what it takes. If I may say so, sir, she left all of them waiting for Matilda—on the runway of broken hearts."

"How very poetic of you, Seymour. Is that how you wrote it up in the report?"

"No, sir." His cheeks were turning pink. "I just thought I would...throw it in."

"I see. Well, throw it out. What else?"

"She tries very hard to excel. She seems to have a great deal of endurance, sir."

"Essential," said Hamilton. "Tell me, how did she do in the self-defense and offensive action?"

"A bit shy, sir." Seymour ticked off the negatives. "Hasn't made up her mind yet whether or not she wants to kill. I think she would, sir, but—well, she's a bit of a rum one, if you know what I mean."

"Unpredictable, Seymour?"

"Yes, sir." On an impulse, Seymour had asked her to load his revolver. Within seconds, he had sensed she could use it: she was pointing it at him....

"Go on, Lieutenant."

"Well, sir, under actual conditions, Wren Sinclair could stand up to the best of them. In that case, we made it absolutely clear to her that one chance is all she might get."

"Quite right," murmured Hamilton, who loved nothing better than a victory. He would need one, in France. "What about her French?"

Seymour was reading her bio, rife with mysteries. "Fluent." The Lieutenant had found the page. "From all reports—"

"—yet SOE was not able to validate any schooling for it."

"No need for it, sir. The vicar taught her. Perhaps he was suspicious of British standards. Being part Egyptian, I would say his actions were understandable."

"A logical deduction, Seymour." Egyptians were not normally acceptable to Westminster Abbey. "His heritage part of the Church Record, is it?"

"Family secret, sir. Edward Crewe, her father, is the son of a British officer...Egyptian mother. Happened during the Cairo Uprising."

"What about the girl's mother?"

"English and Maltese, sir."

"Hmmm. Interesting. Well, of course, the question is not how well their daughter speaks French, but whether she'll pass muster while doing so, against the agents of the Gestapo in Brittany."

"Yes, sir, I agree."

"Churchill," Hamilton said, "is of the opinion that our last fifteen agents were doomed to death before they left England, under the assumption that training—memory, habit, and clever acting ability—constitutes an agent's reasonable bet. It does not. For example," the Commander revealed, "the back-room boys have determined the Germans are advanced in the detection of accents. *Abwehr* may recognize immediately a British woman trying to appear French, or even a French woman trained in Britain. Certain attitudes and patterns of behavior, Seymour— mannerisms of speech and conduct—simply cannot be faked."

"Yes, sir," Seymour acknowledged. "I can see that."

"If you can see it, so can the Germans." Hamilton's first loyalty was to himself, a fact pleasing to Churchill, who was of the same cut. If mistakes had been made, he was not going to repeat them. "'What one man can invent another can discover,'" recited Hamilton to Seymour, quoting Doyle for Holmes.

The Baker Street Irregulars, one of myriad civilian agencies, named tongue-in-cheek for their address at 221½ Baker Street, made famous by Sherlock Holmes and Dr. Watson, had been taken over by the Boffins, the shadow men of counterespionage. Occasionally, thanks to Bridley, the Southampton office had been known to raid them.

"By the way," Seymour asked him, "where is Bridley?" He would need him by tomorrow night for the signature. Neither man knew. Hamilton told him he might check with Lieutenant Parker.

Conrad Parker: Keeper of the Codes.

The Lieutenant's brown eyes flashed with hard recognition. His own recommendations had disappeared into the shuffle on Parker's desk. From now on, Hamilton assured him, this mission would stay their mission, and free of red tape. Requiring an agent of a different stripe, it brought them back to Valerie Sinclair.

"I've never met anyone quite like her, sir," the Lieutenant had been trying to put his finger on it, "but I'd say it's the way she thinks. If I may say so, sir, her logic is definitely...*peculiar.*"

"Call her a spy," Hamilton said.

"Before you make your decision, sir, I think you should see something that came in today." It was a photograph. "I'm sorry, sir, but I'm afraid it's Mary Gladstone...."

She had been missing since Christmas.

Sent by *Abwehr*, German Intelligence, and salted with cinnamon, the packet had arrived from a blank address in London. Postmarked Marley Square, a commercial banking district, it had proved impossible to trace according to the rider from Blackstone. The spice, enclosed as an insult, was a reference to the British Tea & Mercantile Company, a firm answerable to the Admiralty.

Hamilton felt his jaws tightening.

"Obviously, she's about to be executed."

Hamilton looked. An 8 X 10 enlargement of the photo taken by the Gestapo, it was the picture of a creature in pain, of a naked woman, mostly skeletal, with lifeless black hair, and forced into an upright position amid tufts of dead grass. Her wrists and ankles were scarred with lesions from months of chains and handcuffs, and her eyes had retreated into secrets so terrible he could not follow them. The long translucent hand, extended forward and positioned to cover her sexual parts, connected her to a world forsaken through the eye of the Wollensak lens, which had delivered her back into this room. Seconds later, the shot would have rung out. Its sound in his mind was all that was left of the bravest heart he had ever known.

Hamilton had sent her, and struck out. He needed a hit.

The younger man continued to stare at the photograph.

"It's a hard call, Seymour, and seeing this picture won't make it any easier." He had seen others. "I should be remiss in my duty if I failed to send the person most qualified." He paused. "There may never be a more important mission!"

"Yes, sir!"

He had taken her to Leed's for late tea the day before she had climbed aboard a moon plane, strapped to a parachute. She had just had her teeth cleaned, and she was all smiles...

Hamilton had waved her good-bye.

The room was quiet for a moment.

"I see it this way," said the Commander, returned to business. "As you have correctly observed, Seymour, Valerie Sinclair is a queer fish. After two years on ice, she may not be too happy with us. Whatever she expected the first time, I can assure you that it wasn't Gilbert and the Ferry Pilots, even though we kept our part of the bargain."

"Yes, sir. You may be right. I seriously question if Valerie Sinclair would agree to anything at this point, unless she thought there was something in it for her."

"Exactly. She'll accept the commission of course, because there's no way around it. However, one never really knows, does one? We don't want any surprises. Should she see it as already decided, and herself merely as a pawn, we could find ourselves with a problem."

"Trouble we don't need," said Seymour.

Hamilton was covering the bases. The mission had already started. It was too late for a replacement.

The Lieutenant looked worried.

"Relax, Seymour. Fish never bite on a northeast wind. She will set the hook herself, once she hears we're throwing in a partner."

"The French agent, sir?"

"Sinclair's a *woman*, Seymour."

"Yes, sir, I know that. But she *is* a bit off the wall, sir."

"Precisely, Seymour. Well put. But you see, it's the very nature of this candidate, exactly those differences, that can even the odds."

"Sir?"

"Her photographic memory, Seymour. Have you forgotten? Carrington's told me it's as though she lives inside of it, like a skin. Whatever it is, it appears to be something more than just simple memorization. We really don't know how it works, but it does look as though it may point to some other personality—which is exactly where we intend to take her." Hamilton tossed him the lighter. "Her cover, I would think, could be our best chance yet for a real shot." Sinclair's new name, not yet released, would be assigned by the Free French once her acceptability had been determined.

"Speaking of that, sir," the Lieutenant clicked the lighter, disappearing behind blue smoke, "she knows the area around Brest from spending holidays there with school friends."

"Very good, Seymour." He retrieved his lighter. "I keep thinking," Hamilton confessed, "about that stolen car." Could the Lieutenant have missed something? "Any prior record of her having used a gun?"

"Yes, sir. Her husband taught her, before Dunkirk. Since they lived in Dorset, considered the likely place for a Jerry invasion, he made sure she knew how to handle it."

"Is that her own story, Seymour? Did you check?"

"Checked," the Lieutenant said. "We ran it through Scotland Yard. She's clean. Several other things, some hearsay we got from her father, was that she'd beaten up some boys who had challenged her, and that she'd run away from home—"

"Because of the boys?"

"No, sir, because of her father. Some years ago, it seems, his parishioners presented him with a church car. A Morris, I believe. He refused to let her drive it."

"Did she know how?"

"Apparently she did, sir."

"I see. Well, that's something, isn't it?" Hamilton might have plans for the father. "Let's get back to the guns. Do you think then, given a few hours, she could master regulation side arms?"

"Definitely. But you see, sir, the problem—"

"What is it, Seymour?"

"Well, sir, she's had very little practical experience."

"My point exactly: She is an unknown. Therefore the Germans have no dossier on her." He looked up. "Would you not agree, Seymour, that Sinclair might come straight about—with four days of Commando training at Achnacarry?"

"*Achnacarry,* sir?"

Achnacarry Castle, in Scotland, had been turned over by Sir Donald Cameron to the Royal Navy: specifically, to Lord Louis Mountbatten, who was head of the Commandos. Up to now, females had been excluded. Hamilton would have to use his clout.

Seymour said: "That might work at that, sir—if you can swing it. But it would be cutting it rather fine. I would like to see her get more time."

"There is no time," retorted Hamilton briskly. "As matters stand, Commodore Blackstone could cut the cards to other than our favor. Besides, I couldn't very well object when he reminded me that some of our own pilots have had as little as nine hours flying experience."

"Yes, sir. She will be air-dropped then?"

"Not if I can help it." Hamilton was firm. The Commander had looked to something new under the sun, his Lieutenant with him, and they had found it: in this hunter-child's body, and in the unsearchable swift potentials of her mind. A Proteus, she inhabited this room where so many had come before, and through whose doors, so many had departed, and died. All of them were women, yet none of them were her.

"Tomorrow I will call Wren Sinclair myself and set the appointment. If selected, she will have to volunteer. This must be her decision, as well."

Seymour nodded.

Hamilton, struggling, was tightening his tie. "Oh yes, one little item, hmmm? Should Parker contact you requesting the full pre-Mission Report for Blackstone, tell him the entire matter is in the hands of General LeClerc. By the time they get through that seawall of suspicion," nice phrase, noted Seymour—"we should be off and sailing."

"Yes, sir!"

He would tend to it, on the run.

"Sir, if Commodore Blackstone calls—?"

"Take care of it, will you?" Hamilton threw on his raincoat and was out the door. "And see to Loot's transfer."

"Got it!"

Her eye was on the bird.

The same seagull, tired of garbage, who had checked her out the other day, sat atop the splintered pile at the end of Dockyard Row, peering into the water and trying to find some fish.

She wondered how he was doing.

Grasshopper Bay was awash with high swells surging over black rocks from the prows of the hospital ships that were coming in from Normandy, where blood was running into the sea. In listing the ships Valerie noticed that most of the LST's and LSP's that had been there the day before, had now departed. Lieutenant Carrington, who had business to attend to on some of the others, had told her not to expect him until the following morning. She was just about to lock the safe, where the TOP SECRET information was kept, when the telephone rang. Sinclair snatched it off the hook. "Lieutenant Carrington's Office. Wren Sinclair here."

"Is Lieutenant Carrington there?" The voice sounded familiar.

"No, sir, not at the moment."

"Good. This is Commander Hamilton, from Southampton." She could see it, behind the voice, giant shipyards bristling in sunlight a hundred and fifty miles up the coast. "I visited your office yesterday and was very impressed with the way you carried out your duties."

"Thank you, sir. I am sorry, but Lieutenant Carrington is not in the office."

"Just as well," said Hamilton, "it is you with whom I wish to speak. A matter of some urgency, you see. Listen carefully. Meet me tomorrow at 1300 hours where you usually take your lunch...Dorothy Cafe, yes, that's it. Now, not even Carrington must know about this. I shall be wearing my uniform. A corner booth is reserved where we can talk undisturbed, and our conversation must not be overheard. Do you have that?"

"Yes, sir."

"Not a word of this to anyone, do you understand?"

Valerie stared at the phone. "Yes, sir."

"Fine. I know you can be trusted. See you tomorrow, then. Good-bye."

"Thank you, Commander," Valerie Sinclair said. "Good-bye for now." She said it as an afterthought. It was more like a question. She turned then, and saw the safe already secured. Gathering up her purse—what in the world could he want?— she switched off the lights, locking the door. In the Administrative Offices of Grasshopper Bay, the upper windows were turning dark. She walked downstairs and made her way across the yard, digging out her pass....

"'ello love, what we doin' tonight?"

"We?"

The guard wanted to chat. She left him hanging and entered the street. Wind flapped at her skirt. She crossed over, walking along the promenade to her flat. She had worked later than usual, and the long English day was at its best. Weymouth glowed in its beams of sunlight spearing in from the sea. Her thoughts went to the call from Commander Hamilton.

Would he be on to her about the Lea Francis?

Had he told Lieutenant Carrington? Could that explain why Carrington had been acting odd? In the cross-country, they'd told her to get there—they hadn't told her *how*. That bloke who came in second had probably filed a complaint. See you, Harry. Valerie wadded her guilt up in her chewing gum and tossed it in a can.

Twilight bathed the streets.

Suddenly, she felt she was being followed: nothing concrete, just a feeling of apprehension. She looked back. Did she see a man in a dark coat, slipping behind a shelter on the promenade—just there, where the Queen Victoria clock stood? After that strange conversation with Commander Hamilton, one could imagine anything. She turned and continued walking. It was still a good fifteen minutes to her flat. Daylight, which had filled the streets, disappeared from the horizon.

Darkness had come.

There seemed to be fewer people around. A wind had risen.

Actually, what with papers flying, all she could see was a man in a trench coat, walking, some distance ahead.

She heard footsteps behind her—this time it was not imagination! She was definitely being followed. She must not continue walking along the front. It was too dangerous!

Now, even the man in the trench coat had disappeared, probably into a side road, which led off the main one. She must do the same, before the follower caught her up. He must not discover where she lived!

Trash rustled along the curb. She rounded the corner. Footsteps echoed from cribs of stone. She passed the man in the trench coat. He was wearing a wide-brimmed hat. Shadows concealed his face. Hurrying forward, she got an eerie feeling:

He didn't seem to have one!

She reached an alcove, stepped inside, and looked back. Her pursuer had appeared at the corner, in a dark coat and tall. He was reaching for something in his pocket. Was it a gun? He would have to pass the other man before he could get to her. Instead, he donned his cap and opened the door of a limousine.

A bus was coming. She pushed out of the alcove and crossed the street. The man without a face, standing amidst the stones and stairwells, seemed to have vanished.

She boarded, and found a seat. The bus accelerated. Behind it, following at a safe distance, a silver and black limousine was keeping it in view. Her pulse was racing—she had to get her breath! She wiped at her hair, adjusted her clothes, and looked back…at empty streets. She felt such a fool! Five minutes from the downtown area, she was soon among happier surroundings.

She stepped off the bus, and onto the esplanade, making her way back to the Gloucester Hotel. Adjacent to the Royal, the exquisite luxury of the place had not been dimmed by the demands of war. She remembered parties she had attended here, hosted by the Household Cavalry Regiment—chaps who knew how to treat a girl—Protectors to King George VI. She entered the lobby and approached the front desk.

"Do you have a vacant room?" she asked the receptionist.

The older woman, who was carefully groomed, put down her magazine and looked up. "Just one left, Miss, number thirteen. Seems that no one dare take it, with that number." The thick Irish brogue left the rest undeclared.

"I'll take it," Sinclair said.

"Eleven 'n sixpence then, 'n may the ghosts not find you."

Sinclair paid for the room. It took most of her cash. With ghosts, it should have been cheaper. The Gloucester was still the Gloucester. Well then! She would enjoy a hot bath! Having collected the key, the girl paused for a moment at the magazine rack. She glanced over her shoulder. Outside in the street, fog was rising. Valerie felt chilled, she could feel it...

A vibration of some sort...

She turned then, and headed for the stairs.

The Spy looked.

Frustrated, all he could see was her legs! Squinting into the lobby, the mysterious figure in the trench coat touched his driver's shoulder. "A clean hit, Ryan," instructed his employer. "We do not want any witnesses!"

Ryan nodded, his powerful jaw muscles clenching in the efficiency of the thought. If you walked into a bar and saw Ryan, you wouldn't want to drink there.

It was looking like a scorcher.

Yielding to a hot sun, the veil of mist was burning off the harbor. Valerie opened the windows. She liked having the office to herself, it gave her a sense of belonging. Someday, she would have her own. She had checked out of the Gloucester, where she had enjoyed a solid breakfast. The world was making sense again.

Lieutenant Carrington called, still delayed, informing her that he was expecting an envelope. He asked her not to open it. Shortly after his call, it came in. It was from Hamilton. She held it up to the light, couldn't see what it was, and placed it neatly on his desk. The morning passed—strangely, there were no calls—and she was able to finish her files. At 1245 hours, Valerie locked the office, walked down the stairs, and hurried across the yards to the gate, where the guard waved her through. She missed the broad accents and lewd whistles of the friendly American troops, whose loud voices had carried laughter through the streets.

She entered the Dorothy Cafe, and looked around.

Commander Hamilton was already there. He came over immediately and escorted her to a back booth. "Well now!" the

Commander said briskly, after they were seated. "Unfortunately, we all have to eat." He had skipped breakfast. "You don't suppose they might have bacon and eggs, do you?" He stared forlornly at the card. Sausage and Mash? It was one of two. "Let's see, the fish sounds good...." One left over, from Tuesday.

A nature lover, she could see the fish swimming: "The fish? Yes, that does look good, doesn't it?"

"Supposed to be food for the brain, and all that—" He paused, embarrassed at the platitude.

Valerie waited.

The Commander placed their orders. They chatted awkwardly until the steaming platters arrived. When the waitress had gone, Hamilton said: "The reason for this meeting is too important to be discussed over the telephone. However, before going into it, I wanted to make sure that you have a proper lunch."

He had come, prepared to deal.

"Thank you, sir." They could have had a proper lunch at the Gloucester. She poked at her food, searching for some good bits. Hamilton's first priority was the mission. He had to find out if she would go. He looked up. "Now, for the trip I have in mind for you...."

"For me!"

In response to her startled words, he waved her silent.

Customers were looking and he concentrated on his plate. Valerie's fish had turned into a skeleton. A trip? What kind of a trip? Something good? If they were sending her back to the Ferry Pool, they could forget it! The customers were making their way to the door. Hamilton watched them go, thinking how best to phrase it. "Lieutenant Carrington will be out for the rest of the afternoon. This being the case, I have planned to meet with you in his office after lunch. Think we can arrange that?"

"I'll be there," she said.

The Commander ordered tea. Waiting for it to arrive, he gave her orders, work to do. Finally, he put his cup down, and smiled. "Tell me, Wren Sinclair," Hamilton said at last. "If your country asked you to do a very special thing, something that nobody else had ever been able to do, and you found out—from me, for example—that you could get an officer's commission in the Royal Navy, just by doing this thing, would you?"

"I don't think so," she said.

"My thoughts exactly," observed Hamilton, trying to recover. "Why, indeed, should one give one's life to one's country, unless one's country is willing to give something to one's life?"

"Yes, sir. My thoughts exactly, too," said Sinclair.

"Well, now," said Hamilton, "we seem to be getting somewhere. Let me tell you what I have in mind..." As the meal progressed, he lowered the boom...

Oh, blimey!

"What I mean is," Hamilton said, "is that you certainly wouldn't want to do it...without the glory, would you?"

Sinclair was chomping on a bone. The bait he had offered at the end of his hook was suddenly missing.

"I wouldn't think so," she said.

Seymour had her right!

She had doubts? He would defuse them. "The reason we sent you to Northwest England," he stated, "was to acquaint you with basic military procedure." As Gilbert's secretary, half her time had been spent polishing her nails. "Also, because what we initially had in mind for you, and still do, is of such import and has taken such an inordinate amount of planning that it became essential, early on, to keep you out of harm's way"—he glanced over his shoulder, lowering his voice—"until we were ready, you see, to bring you into it." Churchill had made him wait. In the British view of war, where the means justified the ends, Hamilton was earning his pay.

She was staring at him, her lips partially open.

"More tea?"

Double whiskey?

"No? Of course, one would still be called upon to volunteer. For security reasons"—she was coming—"we were not able to tell you until now. Naturally, there will be battle pay in it for you. We're terribly sorry, you understand, about that little matter with the Ferry Pilots, but—"

"Say no more, sir!" All was forgiven. Gilbert, forgotten.

Hamilton arched an eyebrow. "Are you all right, Sinclair?"

"Yes, sir. I'm sorry I shouted, sir."

"Tut."

They needed her!

"Glad to hear it," said Hamilton, and he tied his fish to the boat. "Well then, just to bring you up to date, your safety and well-being, as I said, have become of the utmost importance to us. Should you have any problems, any problems at all, you see, I want you to feel absolutely free to share them with me." He was thinking of Loot.

"Thank you," she replied. "I will."

She looked at him. There was something clean about him, something decent. What is more, he had the power to help her. This above all, he had just made clear. From this day forward, she would take him at his word.

"Well, now that I think about it, there *is* something that's been bothering me, sir." Suspicious, it sprang to the top of her mind. "It's about what happened to me last night...."

"Last night? Indeed!"

"Yes, that's right." She told him of her encounter with the man in the trench coat, who didn't seem to have a face, and of the mysterious driver: tall man, dark coat. Her decision not to go home, she saved for last, trying to make light of it. The Commander listened intently. She finished, staring into her cup.

"Can't recall his face, you say?"

Sinclair shook her head.

"You mean, you didn't *see* it."

"No, I mean, he didn't *have* one."

She was sticking to it.

"Well now," the Commander observed, "trench coats are not to be taken lightly, especially in the summertime." She hadn't thought of that. As for the man's face, he concluded, he had probably been backlit, leaving her looking up into a light. *A mask?* Her descriptions, sharp as snapshots, clearly identified the man as foreign. Certainly, not one of his. He thought of Parker. Blackstone up to something? Something he didn't know about? Could that something be a someone? Could that someone be The Spy?

Something had entered into Hamilton's thinking....

"It's nothing, I'm sure, but..."

Commander Hamilton checked his watch and reached for a cigarette. He clicked the lighter, returned it to his pocket, and said simply, "All precautions for your safety must be taken at once. At *once*," he emphasized. "I'll assign a man to your flat."

He called for the check. "In fifteen minutes then."

He walked out of the cafe.

Valerie waited a few moments, then arose and returned to the office. Was she really in for a commission?

Ruddy luck, what!

She crossed the yards, sidestepping cable. The sun was blistering; and she made a note to get some Coppertone. She thought hopefully of Blackpool. Battle pay, he had said. Was she really going to war? A trip, he had said. Was she being transferred to Ireland? Were they sending her—but where *were* they sending her? At least, she gathered, he would follow her to the office in fifteen minutes or so, for security reasons. And then...well, then she would know.

She would get a tan! Sunglasses, too!

During lunch, he had asked her to have the detailed French maps available. These would show them where the Allied units were presently fighting. They were certainly not fighting anywhere near Ireland. She unlocked various cabinets, removing secret scrolls. Maybe he would send her to Africa, or Lisbon. Within minutes, what he had asked for was ready.

Hamilton was coming up the stairs.

He knocked quietly on the door. Upon entering he put his fingers to his lips; then walked to the windows, near to where Valerie stood. He leaned over, and looked out. He closed them. There was no window immediately above or below them. The Commander felt along all the undersides of the desks, the windowsills, and the mantelpiece. Before the war, Carrington's office had been part of a suite of a luxury hotel. Joining her on the far side of the room, where the maps were, and where the two of them could not possibly be seen, he said: "You may wonder why I am taking all these precautions, but believe me, sometimes even walls have ears."

"I understand, sir." There were placards all over the place. She walked over and looked down into the wastepaper basket. "Bugs, in this office?" She looked up. "I think it safe to say, sir, that one can trust Lieutenant Carrington."

"Umm." Hamilton nodded.

Valerie smiled, she was loyal.

"But one never knows, what? Well, I am going to put the cards on the table and tell you exactly the problems we now have in France."

France?

"Yes, sir."

He cleared his throat.

"There has been great difficulty keeping in touch with the French Underground—air raids, electronic interference, that sort of thing—and now that we have a slight foothold in the country, the help and knowledge of the French would be invaluable."

"Yes, of course," the girl replied.

"In spite of large German forces being held at Calais, the plans found on a dead British officer—we washed up one of our own, you see, on a Spanish beach—indicated the main invasion would come just there, at Calais. To throw off von Rundstedt, hmmm?" He had unrolled the map—"Put that inkwell on it, will you? Thanks. The Germans are piled up here"—he pointed—"consequently, the American, Omar Bradley, and his divisions at Omaha and Utah beaches have not yet been able to move inland and capture Cherbourg"—pointer, sweeping north—"Montgomery, in command of the British and Canadians, had much better luck at these beaches, managed to move inland but they have been stalled near Caen for over two weeks."

"That's a long time, sir."

"Indeed! But we had an overlap, you see. During those first six days, 'the Fairway'—that's the path of entry for the ships—closed at 1630 hours, before dark. Gave our chaps a chance to get home before the nightly U-boat activity. Supply and deployment got bottled up, and they are still trying to sort it out. Monty tells us the Germans are blocking the advance with tanks, artillery, anything that can be mustered."

"I have been of the opinion that General Montgomery is very cautious," said Valerie, quoting Carrington, "and will not risk getting his men killed if the odds are too great."

"That's your observation, is it? You should hear Eisenhower's. Now then, one of the things we need to know—and fast—is how much time do we have? How much longer will the German 15th Army be fooled into thinking our main invasion, under Patton, will come at Calais?"

It was Operation BODYGUARD. She knew that Operation OVERLORD was Normandy. When Hamilton had asked her, she had lied....

"I have no idea," she murmured.

"Of course not, of course you don't my dear. But these issues must be addressed. Even more important, is to find out where the launching platforms are located for their flying bombs."

"The V1's, sir?"

"Exactly," Hamilton said. "We know they intend to go all out with it, to launch against us en masse, in an effort to finally destroy our cities. The V1's are already falling, and you can imagine the uproar, should the public find out that even deadlier ones may be on the way. So you see, we must take care of the matter at once."

"At once...of course, sir."

"However, there's a bit more to it than that." His tone had changed, the room seemed to have grown quiet. Valerie was aware that it was difficult for the Commander to speak. Like all good Operatives, it was hardest for him to share what he most needed to reveal. "We suspect —" he took a deep breath —"a weapon even more ominous —not necessarily this atomic thing that Einstein and his people are tinkering with —but something more immediate, and awesome, in terms of Britain. A weapon that, if deployed, will render us absolutely defenseless against it."

"You mean, worse than Coventry, sir?"

"Yes, perhaps so." Hamilton cocked his head. "Yes, if deployed, most certainly...worse than Coventry."

Fifty thousand homes destroyed, four thousand victims...

Valerie felt her blood run cold.

She looked up at him, as if for assurance, and his eyes were grey and calm. He held death in his mind, where truth was; and she could not know it. By the eve of Coventry, MI.5 had cracked the German Enigma Code. Informed of Berlin's plan to destroy the city, Churchill had opted to sit tight, rather than tip the *Luftwaffe*. Withheld from the public, this "nondisclosure" had been safely filed away with Blackstone at Bletchley Park. Smacking of gingerbread and Gordon and Lewis Carroll —officially, the Government Code and Cypher School, or "Golf Course" —this Victorian estate north of London formed the last refuge for survivors from the world of Palm Beach suits; sexual pariahs who had been flushed out, or reluctantly recruited, by the demands of war: men like Alan Turing, who had deciphered the German Enigma, and James Bridley; delicate and creative men from the fashion, film, and theatrical districts, who were its undisclosed, often embarrassing, *cohabiteurs*.

Bletchley had seen red.

"Why, those ponces are no better than the bloody Indian snakemen down at Blackpool, sir!" Commodore Blackstone had blustered. *Snakemen*. Men with tattoos, he'd meant: Cockneys and concessionaires and that sort. Blackpool, by the sea, favored by shopgirls like Valerie Sinclair, who had delighted in its summers.

"Sir?"

A few seconds had passed. He had been thinking of something. Neither of them had moved. He was describing the monster, made of metal; information so terrible that even as he spoke, he himself could be suspect. Resumes could be rigged, changed..... Then what of hers? "Under pain of death," Hamilton now reminded her, "you have recently signed the British Official Secret's Act."

"Yes, sir." She had?

He waited.

"Mum's the word, sir."

Through the closed glass, sunlight was beating; shadows crawled along casements. Sinclair was thinking. "But what kind of a weapon, sir?" Her voice was little more than a whisper.

"One that could cause us to lose." He looked at her coolly.

"To *lose*?"

"Exactly."

My God, he *meant* it!

"Something exceedingly massive," Hamilton said. "Rocket-oriented, directional beam, we suspect...some new principle. They call it 'the Waterfall,' between forty and eighty thousand tons. We suspect they have at least *fifty* of them, and that they will launch before August."

Aware that Von Braun and his teams were accelerating the knockout punch, Hamilton knew the British must find it first. Insisting it a *rocket*, he had just removed her from further consideration of it as the world's first Atomic Bomb.

"We have to locate it," she was hearing, the voice an echo. His words, carefully selected, were skirting an abyss of horror.

She was starting to feel frightened.

The Commander placed a reassuring hand on her arm. "There there, my dear, we'll take care of it, of course."

"We will?" Her eyes were wide.

"Certainly. That's our job: to resolve these darker mysteries of the war. At the same time, we must discover the *locations* of their laboratories and launching pads. It is our duty, you see, to make certain they do not reissue."

It was also to their interests.

In a surprise move, Whitehall had cut a deal giving General Dwight Eisenhower, the Supreme Allied Commander, full control over the R.A.F.'s Joint Weather Command. In exchange, Ike had agreed to place General Omar Bradley's 1st Army, presently in Normandy, under the direct control of Britain's Field Marshal Bernard Montgomery. With Mountbatten out of the country, and with Air Boss Tedder minding the fort, David Hamilton had been called in as a Special Aide by Churchill himself, on that one.

"You were saying, my dear?"

She was aware of his hand. The man's strength flowed through her like a current, bringing warmth and trust.

"So you see?" He released his grip.

"Of course," said Valerie. She wished he were still touching her.

"Now, Sinclair, this is where *you* come in."

"I?" said the bewildered girl. The excitement of the Cafe was wearing off.

"Yes, you," stated the Commander, "if you will agree to help. I understand you know the countryside of France extremely well, especially that part of the coast of Brittany we are most interested in—*Brest*, is it?"

Valerie nodded, she remembered: *wearing a proper coat, she had been hiking through long fields of wheat, fiery rows of poppies, bright as Mayfair lipstick.*

"You're fluent in French, is that right?"

"*Oui…sir.*"

"I see from files that you also have something else going for you, something extremely rare—a photographic memory, is it?"

"Yes, sir," she replied, raising her hand against a rush of sun, "but I never really thought of it as being very important."

Click!

Hamilton turned around, he was holding the pointer. "My dear Sinclair," said the Navy man, "you must not underrate yourself. It may be necessary to memorize complex formulas—schematics, equations, those sorts of things. It is *you*, you see, who have exactly what we need, far more than many agents whom we have spent months training." She thought of the cross-country. "We have already sent several men, but they've been unable to get through, to contact the Underground." He knew that the "several" were many; and he knew that they had been shot. He had a quick glimpse of the raped and mutilated bodies of female agents, bullet holes through their heads—photos shown him by Seymour. "Female agents, of course, have been out of the question." He paused to gauge her reaction. When there was none, he continued. "After so many failures, I thought of you, of your young innocent face, your good looks, your fluency in—"

She beamed.

"Cars."

"Bloody RAFs," she muttered.

"—your loyalty to the Crown." A bit for officers, that. The fish was in the boat.

"My country is my life," she reminded him, recalling she had read it. "I would do anything—"

"Exactly. And now you can. When you first came to Southampton to be trained for your job in this office, the people who met you at MI.6 assumed you were a child, dressed in adult clothing."

"A child?"

"Not in terms of your...efficiency, of course." He stared at her. "I wish I could have been there to meet you that day, a lot of valuable time might already have been saved."

"How kind of them to speak so well of me," said the girl, with uncertainty. "I can hardly believe they...liked me so much." She was embarrassed she had looked so young.

"I am sure their praise was well deserved," amended Hamilton. "I must say, you have a beautiful fair complexion. However, if we darken your skin with our special makeup, a little nip and tuck, as it were, you could easily pass for French." He stepped back, appraising her like an artist. "Let's see, a college student or"—gently touching her chin, he turned her face up into the light—"there now, that's better." He took a closer look. "Grade school...hmmm?"

As the plan unfolded, Valerie felt more and more intrigued; although, admittedly, apprehensive. Not for the world, however, would she have let the Commander know.

Hamilton, as though divining her simplicities, said: "You know, Sinclair, it is entirely up to you whether or not you go on this mission. It is strictly voluntary. I am not saying you *must* go." He moved closer to the window and stared out at the docks, as though searching for another candidate. "Should you decide not to of course, we would still like to retain your services in this office, where you have proven yourself to be a most capable assistant to Lieutenant Carrington." The point was not lost on her.

"Something, Sinclair?"

Valerie shook her head.

Hamilton relaxed a little, but he did not intend to lose. He jabbed at the maps. "It is extremely dangerous, and you could be caught by the Gestapo. On the other hand, although you lack experience in espionage, your very look of innocence, of helplessness, shall we say, should make men want to come to your aid, to...ah, 'protect' you."

She blushed.

"The 'child spy,' you see."

Her dossier at the War Office was already starting to fill. It had begun with Mrs. Churchill....

Hamilton was looking at her. "Well?"

"Well, I do have a bit of trouble in ordering drinks sometimes."

Whisky double, please.

"There! You see? We are banking on this in helping you to outwit the Jerries. In fact, I feel the most observant German would not be in the least suspicious that you were anything other than what you purport to be—a young French girl."

She had it now: this was the trip.

"If you think I can pull it off," offered Valerie. "You know, when I was growing up—even today—I look such a kid—"

"That is what we are counting on. In any event, we know you are most capable. The loss of your husband was a terrible blow, and yet, it did not stop you from getting yourself a job, looking after your young son, making the best of things. Importantly, you have joined His Majesty's Navy, a most commendable action."

"Yes, sir. I—"

"You know, Sinclair, the more I get to know you, the more I feel you have what it takes to pull this job off successfully. As for your late husband...well, life must go on, you know."

Valerie said, "He's gone, isn't he?"

"Quite so," rasped Hamilton.

"I still have my son."

"Who will no doubt serve the Crown well, once he is a *man*, of course," Commander Hamilton said. "British Naval Intelligence is the best in the business. You see, one must expect danger in this field, and be prepared. The plans for the mission are well laid." The confirmation had come in that morning, from the Office of General LeClerc. In their deal with Blackstone, anticipated by Hamilton, the French had called on *Egalité*: Hamilton had used it as a ramrod, to guarantee her commission. "I think you should know, you will be accompanied by a Free French agent."

"Yes?"

"Yes," said Hamilton, "another officer. You will be turning the schematics over to him, you see, for transforward to us once you commit them to memory."

It was Blackstone's condition.

"I am so glad that I will have a companion," said Valerie, absorbing it all in small bites, the way she would nibble an apple.

They were quiet for some moments while Hamilton enjoyed a cigarette. The horn of a tugboat cut through the hot stillness of the afternoon.

"Do you feel comfortable about the idea?" he asked finally.

"You mean, in pretending to be a kid?" she laughed.

"In pretending to be a *child*," he said, firmly. "How do you feel about it?"

"Fine," she replied.

"You're willing to go then?"

"Yes...certainly."

"Good, then I have confidence in you." Hamilton produced a document from the inside of his coat, and handed her a pen.

"Sign here," he said. It was the volunteer release form, absolving SOE from responsibility.

Sinclair signed.

"Welcome aboard."

"Thank you, sir!"

She was in.

"Now that you have agreed to help us there is no time to be lost." He pocketed the document. "Tomorrow, I want you to take the early morning train to Edinburgh. I will meet your train. From thence, we will proceed by car to Sir Donald Cameron's place, where the British Commandos are trained—American Rangers, too."

"Yes, sir."

He put out his cigarette, and flipped through Carrington's desk calendar. He stopped and read, then looked up. Apparently, whatever he'd discovered did not concern her. "You have a French Christian name which fits in perfectly with what I have in mind. Your cover, you see. When the time comes, we will assign you an appropriate French surname to go with it." He looked at his watch. "So then, shall we call you 'Valerie'?"

"Please do," she said.

"It is now 1450 hours and you are relieved of all duty. I want you to go to your parents' home in Newton Swyre. Naturally, you will want to spend this last evening with your son, and the other members of your family."

"Yes, sir. I'll just stop by my flat, sir, to pack up my things."

"It's already been done."

"Done, sir?"

"Done."

"Yes, sir." The navy owned it, she supposed they could take it. Well, she still had a few of her old outfits at home. Several business suits, from the Royal. Her red dancing dress, packed away by her mum. Clothes that her father had given her, things that her mother had saved. The blue robe...

"Now then," said Hamilton, "about your parents—"

Valerie heard him, she was thinking of mothballs. Smelled like old admirals, they did!

"Your *parents*, Sinclair."

"Yes, sir!"

"You will tell them that you are being sent to Southampton for further training on your present job. As for Lieutenant Carrington, we'll take care of that on this end. Any personal items in your desk?" She opened the drawers, and looked. There were just a few, she put them in her purse. She found room for her husband's photo; she would give it to her son. Hamilton watched her, but kept his thoughts in check. "Can you get a bus or train to your home?" he asked, as an afterthought.

"Oh, yes. There is usually one on the hour." She finished with her purse and looked up. She felt strangely drawn to this man, as though to a mystery. Still, they were as unlike as chalk and cheese.

"You think you can handle it then, do you?" He was locking the desk. "You'll be wanting to catch the early train to Scotland. That's tomorrow."

"I'll be on it, sir." She bent down to adjust her stocking. A run was starting. It had caught in her shoe.

"Hmmm. By the way, be sure that you wear your uniform, but bring some civilian clothes with you." *Was this bloody woman listening?* She was still bending over. "I say!" Hamilton stooped, so as to get her eye. "After tonight, Valerie Sinclair, as we have known her, will have disappeared into the history books."

"Yes, sir."

"Well?"

She straightened up. "Right, sir," she said a little breathlessly. Damn! There went her last pair of stockings! "I'll be going now, and catch the bus."

Hamilton glanced at her legs.

"Jolly good. Well then, good-bye, Valerie. I'd say you've made the right decision. I shall be waiting for you in Edinburgh. Leave your keys with the guard."

"Yes, sir."

He turned on his heel and strode rapidly out of the office. She could hear his footsteps disappearing down the stairs. "Thank you, sir." She looked up. A photographic proof had just appeared; hanging out to dry. She had not meant to take it. Still wet, it was the darkroom print of a full Commander, Royal Navy. Jabbing with his pointer, neatly framed, he was issuing instructions....

She was to go home, and tell lies.

* * *

38

"Up easy, girl!"

Valerie smiled at the bus driver. She wondered if he was single. The door whanged shut and they were off. A cataract of clouds covered the sun, leaving its recipients suffering from the humidity that had fallen over the countryside where citizens, dabbing at foreheads with handkerchiefs, moved like slugs. Cars and jitneys bounced over threatened terrain, traveling across England the way pain travels along a nerve. Being British, the passengers sat apart. To the south, where the coast curved, waves of heat billowed from the tar sealed road. She stared out the window.

The bus passed the Gloucester.

She glanced back, but the cause of her uneasiness wasn't there.

Valerie closed her eyes, remembering the Royal. She heard the orchestra playing, the assertive baritones of the officers, asking her to dance. As she moved about the floor, her reverie was interrupted by the shrill and irritable voices of two small children, across the aisle, struggling with their nanny burdened with bags of white-papered packages, reeking of offal and fish. To calm them, the nanny was getting them to chant "Humpty Dumpty."

ABBOTSBURY, the sign said....

Famous for its swannery. Round and round went the royal swans, in endless circles of stillness, like the women, having nothing else to do, who came to watch them. Could one cook them, like a goose? Weren't their feathers coated with grease? She wondered if swans were good to eat.

Maybe the necks...

There was no telling what she might have to eat in France. Her thoughts returning to the Royal, she wished for a cigarette. Clementine Churchill had sent her a nice letter, on paper that smelled of jasmine, remarking she would see what she could do in recommending her for a better job. It had been some time, she still hadn't heard.

She scratched her nose.

As the country flew behind her, photos of the Dorset Coast, called locally "Golden Cap," filled her mind; and she thought of the vicarage: the sheer and dangerous slope of grass that ran down to the cliff. Blocked by a hedge, roots crawled over the edge to a straight drop of five hundred feet. Once, when she was ten, she had fought her way through, emerging on the lip of the precipice. She took pictures of it. After, she had stared at the slow-moving waters far below, white-topped breakers smashing into the rocky channel coast.

Children do that.

Climbing down fifty feet, she had climbed back up.

Actually, nothing had been too daring for her to try: if the boys could do it, she could. If they called her bluff, she would leave them standing. Later, fierce fights ensued, after they stole two of her mother's chickens. Her mother, Alma, had got them as chicks through a mail-order advert, appointing her daughter their guardian. Valerie felt honored, but after studying the mental processes of the birds for a few weeks, she had concluded that their brains were still waiting to arrive in the mail.

When she walked into the vicarage, Newton Swyre, her parents—Vicar Edward Crewe and his wife, Alma—were having afternoon tea. Surprised to see her, she could sense their irritation. Strangers, friends of her mother's, were on hand: a plethora of voices. Hurried introductions...names lost in the air. "Mama!" Brian, her little boy, fighting his way through a sea of legs, ran towards her shouting, "Are you going to take me back, Mama?"

She could see her father, standing darkly in the doorway. "Yes, love."

But the boy would be safe, here at the vicarage, away from the rockets and explosions in the cities: the children must be protected. Besides, Lieutenant Carrington had insisted—oh yes! her mother made that clear—which got her guests talking about the navy again. A woman Valerie didn't know asked her where they'd be sending her next. Word for word, the girl parroted Hamilton's line. Weren't the bombs still falling at Southampton? No, Valerie assured them, they were falling on London.

Fans fluttered in the heat.

Brian, heavy with ice cream, was put to bed for a nap. The grownups prepared to play cards. Annoyed that she had not called first, her parents attended to their invited guests.

Valerie walked alone over to the church.

Bushes of yellow gorse pushed in upon the road, heavy with the smell of summer's heat. Old oak trees, gnarled from centuries of British history, stood massive sentinels to the eerie trilling of birds. Where the branches joined overhead, the country road seemed particularly narrow. Then, the sun would come streaming through, between the gaps of the leaves, sketching cobwebs on the slate of a child's frightened mind. The air today was tasting hot and sweet, magnetic as if touched by a current. She licked her lips. Could the beams of light, high in the limbs spearing through the tops of the trees, curving down the coast, be the reason "Golden Cap" had received its name? She stepped to one side—into the leaves—and listened. A face was there. Except that it wasn't a face. Trying to photograph it, it was gone. A voice...

It will move through the trees....

Valerie returned to the road, not daring to glance sideways at the *Inhabitants*. Within the grove, bronzed with sepia, shadowy beings were standing in the sunshine. Silvery at twilight—they were waiting to play with her. It was because she had to go away, she told them, but she had not told them why....

For security reasons.

She glanced back towards the house. Voices were drifting across the field. Someone was laughing. Valerie squinted. A sound, like wind. Thirty feet up, a giant rook exploded out of the branches, and flapped across her path!

Click!

She passed a rotted bench where the road bled away into slippery sheets of grass, tumbling down to the edge of the cliff five hundred feet above the sea. The church, tarnished with time and the weight of childhood memories, loomed out of the dusk as ominous and threatening as a forbidden book—possibly one of those by Frank Harris, Havelock Ellis, or Rudjer Boskovič that her father kept locked in a special cabinet in his bedroom.

But there was something about her father's books that he didn't know. She thought of them as genies, hiding in a box from which they jumped forth at twilight, just before dark, to gather in the secret places of the woods, fearful and forsaken, or to crowd forward about the walls of the church, the sight of which was now causing dread to swell in her heart....

It was where death lived.

She entered the vestry, found a seat, and turned to the wall on the right. There, on the Roll of Honor, was the name of her brother. In alphabetical order, a short list of the living, the longer list, of the dead. Names of local young men mostly, navigators and cadets: Battle of Britain pilots who had gone up into the cold, dark, terrible air. Next to each name killed gleamed a cross, polished in brass, and down near the bottom, the name of Basil Sinclair. Her mother had explained it. Though he had not come from this parish, her father had made the arrangements. Valerie, who had not been consulted, considered it a personal intrusion.

The vicar meant it as a surprise.

She recalled the day she received the dreaded telegram that read, "THE LORDS OF THE ADMIRALTY REGRET TO INFORM YOU THAT YOUR HUSBAND BASIL SINCLAIR IS MISSING, BELIEVED KILLED ON WAR SERVICE." Her father had talked with her at length. Afterwards, he had told her, "You must remember, my dear, in a war like this, *no one* is privileged."

"Yes, Father, I've noticed."

Bombs had fallen on the small town of Bridport.

Still in the church, the candidate said a short prayer. She closed her eyes. "Please, God, if you love me, be with me on this mission, and help me...to..." Tears came, words would not follow. In her heart, she knew prayer could not deliver her and neither could their God. The horrors of Hitler filled her future—there, in its ashes, where she would walk.

She got up and walked out of the church.

She saw the sun dancing, and it was like a disk—two disks shimmering, blue-grey silver rimmed with gold—and she intentionally let it burn her eyes for a few seconds. A third disk emerged from the second, vertically, and at right angles to the first. The south poles joined. She blinked, and uncrossed her eyes. The two suns slid back into one. It was how she took pictures, her film from the world. She knew she was different. Were there others, photographers she didn't know about? She slogged along kicking at weeds, stumbling and feeling crazy, and wanting not ever to return.

She arrived back at the house and opened the door and walked into the room where Brian slept. She sat down on the bed and put her arms around him. He was already awake, and he looked up at her. "Mama, why are you so quiet? What's the matter, Mama? *Mama!* Grandpa hasn't been saying his prayers."

The child spy...

She looked lovingly at her son.

"Mama, please. Please may we go?" asked the small child.

"I am sorry, darling. Perhaps soon. Give Mother a kiss." She dug in her purse and handed him Basil's picture, the photo of his father. "Guess who *this* is," she teased, her voice musical. Her son sat up, clutching it awkwardly. "Oh, we have been here a long time, haven't we? You are right, dear. We need not be quiet any longer. You have been a very good little boy."

How could she leave him here?

Invited to spend the night, she accepted. The needs of the guests came first, but they were either already gone, or leaving, and she went into what used to be her room and closed the door. Brian slept with her parents, and she had packing to do. Her room had not changed, and neither had their lives. She looked at the box radio, placed next to the bed by her mother, for her visit. From a distance, she could hear the whispering of the sea. Valerie listened. They went to bed with the chickens out here. She pulled the blackout curtains and set the alarm for 500 hours. Pre-dawn busses lay ahead. She clicked off the light, undressed, and got under the covers. The sheets, which had lain unused for months, smelled like dead bibles. In some terrible and sad way, the vicarage had reclaimed her again. Would she ever be free? They asked her to sleep in her own bed, but she didn't have one anymore.

In the dark, she thought back to her father's bedroom, just down the hall; and to that secret cabinet, long ago. Thumbing through his prayer book, she had discovered a key, buried in its spine. Her parents, gone on holiday, had left her at home for the weekend. She had read the books, beginning with Frank Harris, devouring all five of his volumes. She read the other ones, too. Edward Crewe, she discovered, had tried to lock up evil. But in locking up evil, he had locked up truth. By protecting her from it, he had denied her the knowledge to know it; and she had torn it out of his cabinet with the furious and starving hands of her mind. The afternoon's meeting with Hamilton came back to her. She had it within her; she was going to *be* somebody! The history books, he had said.

Really?

Valerie reached over, she turned on the radio. In coveralls, live from the floor of a factory, the fist of Vera Lynn was swinging at the nation, giving Hitler hell....

Heute Deutschland, Morgen Die Ganze Welt!

Clocks were ticking....

Time passed. She kicked off the covers, as though ready for love. Her eyes had closed in sleep. At the edge of the vicarage, a limousine had arrived. Silver and black in the shadows, it trembled like a cat. Leaves were blowing, and the curtains moved. The programs changed. Music came on. Sinclair rolled over. There, from the nightstand, aglow in the darkness, sweet in their singing and brazen with mourning, the Second Welsh Fusiliers marched steadily past her bedside....

Piping her to glory.

II

Scotland was hot!

Commissioned before midnight, an officer now, Valerie Sinclair arrived in Edinburgh wearing her W.R.N.S. uniform as Hamilton had instructed. Rockets, missing the tracks, had exploded along the way, and she realized that Germany could still win the war.

Adrift in the terminal on this Saturday afternoon, some kids were eating popcorn. They were stuffing it into their mouths while dropping a good portion of it, and some birds had got in somehow and were following them around. The trails of kids, popcorn, and birds had created a barrier in the middle of the platform which people were carefully sidestepping in order to get where they were going.

The birds, keeping a sharp eye peeled for shoes, had accepted Sinclair into their midst and were sticking close to the smallest kid, who was holding behind the rest of them like an anchor. Dragging a sweater with one hand and spilling popcorn with the other, he was trying to tell the others up front that what he really wanted was a candy bar. Valerie, who had just decided to buy him one, suddenly jumped upon hearing the voice behind her, causing the birds to run out in all directions, like water leaving a drain.

"Good journey, was it?" He picked up her bag.

"Yes thank you, Commander." The kids were getting away! She had hoped they would lead her to the vendor.

As they walked through the station yard, Valerie trailing, he informed her of her new rank. "You're a Lieutenant," Hamilton said over his shoulder. "It came through this morning."

"I *am?*"

Valerie caught him up.

"Better pay and privileges...hmmm?" He steered them around a group of Hindus, wrapped in white and thrusting up posters of Gandhi. Sinclair, interested in such things, wanted to stop and read the messages, which seemed to be printed backwards. Hamilton, muttering something about radicals, pulled her away. "Papers all signed. Looks better for the Record, you see..." What he didn't tell her was, "In case you don't come back."

Lieutenant Seymour had tracked down Bridley. James was going out of the country, no one knew where, but Seymour had managed to track him to his favorite bar, the El Flamingo, where Bridley was about to be flattened by an irate Irishman who had caught him wiring the urinal in the men's room. Quickly measuring the situation, and sensing Bridley's imminent doom, Seymour had swung first. The Irishman, being a fair chap, had flattened Seymour instead, whereupon Bridley had promptly come up with the requisite signature.

Valerie Sinclair was approved.

"By the way," purred Hamilton, "Lieutenant Seymour sends you his warmest regards."

"He *does?*" She liked Seymour. He had let her hold his gun.

The Commander looked over the tops of heads. "Ah! De Beck!" Dressed in the rich blue of the Free French, her French counterpart was opening the door of their car. It was Hamilton who had selected this officer, known to him, and recommended by Commodore Blackstone.

The two Brits approached. "Lieutenant Sinclair, Valerie, this is Pierre de Beck, Captain, Free French Forces—your partner on the mission."

"How do you do?" Sinclair said.

The Captain, perceiving her to be extremely young, noticed she was wearing uniform of rate, not rank, which he attributed to some clever trick of Hamilton's. De Beck, smiling warmly, said "Avec plaisir."

"Enchanté."

The two spies shook hands.

"Pierre is from the area where you will be going," Hamilton told her. "We are hoping, you see, that one of you will get through."

"I am certain we both will," said Pierre.

Now that she had met the man into whose hands Hamilton had placed her, she felt a renewal of purpose. De Beck spoke excellent English, though with an American accent, and he seemed to know what he was about. Valerie judged him to be in his late twenties, five feet ten, dark hair and eyes, and very good-looking. Stowing their gear, Hamilton and the girl got into the back of the car. De Beck proved an excellent driver, and Edinburgh soon disappeared into the Scottish hills. The Commander ordered conversation held to a minimum. It was thinking that he had to do.

With the air cooling in late afternoon they stopped at a hostelry to eat. Sinclair, glad to be free of the Dorothy Cafe, thoroughly enjoyed the courses, especially one that arrived at their table on a pewter platter, smoking and garlanded with sprigs. Bear meat—what else?—as must have been obvious to any hungry person. Valerie felt a reverence, for it seemed fitting—here on this eve of Achnacarry, as it were—to commemorate this primitive place with practically raw meat of its ancestors. Hamilton, respecting her strange grace but finally clearing his throat, started dishing it up. Sinclair licked her lips. Dabbing daintily with her napkin, she could see the furry monster in the flames, its great fanged jaws roaring at the moon.

"Like the veal, do you?"

Valerie nodded, she jabbed with her fork.

Hamilton ordered after-dinner drinks. Burning logs casting shadows on their faces, the men talked. Sinclair wasn't sure what was in the glass, but she slugged it down. Maybe it was malt. After two, she felt replete. Pierre, she learned, had fought at Dunkirk; both officers had seen battle together. Was that why Hamilton had selected him?

Valerie stared into the fire, warming her hands.

The fireplace made her sleepy; the car made her cold. Even

in June, evenings were chilly in the Highlands. It was after dark when their car passed the depot. Seven miles on, de Beck pulled into Achnacarry Barracks. A black smudge covered the heavens and the lights were yellow, the way they are in camps. A soldier was waiting at the desk. The Commander hurried them through Reception. Once cleared, he turned to the Frenchman: "Breakfast is at 600 hours. Good night, Pierre. You know your billet."

With the Frenchman gone, Hamilton escorted the girl to her quarters. At the door, he told her: "Your training starts in the morning. Remember, your time here is not to be wasted." Having delivered her, he spun on his heel and disappeared into the hallway.

"Good night, sir."

Sinclair entered the room and kicked off her shoes. She threw the switch and dropped her skirt. Off with her blouse, her panties and bra. Flapping out her blanket, she looked out the window. There was a clothesline. Men's underwear hung down into the humid night.

Stiff as iron.

It is something she hears: the snap of a lock, a loudspeaker... a language. It is something she listens to: drifting through the dark, welling up from the subterranean fountain of military life—the secret and violent hush of morning. Alerted by the yapping of the camp dogs, sopranos in pitch blackness, footsteps move along the corridor:

The Spy arrives before dawn.

Click!

Ryan and the limousine hidden in thick woods beyond the security fence, her camera jammed! Unphotographed, the man without a face evaporated from her consciousness as explosive knocks on her door pulled her out of vanished dreams:

Into the hot, rising sun.

It was 530 hours.

She took a fast shower which helped her wake up, got dressed, and reported for breakfast. She was wearing a man's naval battle dress, which Hamilton had arranged. It was the smallest size the Commander had been able to find, and it had been waiting for her in her room.

The Commander was also waiting.

Pierre joined them. What a break for me, he thought. Throwing the girl a warm smile, he made sure that she got it. A Swordsman, he liked them young.

Breakfast was a fast affair. As they came out of the mess hall, they passed two American Rangers leaning up against a wall. "What'n the hell?" She was the first female ever. "We got *kids* now?" and he turned and spat tobacco juice onto the grass.

They reported to the firing range.

"Valerie," said Hamilton, "this is Sergeant Llewellyn, a crack shot and a good Welshman! He will teach you how to handle a pistol, and how to kill a German at twenty yards. Actually, you will not be taking guns with you." He pulled her aside. "As a French student you see, you would not be carrying one." He released his grip. "Ready, Sergeant?"

"Aye, sir." The Sergeant produced two guns: a German Luger and a Schmeisser machine-pistol, much preferred by the S.S. "Firing either of these babies," he pointed out, "is something you were not taught when you joined Naval Intelligence." Commander Hamilton coughed politely, and Llewellyn made a mental note. Officially, Valerie Sinclair was not here. "This one," said the Sergeant, "is the standard Luger automatic, .30 caliber—"

She observed.

"—nine bullets to the clip." He slammed the clip home and handed it to her.

Valerie proved an exceptional pupil. Acquainted with guns, she gained an understanding of the powerful weapons quickly. Hamilton, hands behind his back, watched with interest. The Schmeisser proved to be the more difficult. "Yes," said the Sergeant, finally, to the Commander, "I'd say a four-inch group at a hundred yards was respectable."

Rifle practice followed: German guns and Allied. Valerie lay flat, propped on her elbows in the hot grass, her cheeks burning and her head ricocheting from the explosions.

"No no, lassie! Do what you did before. *Squeeze* the trigger!"

By noon, hands burned raw from the gun oil, the smell of the powder had her reeling.

"Come along, my dear, we will have a spot of lunch now."

"Perhaps she's had enough for one day, sir," offered the instructor.

"She is not here to be spared," Hamilton snapped crisply. "She'll pull a full twelve hours, along with the men."

Valerie appreciated the Sergeant's kindness and wished some of it would rub off on Hamilton. She turned towards him, trying to hide her bleeding hands.

"I know, I know," he said gruffly, "but I want you back alive. Learning and talking about violence here, where we are safe, is entirely a different matter from being faced with it. If ever in that position, you may surprise yourself."

They reached the mess hall and found a secluded corner.

Valerie's hand trembled as she tried to hold the fork. Hamilton, eating at his regular rate, said: "I speak from experience. On the Dieppe raid, code-named WEYMOUTH, I was an observer. All bloody hell broke loose when we landed. It was a very tight corner."

"Yes, sir." She could see the towering clouds of black smoke. "That was Number Four Commando, sir? Lord Lovat?"

"That's right. His orders were to knock out the German battery at Varengeville. The battery was utterly destroyed. A hundred and sixty four men took part in the raid. Fifty killed. The Germans lost three times that number. Pierre, you know, was wounded."

She hadn't known that about Pierre.

"Yes, he was a bit more fortunate than the others. Went in with the Canadians, you see. Second Canadian Infantry, the six battalions that attacked Dieppe itself, caught it point-blank, nearly four thousand dead."

"How awful," she said. She waited.

Hamilton dabbed at his mouth.

"And the Navy, how many?"

"One destroyer, some landing craft, five hundred and fifty men killed."

"All those men..." she said.

"No, by counting the German dead, we could measure their strength. That way, you see, we were able to know exactly what we'd be up against. Our recent landings in Normandy, of course, have been the result." Hamilton finished his lunch. "Ready?"

"I met Lord Lovat...." she started to say.

"That's nice. Come meet the man who trained him."

Walking back to the firing range, Valerie said, "You might have been killed."

"I know how to take care of myself. I received the best possible training yet devised, right here at Commando Headquarters. After Dieppe, I volunteered for the Naval Commando Unit. Unfortunately, I pulled a leg muscle, shortened a tendon...you know. This special unit has to be A-one physically. I'd received training in police science before the war, so I ended up in Naval Intelligence."

"I'm glad you pulled that leg muscle."

"Some things are meant to be," the Commander said, and he rousted Sergeant Llewellyn from his cigarette with a snap of the fingers.

Gunnery instruction went better. They gave her some salve for her hands and a pot of cold water to cool them. In late afternoon, the guns were put aside for a simulation on how to cut throats.

"What a ghastly business," the girl remarked.

"Business is business, my dear. But we've run our course for the moment, have we, Llewellyn? Good! Almost time for supper. Ah, here comes Pierre!"

The Frenchman, who had been running refresher courses elsewhere and who had been chatting with the Sergeant, now approached them. "How are you feeling?" he said to the girl.

"Aching all over," Hamilton replied, "but she's not going to admit it. Both of you meet me in the dining room at 1900 hours." Valerie nodded. She had moved to one side, and was limbering up.

Out of her earshot the Frenchman confided: "Sergeant Llewellyn has just been telling me what an excellent pupil she's been."

Hamilton lit a cigarette.

"You know, Commander, when you first told me that a girl would be with me on this mission, I had my doubts. I thought another man might have been better."

"They don't come any better," snapped Hamilton. "She's fluent in French, and has a lot of heart."

"I'll say," said Pierre, eyes glued to her bosom. Valerie caught his look and turned to the Commander.

"Feeling better? Good! Now we must give you time for a soak in the bath."

What bath?

Sinclair relaxed in the shower, wondering what to wear at supper. She'd packed the red dancing dress, along with a pale blue suit, and had planned to wear the dress. She had also brought her turquoise Egyptian gown. It reminded her of Cleopatra. Well, she would leave it in the valise. The blue suit, too. She stared down, dismayed at what was in front of her: big boobs were such a bother! She had finished her shower and was just drying off when there came a knock at the door.

"Yes? Who is it?" she shouted through the steam.

"The orderly, Lieutenant. I have your uniform."

"My uniform? Oh, yes. Would you put it on the cot, please?"

She heard him do it, the door closing behind him.

Dropping the towel she rushed naked into the room, her eyes fastening on the two wavy gold rings, the precise cut of the cloth, the skirt, the eight gold buttons on the coat. With a squeal of delight, she tried on the hat, her fingers running over the embroidered laurel leaves.

Screw the dress!

She got into the uniform quickly, hoping it would fit. It did, perfectly. She stood in front of the mirror, turning this way and that, and blushing, staring at the woman she had dreamt herself to be:

An Officer, and a Lady.

She sat down, dabbed at her eyes with the Kleenex, and applied her makeup. Brushing her hair, she suddenly stopped. She leaned closer to the glass. For a long moment, Lieutenant Valerie Sinclair studied the sombre image in the mirror. Then, ever so slowly, she grinned....

"Smashing!" she said.

David Hamilton was waiting for her at the entrance to the dining room. "None the worse for wear, I see. And your new uniform, hmmm?" He stood back and admired it.

"Yes, sir. That hot shower did the trick," she acknowledged, "and thank you for the—"

Hamilton nodded.

"—uniform." Her hands hurt like hell.

De Beck joined them in the dining room, complimenting Valerie on her appearance, as well as on her commission. Privately, he wished the Commander was miles away. It had been a long time since he'd met a girl who attracted him this much. A *Lieutenant*, to boot. And to think...

They would soon be alone together in France.

In the annals of the British Empire, reported by Rudyard, the dawn comes up like thunder; but at Achnacarry Castle it wasn't thunder that men had to deal with on a morning—but death. To Valerie Sinclair, death was something that happened to somebody else.

This position was soon to change.

By lunch of the second day, she had learned how to kill with the knife and how to use the rifle butt as a weapon. In the afternoon, the carotid, how to break the nose, how to snap the human neck—the most vulnerable part of the skull—and what nerves to crush...German, of course. By twilight, how to puncture his heart. By supper, how to rupture his spleen.

It was dark, and exhaustion blazed in her brain.

In the dining room, the men seemed to be enjoying the evening meal. Hamilton helped her to cut the meat, because of her hands. Valerie waited until Pierre finished, and when he left, she said: "I'm not at all sure I could bring myself to kill anyone, unless, of course, I *had* to." She thought of the teachings of her father, and now she might be called upon to take a human life. In running from death, she had run towards it.

It was as though Hamilton could see into the window of her mind. "The first real knowledge most men ever have is the knowledge that they are dying," the Commander said, and he filled his plate. "Even so, for them as well as for us, death is an unfathomable darkness..." Valerie, who was sipping her milk, spilled it. "As I said before, when it comes to a German or yourself, there will be no time to think, or to be self-sacrificing. You will cause him to die by whatever method you are learning here. The German soldier is formidable and brave. To *kill* him"— and he speared the meat—"is merely a matter of what's appropriate at the time."

Valerie stared across at him and suddenly didn't wish to eat. The dining room wavered and withdrew, reverberating like the distant *splat* of bullets; like the overloud voices of a dream. Fatigue, with a mumbled excuse, pulled her from the table and hurried her to her room. There, safe from Hamilton's scrutiny, she sat on the edge of her cot, shuddering with horror. Exhaustion seeped into the corners of her being, wretched nausea; and deep, explosive shocks.

The Spy was still in Scotland.

The hours passed, and she was aware of being cold. Dawn with grey face, with pocked Commando visage, leered at last above her bunk. She awoke, and tried to focus, then crossed her eyes, as though staring at some rapidly moving ghost. She staggered out of bed, feeling drained of all desire except to return to it.

Breakfast and scalding coffee got her heart started. The Commander was not yet about, though Pierre was soon in attendance. Not a bad sort of chap, really. And he seemed genuinely interested in her. She acknowledged the Frenchman with as few words as possible. She was too tired to talk. Too tired, even, to chew.

She poked wearily at her breakfast.

All around her, beneath the cold lights of morning, the cacophony of men pressed inward upon her brain. The sounds of eating, cursing, and hard male laughter crashed against her ears, welling up like cigarette smoke, evocations of a terrible strength. Somehow, she knew, it couldn't be any other way: they were here to cut throats. They were here to be hardened in the way that iron is hardened, to become lethal as steel. But Valerie wasn't made of steel, she was made of woman. Like a car, being wrecked, she was running out of gas. Here because of Hamilton, that fact seemed to be lost on them. Commander Hamilton would help her. Hamilton would understand...

Hamilton was coming through the door.

"Good morning!" he said, rubbing his hands briskly together and commandeering the seat next to her. He poured himself a steaming cup of coffee.

Her prayers were answered, he was smiling at her.

"Well now," the Commander said, glancing impatiently at his watch, "ready for another go, are we?"

Fast Machines!
Bugatti, Hispano-Suiza, and Duesenberg: their clutch and gear systems. How to hot wire and steal a Mercedes Benz. Trucks: what they contain and where, what they can do, and what you might have to.

Next, *the Body*, also a machine: how to use yourself as a fulcrum, how to break arms, how to cross a river with a rope.

Lunch!

In the afternoon, how to get through barbed wire, and where to cut it…ducking live ammunition.

Rat-atat-tat-tat-tat-tat-tat Rat-atat-tat-tat-tat-tat-tat.

Two and a half feet above her, a stationary machine-gun lays down a steady, unwavering blanket of bullets. She has but to raise her head to have it blown apart. She gets caught in the barbed wire, starts to clear herself and remembers at the last moment—death is no longer happening to somebody else. It is inches away! Eyes fearful, hugging the earth, she becomes a part of it. She curses, she waits, she rips herself loose!

Rat-atat-tat-tat-tat-tat-tat…

Valerie's heart was in her mouth as her belly scraped on the clay.

Minutes became hours.

"Here is a rope," a Mr. Groggins said, "here is the grappler on the end of the rope. And here, come over here. You see up there? That is a cliff."

She squinted upwards at the giddy height, into the blind eye of the sun. It was not at all like the cliffs of Dorset. Looped with barbed wire, there was something different about it: the way that steel is different from rock.

"Climb it!" Groggins said.

She stared at her raw and bleeding hands.

"Try spitting on them," Groggins suggested.

Later, after she had skidded and crashed a dozen times, after she got over the barbed wire and learned how to "sling it"—and got to the top—Hamilton informed her, in her case, that the rope would first have to be stolen: probably, a French clothesline.

Commandos instructed her.

An hour went by. Bridges were built, using human bodies: ascending vertically, geometrically, forming ladders. The sun was sputtering. She glanced up. It was like a bola.

Time for tea.

Hamilton walked over to the Staff Building. Not invited, she stared after him. Groggins pointed a stubby finger. She had a lecture to attend. It was half a mile and she would have to run. Pebbles flew from her heels and the dust had her dizzy. She arrived, neck hot from sunburn, and joined her unit.

"You're *late*," her instructor announced, "go back and try it again." Men laughed and she could hear them behind her. The sun was at her back. Groggins was waiting, he pointed with his finger. "A little faster," he said.

Sinclair flew like death.

Pain was cracking, dry in her throat. "That's enough," she heard. Stumbling, she fell into their midst. They had gathered at a tarn without water, dry gulches bleeding up over a rise onto a field of blistered rock. The men made room for her, and the sweating girl tucked herself in.

A review of garrote, she sat among stranglers. Surrounded by sun-blackened faces, flaring their nostrils, she was seeing what she had come to learn. Invisible to their speaker who was standing on a ledge, the men were looking at her with bony eyes, stripping her of her clothes with slitted thoughts. They were enjoying it: nailing her, brutally and at once, the way a big dog moves swiftly to grab a smaller one: locking in, with the first thrust. Some of them were staring straight ahead, and they were the worst. Trembling, arms around her knees, she pulled in her feet, fighting back the tears. The men were grinning. Sinclair waited, tossing her head. He moved closer. Imagining tobacco juice, she turned her head to one side....

And spit.

"Oh! I am so *terribly* sorry," she said.

He wiped it off his pants.

Twilight came, and the hope of deliverance, but night arrives with a *bang*! Hamilton decides to squeeze in an extra hour of night firing. Ears ringing, she skips the late supper, and sleeps in her clothes.

She dreams of guns.

Sunrise.
In the dining room the radio is blaring.

Deutschland wird entweder eine Weltmacht werden, oder nicht! Die Welt ist nicht eingerichtet für feighe Nationen!

roared the Reichmaster, leaning into the ganglion of microphones and nodding three times between sentences.

*Starke liegen nicht in der Verteidigung, sondern im
Angriff!*

"According to this morning's BBC report, quoting the
Home Office, more than 30,000 people were killed
last night in one of the worst raids on London. His
Majesty, the King, traveled to the East End to comfort some of the grieving people. From the Northern
Registers, the temperature in the Highlands is 81
degrees, as of midnight, with clear skies expected. In
other news, following last Wednesday's meeting of the
House of Lords..."

Hitler again:

*Unser Feind Nummer Eins ist England! England kann
uns nicht widerstehen! Amerika wird uns nicht
widerstehen! Das Grosse deutsche Reich...!*

"Oh yeah? Fuck *him*! Who, the King? Fuck him, too!" An
American Ranger turned off the radio. It was on a shelf, at the
end of the dining room. Hamilton was telling the man's officer
what a great sport the King was. Sinclair looked at her tray:
any meal could be her last.

It was her fourth and final day of training.

"So then!" said Hamilton, arrived at the site. Behind him,
hot sunlight welled along the crag. "Come over here, Lloyd—
that's a good fellow. Now Valerie, this 'German' has a gun. You
need it. How are you going to get it? The moon is full and our
friend here is on guard duty. McGinty?"

McGinty, the Senior Trainer, showed the girl what could
be accomplished with a large stone if the intended victim were
unsuspecting and no other weapon were available. He went
through the method of obtaining the gun from the German,
over and over again. Then a dummy was used to enable her
to hit with the stone so that it would put the victim out. How
to hit in another, a vital spot, to kill him. The difference, it was

explained, was the Geneva Convention. It was further explained that following the Commando raid on Vaagso, in Norway, code-named ARCHERY, Hitler had directed that all Commandos be shot on sight.

So much for the Geneva Convention.

"The choice of one is not a choice," the Trainer explained, and he ran her through the demanding exercise until her legs trembled, and her body staggered from the overkill. At last, Hamilton and the Trainer were satisfied. Stewing in her own sweat, she stank like a Brighton whore.

"Well, Sinclair," said the Commander, "I think you are nearly there. Do you not agree, Sergeant-Major?"

"The lass will be a fighting man yet, sir," the Trainer acknowledged, grudgingly.

Valerie glared at them both.

Lunch was canceled; the world was a blur.

The blur was the sun in her eyes and the place was a wide ring where the heat shimmered upwards from the dust. Spectacles were put away and watches were removed from wrists. It was the hand-to-hand combat zone, the "dessert" of the death camp, and the customers looked hungry:

It was her on the plate.

It began simply enough—slowly and carefully—how to encircle, where to grab, the mechanics of the throw. The chops, in slow motion—the rock-hard repetition. By late afternoon, she was half-blind from the sweat and half-choking from the dust of the ring. "Have it now, do we?" asked the Trainer.

She nodded numbly, fumbling with her belt.

Hamilton had been bothered by the girl's words in the dining room: *I'm not at all sure I could bring myself to kill anyone.* The words stuck in his craw. It just wouldn't do. Thinking about it, he tapped deftly with his riding crop and pulled her partner aside. "A little walk, you see..."

Valerie saw him interceding. She was grateful.

When they were a few yards out of hearing, Hamilton clasped his hands behind his back, leaned forward, and said to the soldier: "Knock the hell out of her."

"Sir?"

"You know *how*, don't you?"

"Yes sir, but..."

It was an order.

"Do it," the Commander said, "let's see what she's made of."

"Yes, Sir!"

"Ring time!" announced the Trainer. The men who were watching walked over and stood around—American Rangers and British Commandos—tough, gaunt-looking men with dark eyes and unshaven faces. The sun was like a wheel and she was suddenly in the middle of the ring, facing a swift-looking man who wasn't smiling.

"Give him hell, Lilly!"

"Ten bob says he takes her."

"You're on."

"All right lads, this is the real one now!" The Trainer circled the ring in a half-crouch, clapping his hands in rapid encouragement. "Give it your best!"

Hamilton nodded to her from ringside.

Valerie assumed the position.

The first blow with his foot to her head caused her teeth to crack! She staggered, but kept her balance. They circled. He reminded her of a rooster, the kind of cock you bet on for money. Sinclair remembered him now: it was the man she had spit on, in the strangulation lecture. She lunged. She missed. He threw her down. Up.

The chop!

Her head exploded, and her nose, which was now bleeding.

He hit her again! Her world shattered, like glass! She was in the sand, on her butt! Her lips were numb. He had split them!

The Trainer jumped to stop it! Hamilton held his arm.

Sinclair staggered up! She scrambled free, gaining ground, fighting for time! *Her head cleared…* From the corner of her eye, she could see them standing there. She realized that Hamilton and this damned soldier had made a deal, that… The soldier made a grab! He had her by the wrist.

He was *hurting* her!

Could she take a picture, she would see herself dead. Instead, from the secret place of her mind, reaching out beyond her own body, she felt the grip of The Spy.

Instruction was entering….

Sinclair steadied, staring down the corridor of pain.

She reversed it—and, as though having entered another

world, she suddenly seemed to hang bodiless in time and space. She heard, rather than felt, something snap inside of her and it was like the sudden *crack* of a dry branch. Instantly, it was a feeling that she hated. Therefore, it was a feeling that she loved...

It was the taste of blood.

She spun him!

Her mind had gone cold, like steel, but there wasn't time to think about that either. Her body now thrummed with a murderous joy! Throwing out the book, her fist caught him in the stomach! His breath came out! She chopped! Had he not been the best in his weight class, the blow would have killed him. Stunned, bleeding, off-balance, the man stared at her in disbelief.

She *slapped* him!

Commandos almost never attack from the front: he didn't expect it. Her knee came up! He grabbed himself! His head dropped in agony, and the heel of her hand cracked like a hammer into the base of his neck!

"The Liverpool Chop," noted a Ranger, with satisfaction.

She was roaring and blind from the dust, the sun was in her eyes, and she was going to kill him.

The cock was red-faced and furious. He was hurt now, and dangerous. "I'll bust 'er bloody arse!" they heard him yell. His head snapped back with blood spewing from the ferocity of her fists! Strong arms grabbed his, and hers. She kicked—and shrieked and bit!—at whoever it was who was holding her.

It was Hamilton.

The soldier, his face a sponge, was in the grip of the Trainer.

There was a warm round of applause, and much spitting of tobacco juice. Bets were paid. Water was splashed. The sun was setting. But the Commander, with arms of iron, kept her locked.

"Jolly good. Well then, come along my dear," said Hamilton, aware of teeth marks in his hand, "and let us have a nice relaxing dinner together. Perhaps I can talk you into a drink, hmmm? You certainly deserve one."

He released her, and she spun round to face him.

Delivered with rage, humiliation, and white-hot tears, Valerie Sinclair's answer, exploding in Hamilton's face, echoed away across the dying fields:

"You rotten son-of-a-bitch!" she howled.

Two hours into darkness, and with the shades pulled, the light in the window was still burning. It was in the officer's briefing room, where Hamilton had finally got her calm enough to listen. It had taken some doing. When she did, she understood. The Commander had left strict instructions for them not to be disturbed.

Hamilton said, "We are going down to Cornwall. For security reasons, we will travel separately. Lieutenant Seymour will coordinate. Our launch rendezvous is a hotel called The Red Lion, in Polperro. I want you to take the night sleeper, from Inverness to London, Euston Station. From there, go by tube to the main line station at Waterloo. You'll be able to catch the afternoon express to Falmouth, where I'll meet you. We'll motor to Polperro."

The Red Lion...

"Got it."

Her photographic memory snapped a picture of his instructions, of the complex military directions. The Camera Shop, damaged in the fight, had opened again.

The Commander was off the hook.

"I'll pick you up in ten minutes then."

A cold breeze was blowing. Nightbirds cut dark arches against the scarp of the hills. She waited, shivering on the porch of her billet, with her gear. Above a black and jutting Scotland, a silver moon rode low in the Mars sky.

A horn honked.

She hurried to the car and Hamilton hoisted her gear. Pierre had left earlier, booked for London. There would be just the two of them. Sinclair got in and closed her eyes. Through the gates of the ancient castle grounds the woman who was not supposed to be here was leaving as quietly as she had come. She thought back to that first night following her arrival. The Spy had looked in on her. She had tried to take his picture, but couldn't. Why couldn't she? The Commander, having checked with the man he'd assigned to her flat, and been informed of nothing unusual, had concluded that The Spy had left town.

Sinclair would settle for being alive.

After Achnacarry, which was now a permanent part of her

dossier, Valerie was grateful to be going to Cornwall. Of what she had just accomplished she was not yet sure, nor did she feel in any condition to evaluate its use in the future. For now, there was no future: just fatigue.

Hamilton drove her to Inverness, where he handed her an envelope of tickets and travel cash. He reached over and opened the door and she stepped out.

"See you in Falmouth." He saluted her with his finger, she returned it, and he drove away. Shouldering her gear, Valerie walked into the terminal.

Beneath the blue lights, dimmed from the cathedral ceiling, she stood and watched it approaching. Headlight hooded, the locomotive passed the platform, and slowed. The train braked. She boarded and found her sleeper. She undressed, and instantly fell asleep.

Blacked-out countryside thundered past and the cars swayed. She was awakened by the screeching of rails—or, perhaps, by fitful dreams of guns exploding—just in time to have breakfast. The train, its pipes hissing steam, jolted into Euston Station.

There she changed to the fast-moving tube.

She got off at Waterloo, grabbed a quick lunch in the shelter, and connected with the afternoon express to Falmouth. Adept adjustment of the Enigma Code, false information intercepted by the Germans, had gradually steered the deployment of the V1s away from metropolitan London and into the outlying countryside—but it wasn't enough.

Several had fallen last night near the area in which she now found herself. Mountains of rubble, Home Guard barriers, and emergency trucks clogged the passageways; the hastily posted detour signs causing confusion. The machine-gun sound of jackhammers, amplified in the vast tunnels and mixing with the clouds of dust, were discharging out onto the walkways. Wherever passengers were going, they were going in a hurry. Plywood short-cuts led into concrete walls. Men wearing armbands and Dunkirk helmets were directing passengers, up one corridor and down another, to their respective platforms.

Sinclair boarded the train.

A three-hour trip: she would have a compartment to herself.

As they pulled out of London, she realized why Hamilton had booked her to Falmouth, which was beyond Polperro, instead of to the Addison Street Station, which was reserved for military and where she could have connected directly to Devon. Intelligence strategy, darkly hidden, her tickets to Cornwall concealed the real purpose of the trip.

The train was gathering speed...

Some previous passenger had left a copy of the morning's paper along with an underwear catalogue jammed into the side of the seat. Published in Liverpool and dedicated to the Male Animal, it had been shipped in a plain brown wrapper.

Satisfaction guaranteed.

One glance was sufficient. Could that passenger, lurking about the train station, be a pervert? Could that pervert be *The Spy*? Apprehensive since that night in Weymouth, Valerie stared straight ahead, as if watching an invisible man on the seat across from her peering over his paper. Smiling demurely, eyelids fluttering, she zeroed in on his fly.

Spies wore underwear, didn't they?

When it came to education, she certainly didn't want to be left out! Her schedule had not allowed her much time for serious reading. Perhaps this was meant to be. Tossing the newspaper aside, she picked up the catalogue. Checking the aisle, she examined it with interest.

The color-photo section opened up on three middle-aged gentlemen, military types, enjoying whiskeys at their Club. Perched on stools, they were admiring each other's underwear. An arrow, sweeping across the page, was pointing to one gentleman's crotch: "Tastefully tailored in Madagascar Blue." A yellow oval sticker, patterned by the catalogue's art department to resemble a banana, had been thoughtfully pasted over the place — or person, as it were — to whom the arrow was pointing. "Also available in Tropical Tan," the oval announced.

She licked her thumb, and turned the page.

Spotlight on their new Mandrake line: "For those Magic Moments," the advert read, "when your Lothar draws the bath." Something to slip into, if a man dare, when the servant is out of the room. The gentleman in the photograph, a big game hunter type, had a leopard skin over his shoulder and was staring approvingly into a mirror. The hunter's underwear was in Bengal Buff. A leopard was clutching a pair of black drawers in its teeth. A more serious Sinclair sat up on her seat. Things this good usually didn't come her way.

The catalogue was vibrating.

The train, pawing like a leopard, thundered up the singing tracks and over gullies thick with jumbled railroad ties hiding barrels bound round by rusting hoops and blackbirds. The long pull of a whistle acknowledged the British Rail System to be on time. In its wake, clacking all together, the birds relanded in squawking rituals; safe once more, behind their thick protectorate of trees, within the secret Britain of the animals.

Sinclair flipped the page.

The Wildebeest Waistline. Against a background of stampeding wildebeests, thin-legged models in knee-length underwear stood stiffly against fake Roman columns or lounged backwards along the rim-seats of fountains, arms straight with hands flat behind them on the stone, a pose that more closely resembled a group of women confiding things of tremendous importance to each other. Sinclair, who didn't get it, turned the page.

One of the models, forwarded from the fountain, had the next advert all to himself. Crotch cradled in Plato Pink, standing with his open palm thrusting forth like Apollo, blazing blond hair carefully crimped, he was reading a book. Unseen by this Greek god, a unicorn was galloping towards him, head down with horn pointing straight at his Plato.

"Classic Hit," the caption read.

Long underwear followed.

"Snow-jobs in Satin," it began. Sinclair didn't wait. She jumped straight ahead, bypassing the explorer who was showing off his shorts in Igloo White to a roaring polar bear, not stopping until she reached the accessories section near the rear of the catalogue. Bedecked with wall plaques, it was appropriately entitled "Athletic Supporters of the Crown."

While the jock straps from their latest Safari line, in limited lots of Lavender Lizard and Casablanca Crimson certainly *seemed* practical—attached as they were to those billybags in Badger Blue and Rhinoceros Red—it was the two-page spread at the end, The Tarzan, in which no expense had been spared, that was causing her consternation.

Suffragette, she didn't have to take it!

It was the same model who had flopped on the fountain, who had survived the unicorn, and who was now wearing a wig.

Just because three bull elephants were turning up their noses at his Jade de Jane undies didn't give him any right to swing across that pond of crocodiles, using a python for a vine, while grabbing by the throat that poor defenseless lady chimp—who up to that time had obviously been cackling contentedly, and understandably so, in her own pair of Junior Jungle Jim Jockies, the poor dear having done her best to decide between these and the Daring Dan Diapers, in Small, Medium, and Large at manufacturer's close-out prices.

While supplies lasted.

Valerie was calculating on her fingers: a dozen assorted, less discount? She would have to place her order soon. Satisfied with her figures, finished with the catalogue, and rolling it up, Valerie leaned forward and stuffed it into the side of the seat across from her. She was feeling new zip in her thoughts. Her heart thumped with mystery, in tune with the bouncing of the train. Having memorized prices and stock numbers, she had photographed the address: Loincloths of Liverpool.

Why not? Mr. Loincloth's creations couldn't look any worse on her than those issued by her own government, the representative of whom would be meeting her train in Falmouth. Valerie Sinclair got up and went to the ladies' room, returning to enter into a series of energetic push-ups, pitting herself against the movements of the floor. The floor winning, she curled back up into the seat, resigned to her corner and staring out the window.

The girl browsed through the paper, then snoozed for awhile. The express, having pulled out of Bournemouth, was soon flying down the tracks again, fighting its way across the glorious countryside of Poole. Weymouth Harbor had passed behind her to her left. The channel, refracting light, was coming up. Awakened by the banging of the cars, Valerie glanced out the window, looked at her watch, and yawned. Ahead of her, the sun was running forward on the line, and she could see the locomotive. The train was slowing. She opened her compact to do her face. *Bruises...* Gathering her gear, she opened the door and entered the aisle.

FALMOUTH.

The Commander was waiting downtrain when Sinclair stepped out onto the platform. Back from Downing Street, she suspected, he appeared to be trim and rested. She recalled the part played by Leslie Howard, whom she adored, and those famous lines from *The Scarlet Pimpernel*: "Is he in heaven, or is he in hell, that damned elusive Pimpernel?"

She hastened to meet him.

Hamilton stepped out into the sun. "Well now Sinclair, had a good journey, did we?" As her superior officer, Commander Hamilton was about as romantic as yesterday's newspaper— *The Daily Telegraph*, she had left it on the train. He gave her the once-over, making notes. She was looking better since the beating: her face was powdered, and her lipstick bright.

Lips a bit puffed.

Outside the station a car pulled up. The driver, in Free French military blue, walked across the tracks to greet them. Pierre was feeling good. He had just got laid. Valerie was happy to see it was Captain de Beck.

"Lieutenant! What's going on? You look so charming." Smiles flashed in the sun. "I realize I may have asked you before, but may I call you Valerie?" He grinned, indicating the girl with the shake of his head. "Valerie Sinclair, right?" It was addressed to Hamilton.

"Try Valerie *Marchaud*," he said.

Her cover had arrived.

Valerie brightened. "Marchaud?"

The call from General LeClerc's headquarters at SOE had come from the Missions Research Officer, a Major Guy Farvillant, who had determined the name from records: a twelve-year old French circus performer reputedly killed by the Gestapo in the earliest days of the war. Blessed with an exceptional memory, the French child had expressed a grace far beyond her years: a normal attribute with children of the trapeze. Fascinated by her uncanny physical resemblance to Sinclair, Farvillant, genius in genealogy, had continued to follow her, eagerly exhuming dusty histories, until Valerie Marchaud had disappeared. Something odd, about the death certificate—dates left open, witnesses shot instead of the victim. Could she still be alive? Sharing this with Hamilton, the Commander had assured him it wouldn't matter. After all this time, would she still be twelve? Farvillant had to agree. Following further talks with Seymour, the French officer had turned this background, complete with its mysteries, into the girl Valerie Sinclair would become. A man whom she had never met had just renamed her, assigning her to history in the world of yet-to-be.

The candidate had turned Pro.

The Commander pulled them close. Passengers were walking past them. "So then!" It was fifty miles to Polperro. "Shall we be off?"

Pierre picked up the gear.

A breeze tugged at her hair; the air felt cooler.

The Frenchman escorted them to a green Rolls Royce, the result of a dockside deal between Seymour and Bridley, following their confrontation with the Irishman at the El Flamingo. Leased to MI.5, specifically to Hamilton, the car was at the Commander's disposal until such time as the Free French delivered it back to SOE for the exclusive use of General Charles De Gaulle. As part of the deal, the French had insisted on their own driver. De Beck got a chauffeur's cap, Seymour got a black eye, and Bridley had got away. Blackstone would get the bill.

"Together, are we?" Hamilton purred.

Sinclair got in. Luxurious leather and rosewood surrounded her on all sides. Her hand caressed the rich felt. She closed her eyes, breathing deeply of the car's perfume, whose name was power. Blimey, she thought, now ain't *this* the cat's meow.

Hamilton, on whom her reaction had not been lost, joined her now in the back seat, and Pierre closed the doors. Up front, he was fiddling with something. It was a chauffeur's cap.

"Problem, Pierre?"

Pierrre adjusted his cap. "Ready when you are, Commander."

Hamilton lit a cigarette, offering one to Sinclair, who took it like a lady. The Frenchman started the motor and soon had them out of Falmouth. He pulled a hard right, swinging the southern sun behind them, then accelerated. Dark clouds stood distant.

Sinclair leaned back.

The sleek green Shadow sped down the narrow English road. In the back seat, Hamilton had turned, so that he could see her, while addressing them both. "Within a few days," he said, "we will leave Polperro by motor launch to rendezvous with a submarine in the Channel. It will be at night, when we expect the cover of a major storm. The submarine will take you up to Brittany. Once ashore, and in contact with the Underground—the *DSM*, Pierre—they will send us a signal." The Commander paused. It was vital that de Beck understood.

Lé Direction de La Securite Militaire?

He had it.

"Presuming your mission successful, that is, that you get the information—you will be returning on that same submarine, at coordinates to be announced. Or one of you at least, hmmm? Should either of you fail, for any reason, to make your appearance, we will assume that you have either been captured *or*, that you are somehow returning via an *alternate route*." She was listening intently. "In that event, naturally, you will be beyond our help."

"This rendezvous point off Brittany," said Pierre, "where exactly?"

Valerie sat up.

Hamilton threw her a glance. "Two hundred yards straight in, two hundred yard straight out. For the month of July, no currents, a flat sea. You will move in to the beach at a direct right angle to the sub, so observe your route."

"Suppose the Boche intercept the signal?"

"You mean from the Underground?" Hamilton queried.

"Oui."

"You do your job, that's highly unlikely. However, nothing is ever really certain, is it?"

Capture, he meant.

Pierre caught the inference; he had a question.

"No cyanide," Hamilton said, answering it.

Hedges flew past, yellow sun emerging from clouds.

"Why no cyanide?" Pierre now insisted, checking his mileage. "Surely if we're caught..."

"If caught, you could still be rescued," Hamilton pointed out.

"But we would be tortured!"

The Commander silenced him with a gesture. He did it from the rearview mirror. The argument was over. Suicide was out. Obviously, de Beck had expected the last minute issuance of the poison. Sinclair, who hadn't thought about it, had not. She stared at the back of the Frenchman's head, noting a thick neck.

"When you know we're coming, will you signal from the sea?"

"No. We are foregoing the navigational beacon."

"I see." Pierre, mind like a ferret, was mulling it over. No beacon, no cyanide. He looked up, into the mirror. "What kind of submarine, Commander?"

"The kind you can get blown up in, old boy."

"Excuse me, Commander..."

"What is it, Lieutenant?"

Sinclair took a drag on her cigarette, she was planning ahead. "Will we be wearing life-jackets?"

How would she find one to fit her?

"We are not planning for you to *swim*, Sinclair! You will be provided with...whatever is appropriate." *Life-jackets?* He had never been asked that before. "You will leave, you will rendezvous. The submarine will take you to a point just off the extreme north coast of the Bay of Biscay. You will then continue in a Carley float, that's a *raft*, Lieutenant"—she put out her cigarette—"landing you below the village of Lorient—"

"South of Brest," Pierre said.

"Right. Now then, we are assuming you will meet no one on this lonely stretch of beach. If you are questioned, Valerie, you are merely a student...lower form, as it were, at a northern Catholic lycée. Your identification will place you in the School for Orphans at Combourg, near Avranches. Difficult to check, you see? Pierre is a friend, or cousin if you will, and the two of you decided to do some fishing after visiting with his family."

"Who live inland?"

"Yes. Their farm, isn't it Pierre?"

"Our farm, that's right."

"That's good," Sinclair said, "where are the Germans?"

"Intelligence has it that there is little if any German activity near this particular landfall." The latest report, it had come from Blackstone. "There will be Germans, of course. But no significant patrols, major gun emplacements, that sort of thing. The main Jerry movement is towards Caen. Our area is well south and seaward of the Contentin Peninsula, at least fifty kilometers, I'd say."

"More," said Pierre, glancing at her in the glass, "it is further."

"Well, you should know," acknowledged Hamilton. "You see,

Valerie, Pierre's parents are in touch with DSM, the Underground. But things could change. As the Germans bring up reinforcements and strengthen their positions, well..."

They could find themselves in the thick of it.

"Radios?"

"No. Your time will be critical. We do not intend to waste it by encumbering you with radios. Germany, as I have explained to the Lieutenant, has very sensitive detecting equipment, its ECMs. In all probability, the agents already sent were located through just such means. Any questions, Captain?"

"Not at the moment, sir."

"Sinclair?" Hamilton, getting no response, turned. "I say, Sinclair!" She was on her knees, staring out the window. Her rump was up; she was looking good. The Rolls Royce had shot past a flock of sheep, and she was straining backwards. Trying to count them, she was practicing her memory.

Pierre, thinking they were being followed, went faster.

"See here," Hamilton exclaimed, "we have to get this place in organization!" Pierre skidded around the curve!

Thirty-two sheep, three rams, and one goat. She sat back down.

"Tell me, Sinclair, what do you know about what I just told you?" Pierre listened like a buddha.

"Not a thing, sir."

"Good show! Then let's get on down to Polperro. We will meet in the hills tomorrow morning at 800 hours, the cliffs above the beach." It would be easy enough to find, unless one were looking for it. He told them where.

They would arrive separately.

"By the way, there will be a dance at the hotel tonight," Hamilton let drop. Valerie, gawking out the window, suddenly perked up. "You will, of course, wear your uniforms." It was the weekly Military Dance, held on Thursday nights in Polperro.

"Super," she said.

Pierre was making good time.

"It might be nice if the three of us could have dinner together, but there could be a German agent about, so we will sit at separate tables." Seeing their reaction, he at once downplayed. "It is highly unlikely, I must admit, but we do not intend to take chances. Briefings of this sort, you understand, are just too important to be discussed in our rooms. Pierre, you've been registered as Longchamps. Your room, Valerie, is in the name of Smythe.

"Nice touch, Commander."

"Thank you, Pierre. One can never be too cautious."

Smythe...

The Germans, Hamilton went on to explain, were past masters at getting hold of hotel records. The man in the back seat had been around Blackstone long enough to suspect, if not to know, that International Bankers were just one big happy family. Any hotel owned all or in part by German interests, even if corporately concealed, could be accessed by Abwehr's agents. What the Commander had gone over previously with Seymour—namely, that the Germans may be the best in the world in languages and accents—he now summarized for de Beck.

"It is important, you see, not to make the mistake of the Americans, who when they hear an American speaking to them in their own dialect, presume him to be one. Keep that in mind, Pierre. Valerie here was not born in Brittany, you were. Once landed, you'll be wanting to protect her."

"Of course."

"Do it," Hamilton said. The way he saw it, German espionage was synonymous with German business. He could have said the same for the British. Blackstone, a banker, had immediately known that Hamilton was not. But David Hamilton had eyes, as did Seymour, and they would be quick to spot a connection: Bridley, perhaps, having revealed more than he ought. Still, Hamilton was not expecting to run into enemy agents at The Red Lion:

It belonged to the Rothschild Shield.

"Now, should either of you be questioned while dancing, your cover, Pierre, is that you are on leave from your unit. Valerie, in your case, you are on a few days leave from Special Projects, Devonport." That Sinclair was actually *Ships Officer*, not Administrative, Hamilton thought best to down-play. It was unlikely that anyone could tell from her uniform. The girl smiled, she tugged at her sleeves. The miles had flown like silk. Late sunlight poured through the glass, bathing the rosewood that gleamed like a god. Other cars went to other places, but not this one. One didn't go just anywhere, not in a Rolls Royce! Whatever the evening then, Valerie Sinclair was looking forward to it.

The band played "It Had to Be You."

To Sinclair it seemed strange, sitting at separate tables. No one else seemed to be sitting at all. They were dancing. Her glass danced, too. She was enjoying the liquor on Hamilton's credit. David Hamilton, tugging at his hat, was certainly no ladies' man, yet it didn't take him long to arrive at her side. A matter of rank, as it were, his main purpose had been to get there before Pierre. "I will try not to tread on your toes...." he began. Valerie jumped up.

It was suppertime at The Red Lion.

Spotlighted center stage, a young American soldier, guesting with the band, had begun to sing:

> It had to be you
> It had to be you
> I wan-dered a-round
> And fin-al-ly found
> The some-bod-y who...

The Commander struggled with his feet. Sinclair was leading. "If I may say so, sir," she whispered romantically, "this song is my very favorite."

"Quite so," observed Hamilton, glancing authoritatively over his shoulder at the other couples, who were embracing. His mind was on the war, but where was it? To the Commander, the dance floor seemed an unfamiliar battleground. The song ended. Perspiring, he escorted Sinclair back to her table, throwing a quick glance at the double Scotch. Making a lame attempt at a bow, he turned on his heel. A whistling shell was now approaching, landing with finesse.

"May I have this dance?"

"Why yes, Captain, thank you."

De Beck reached for her hand. "Allow me," he said.

The song was *Elmer's Tune*, a fast two-step that Valerie loved, and she found Pierre to be an excellent dancer.

De Beck held her at arm's length. "Where you from?"

"Administrative WRENS, Devonport. Between assignments, actually...yourself?"

"On leave from my unit," the Frenchman answered, in Americanized English. "Theese war, she ees hell, no?" He thought he'd throw in his accent.

Valerie grinned.

She adores me, de Beck thought. As he spun her expertly about the dance floor, she could feel his hand, pulling her close, lightly tracing the seam of her panties beneath the stiff British cloth. As she reached to remove it, it was already gone. The French were famous for their flings. Pierre, no doubt, considered this his last one. Valerie gave him a passionate hug, and threw herself recklessly into the music, finishing the dance.

Her head was in a whirl, she gulped her drink.

After de Beck left, the band returned from their break with another of her favorites. The young American began to sing:

There'll be blue-birds o-ver
The white cliffs of Dover
To-mor-row, just you wait and see...

Valerie, who had not seen a bluebird in years, was thinking of aeroplanes. The couples poured out onto the floor. The Commander was moving towards her. He stood looking down. "I say, dare we have this one together?"

"Yes, daren't we."

Hamilton winced. She accepted his hand.

The voice of the vocalist filled her feet. She wished Hamilton would liven up, as had de Beck. As a dancing partner, she didn't want to lose anybody this tall. Meanwhile, what she and Pierre were most in danger of losing were their lives. By this time next week, they could both be dead in a ditch. Even so, being a Frenchman, he would still probably try to seduce her.

Valerie, dancing with David Hamilton, and loving it, pondered the future. The present, she decided, was better: She was in a man's arms. She would be certain to remember and to hold in her heart forever the pink lights flowing across the floor, covering crowds; the smart look of the uniforms, many of the wearers of which would soon be dead; men drinking and chasing women from the vantage of a busy bar; the pungent sounds of dual languages and clinking ice; rich Americans with their Pabst Blue Ribbon, Hav-a-Tampa cigars, Lucky Strikes, Zippo Lighters, Four Roses—and Coca Cola. The British, too, with their smoking pipes and Scotch, serious conversations, baggy blouses, and moustaches.

The war was a mix.

The music was wonderful. Even Hamilton, for once, seemed close to being happy. The musical arrangements, sharp with brass, reminded her of Glenn Miller. Wasn't he stationed nearby? Maybe the young soldier was attached to his unit. The number ended.

"My dear Sinclair," said Hamilton. "I felt just as though I were dancing with Ginger Rogers."

"Yes, sir," she whispered sincerely, looking up at him, "I feel exactly the same way."

Hamilton shook his head. "Let's go up to the bandstand and get a closer look at the singer," he suggested. He was reaching for his handkerchief.

"Yes, let's."

They walked over, as though searching for their separate tables. "With a voice like that," Valerie piped, "he should certainly have a successful singing career once this war is over." The singer's name, they discovered, was Johnny Desmond.

And, yes, he was with the Glenn Miller Orchestra.

No stranger to fame, Hamilton answered: "The Commander of my last Flotilla, chap named Charlie Crichton, was a movie director—and will be again, I dare say." What he didn't tell her was that she'd had a "screen test" by Commander Crichton two weeks ago, in a routine surveillance film requested by Blackstone, previewed by Winston Churchill. Valerie Sinclair looked up, and smiled at David Hamilton. Awkwardly, and for one last moment, they watched the singer.

Valerie wanted to stay.

"Well now! Interesting I'm sure, but we do have a war to win." He had received a call from Blackstone. Anxious to leave, Hamilton walked her politely back to her table. "Regretfully, I must go now," he announced. Several American soldiers were jostling him, trying to get around him to the girls. "Stay a little longer, if you wish, and listen to the music." His words were lost in the smother of dance hall voices.

"Yes, sir. Thank you, sir."

Touching his fingers to his hat, he was gone.

Pierre de Beck, meanwhile, who was starting to get drunk, had decided that things were going better than anticipated. The mission was right on schedule and they could not have picked a more attractive cohort. The Frenchman, an arrow that couldn't miss, clicked a cigarette to life from his lighter and hurried across the floor, drinking in her sparkling eyes and luscious figure.

Pierre knew he'd had several drinks too many, but why shouldn't he? It was because of his cleverness that things were going so well. Sobriety before a launch was a standing SOE regulation. In Sinclair's case, his superiors, having determined his fondness for young girls, had warned him to keep his distance. Headquarters would be annoyed if they found out, but what did *they* know? They were either playing cards back at Milton Hall Castor or getting over their own Champagne hangovers, at some floozy's flat in Mayfair. *Stupid fucks.* Espionage and the seduction of women were among Pierre de Beck's greatest accomplishments. At twenty-seven, he considered himself a master at both.

He slid into the nearest seat and immediately took her hand. "How about a little nightcap up in the room? The success of the mission depends on it."

That ought to do it.

Sinclair, pulling her hand away, patted his. "Pierre!" she laughed, "whatever would Commander Hamilton say?"

"Who?"

Pierre considered his options: there weren't any.

Foot in his mouth, he would have to get it out. If this British bitch told Hamilton, he could be pulled from the mission. As much as he wanted sex, he would not take it on the sword of dishonor. Besides, good times were coming up. What was England? She would be *his,* in France.

"Sorry if I offended you," Pierre began, his voice thick with remorse. *Piss on her!* "Too many drinks! I'll tell you something,"—he lowered his voice—"no one knows this about me, but for nearly two and a half years I haven't even had so much as a *date!*"

"You haven't?" Her eyes were big.

"It's the war," the Frenchman confessed, he had her now, "the killing." Slurring his words, he needed to make his case quickly. "Do you like poetry? Good. Let me put it to you this way: 'We have a rendezvous with *death*!'" His voice had deepened, taking on a rich dramatic tone.

Valerie gulped.

"'In some forgotten, foreign field'". The words were losing themselves, in the glass.

"That's not how it goes," she said.

"Pardon?"

"Pierre, if you must quote Alan Seeger, at least have the *decency* to quote him correctly!"

"I see," he answered simply. "Well." His cigarette ash had fallen to the table, in front of her. "Excuse me. Not all of us had the foresight to be born in England." Pride, and "Le Marseillaise," shone in his eyes. Staggering from the table and drawing himself up to his full height, Pierre concluded with: "Pray, do forgive me!" His smile was dazzling.

"Sit down!" Sinclair ordered.

Pierre slid back into the seat.

Valerie felt like a heel. God, he was gorgeous! Well, she knew what it was to be without a date.

"Friends?"

"*Bon!*"

"Settled." She would help him. "Too many drinks, Pierre." She was his partner. "And I'm sorry, too. I know I spoke sharply, but..."

"No problem."

Pierre, eyes glazed with tears, stared mournfully at the other couples. Love was for others; he hated the world. Valerie reached over, and held his hand. She remembered Dieppe. He was a hero! What right did she have to judge him? To criticize! For such a man to desire her was certainly a compliment. It was because he had killed so many Germans, she decided, that his conscience was bothering him.

But Pierre didn't have one.

"You mustn't blame yourself, Pierre," her voice consoled. "You did what you *had* to."

"I did?" What he wanted was to get into her pants.

"Of course! I wish that more men would do it."

"You do? I had no idea."

"Pierre, we may soon be in a lot of danger together—"

"—danger is my field," the Frenchman admitted. He was trying to focus. "You're in good hands. I will do whatever is necessary to...protect you." Where was her face?

"Thank you, Pierre."

"*Avec plaisir.*"

Sinclair was becoming impatient, this music was too good to waste. She glanced over his shoulder. An American Sergeant, in the entrance, was signaling. *Me?* She could feel it, where it mattered. He looked the right kind of chap, but she would have to dump de Beck. "I will say good night now, Captain, if that's all right...Captain?"

He hauled himself up.

"But of course," purred Pierre, respectfully. "'All's well that ends well.' Bacon, right? Or is that Shakespeare?"

"Shakespeare." The girl smiled, she got up from the table. "I will see you tomorrow, Pierre."

With a courtly gesture, he bid her adieu.

As Valerie disappeared through the archway, she ran into the American Sergeant who had been waiting for her and who swung her back out onto the dance floor. His name was Sergeant Blumensteel. Short, sexy, and with thinning hair, Sinclair had found herself instantly attracted to him. Winning her heart with New Jersey directness, the Sergeant steered her to a table in the back where de Beck couldn't see them. There was a bottle of *Johnny Walker* on it. A bucket of ice, too.

How fashionable!

The Frenchman, long on tricks and short on cash, reached over and finished her drink. The winning number was SEX, but where was it? Had this been a game of *rouge et noir*, he would not have done too well. "*Fuckum!*" he concluded, his American accent having lost to the real McCoy. He staggered up. Gripping the back of her chair, his eyes swept the hall.

She was gone.

Music was playing.

A sandman's dream, it disappeared around the corner.

"This way," Sergeant Blumensteel said. He said it softly.

Both laughing, Valerie hurried to catch him up. They had escaped Hamilton's security people by an adroit manoeuvre through the hotel kitchen and had made their way undetected through seven blocks of the late crowd to the place where they now stood.

Blumensteel tried the lock, jiggling with the key. The door he was about to open was just off the pantry, at the back of the licensed cottage where rooms were let and where a Fire Certificate nailed to the wall in the name of a Mrs. D. Muldoon warned against lighted cigarettes; and where, from the smell of things, a lot of ashtrays had filled up recently beside glasses of whisky; and where no monkey-business was tolerated, or would be going on, after lights-out. But this, of course, was the opposite of the truth. Sergeant Blumensteel, for one, had rented a permanent room here for when he was in town.

"It ain't the Ritz," he said, "but here goes," and he opened the door with one hand while grasping her tightly with the other. Her smile was hesitant. They were both drunk and they fell into the room. "Over here," the American said, and he pointed to the brass four-poster against spotted wallpaper that seemed to have faces on it. "Like I tol'ya, kid, my home away from home. Just put the bottle on the table."

Valerie said, "Ay?"

Blumensteel drank it straight. They had one each for the road—meaning a double. She wouldn't remember finishing it, undressing in the dark, or when he had turned on the light. Sinclair was staring at his skivvies. He took them off. She shot him in sepia and threw the switch.

"Fall in!" the Sergeant ordered, and pulled her towards the bed. She sat on the edge of it. He pushed her over, and she bit him on the lip. Blumensteel howled. Then, she was kissing him, but not the way they do in Hoboken, so he showed her how to do that, too. He felt her up—and they both went down—and somebody fell on the floor. He turned on the lamp and sat up and scratched his hair. There wasn't much. It was that moment of drunken delight when a man can look at a woman and see himself, and she doesn't know it. This one didn't know it because she was propped up like a hinge at the side of the bed, passed out.

A minor setback, he'd bring her around.

Blumensteel studied his prize. Obviously, she had lied to him: she couldn't possibly be twenty-three. He tapped out a smoke, lit it, and immediately sensed a shortage of breath.

She was a beauty, alright.

Too young for a uniform, much less an officer. Stubbing the cigarette, he turned off the lamp and got back into bed. Not that he hadn't seen big tits on young broads. In fact, Blumensteel, at thirty-two, had seen it all. But this was the first time he had seen anyone like *her*. Still, he couldn't tell whether she was faking or sleeping.

"Let's fuck," suggested the Sergeant, breaking the ice and probing for signs of life. He kissed her again, and went down on her, and worked his way up. Nothing!

Nefertiti never moved.

"Piss on this," the American said, and he got up over her. He shook his head. Maybe it was the booze or maybe he needed eyeglasses, but he could swear this wasn't the girl he came in with. Blue electricity seemed to sparkle about her face and she was definitely looking younger by the moment. She belonged in a tap dance class, for Christ's sake!

Blumensteel started to shiver.

Of course, it was stupid, but how was he going to explain this? There was no question about it. He was in bed with a *child*!

Sinclair moaned.

"This is fuckin' crazy," he told himself, excited by the possibility of renewed life, "a dream come true, man," and he moved to the foot of the bed. From there, a good Catholic, his tongue would take them to heaven. "Jesus Christ!" he announced, getting his breath, this was better than that fifteen-year-old from Secaucus! And he didn't just *do* her, he worked at it! There was lots of sweat. It was a hot night, and he was going down on her for the third time while groping for the lamp because something this good has to be seen if a man hopes to get anywhere. His hand found the knob and he turned it. The room burst into light, and the light was like a million needles zinging around in the air. Just out of sight, it was as if he could see things moving…

Valerie opened her eyes.

Some person she should have recognized was bending over

her; he looked the fatherly type. So, what was she doing in France? Better yet, where was this? Faces of the *Inhabitants* were pressed into the other side of the wallpaper, come, not to play with her, but to insure that she was having a good time. Eyes looked down, they were in somebody else's head; and a silly grin swept across her face.

"Got cha!" Blumensteel said.

Valerie drifted on the bridge of dreams, collapsing beneath her, and that tore from her hands the lover sought in a thousand anguished nights of being alone. Wracked by alternating waves of conscious hope and carnal pleasures, she had closed her eyes and her mind had swept away on rungs of trapezed wings as vast as darkened London, sweeping south now to the summer-sweet fields of Lyon, where circus wagons rolled at dawn, their brightly painted wheels bouncing along the ruts of the mistral land, lead wagon silhouetted against the ferris wheel of the sun.

The girl perched on top.

Suddenly the dream exploded, streams of machine-gun bullets shattered on the wagons from a barricade of smoke, cutting down the families of this circus owned by Jews, their horses screaming with the acrobats who fell that day, wagons tipping and falling on their sides; and there, beneath the stacks of corpses piled in the dust, a child's arm was clawing out from underneath the tarp, green-laced costume blotched with blood, flying skirt hooked with splinters. Bullets burst upon her back, one saw her fall, but could the Gestapo be sure? Orders had come, insisting on death certificates. Was the body found, dead and decimated, the same another thought had gained the woods? Valerie could hear someone running, shadows moving through the trees...

The click of a lighter.

France faded, submerged in smoke, and Devon waxed green in April. She had hurried back along the road of years to a place where she had once known peace. The black murk of war had receded into steep slopes of grass where the child-woman sat all alone, widowed and wild with baby, searching the summer cloud banks for the promised face of God.

"Just me 'n you now, baby!" Blumensteel purred.

Her husband was gone, devoured in the depths of the sea.

Valerie was still dreaming, was it his voice that she heard? In the midst of this, she floated. Throughout the night, like beacons to a blacked-out ship, beams of light sliced through the fog. She tried to remember her observations of Sergeant Blumensteel, who had produced a Parker pen and who seemed to be using it to write something on her leg. She smelled cigarettes, and she heard them being lit, but she didn't know who was doing it or where she was. Weren't they on the shore? Poppies blew through valleys of midnight where Brittany bled into the sea. Swimmer against rip-tides, she struggled for air, trying to break free to the surface. Someone heavy, who hadn't shaved, was on top of her. The ashtray rattled, and the lamp went out. Starlight shot through a crack in the curtains.

She drifted.

Blumensteel had switched to a slow, straight rhythm, and he was riding her like a green-broke bull, wild and demented and thundering through the landscapes of the night. Thick-barrelled and snorting, it bucked! The bed rose up to meet him! Slick with sweat, he had fallen off.

Bull without a rider.

"Hey hey! Sock it to me!" What the fuck? He looked. She had folded again. Blumensteel shrugged, and went back to work. Creaking of brass, he was listening...

Was she saying something?

Keep that crazy cobra underneath the sheets. He was trying to put her hand on it! The mongoose was snapping at it, but the cobra would prove the master.

"Ride 'em, cowboy!" the Sergeant yelled.

Her mouth was watering, she was gulping hard. The cobra was searching, trying to find the basket.

She was laying on it.

Valerie was up for grabs, and it was in her dreams. There were no more laws in the world. Anyone could have anybody; all one had to do was *wish.* Just say the sacred word, or touch them walking by. Oh, yes...

They'd come, all right!

Blumensteel, whose hands were shaking, was reaching for his lighter.

Click!

She had returned to her childhood. You could walk into

people's bedrooms that way. Her mother was starving for it, and she was watching the vicar. He preached *love* to his flock, but there was none for his wife. Valerie could walk into his dreams, where he kept a spare bed for her that was his own secret; and one sleepless morning, after she had read the books, she walked in and saw herself there. All around them, flowers were drying in heaps where spiders crawled. He spoke to her from his heart, but his heart was small and he didn't have much to say. She was listening. He, the Egyptian, was reading her pictures from the pages of his sacred scrolls. There, by torchlight, he was removing the last obstacle to her will, a piece of blue muslin: a secret curtain, draping a naked camera, in her birthplace at the vicarage, where he'd chained her to his past.

"C'mon—!" Blumensteel cried hoarsely, "who ya savin' it for?"

The creature in his arms was cold, now hot; and her arms draped gently in unconsciousness above his back. "C'mon, c'mon!" he begged, and she tried to breathe. Time leapt forward, couples got married in the vicar's head; and the knife, that was passion, plunged deep.

Its handle was turquoise.

Tears fell. Not just hers, but tears from all the women in the world. Wearing sensible shoes, and naked except for their sorrow, they arose from the graves of their cities, the most important half of the human race.

She dreamt of Blumensteel.

It was not a dream in the way she dreamt during her waking hours, but more like a series of prints. Desire was on the other side of it, and it was separated by a wall.

Bodies were coming through!

She rushed from the dream.

It was behind her now, and she was on her knees. He would have to do the holding. From somewhere—from this very bed in this very room, she thought—she heard a child weeping, tears so terrible she had stopped running. She recognized the voice, a calliope in the background, the child had a name…

Marchaud!

Blumensteel was rising. Through the wall now, he was getting close. The muslin fell.

She was showing it to him.

"De quoi s'aget-il?"

Love it, baby!

The dream changed and she lay upon the bed of the unknown soldier. The bed was a cage, and the two animals were circling. The mongoose snapped, then shrank back, its mouth and teeth wet from the attack. In the high reeds of the future, and in some other world, there was a movement in the grass.

Above the Pyramids, the lone black star of the Sikh.

Slaves, tongueless—arising from thought—were clawing their way godward until, booming in the final ritual of creation, they were orchestrating through the world that one thin, high, priestly note of prayer, of ulimate rape and rapprochement: the nocturnal, and embarrassing clacking of wood! A twelve-year-old girl was tearing an American Sergeant apart!

His body exploded on the bed!

On the *bed*, not in her body. In those final seconds, blue lights hissing along the brass, strong hands had thrust her aside. The girl lay pressed to the wall, and the wall was between them. Before, in the doorway, something had opened and closed. Later, he wouldn't remember it. After all, it was but the merest moment in his life. A thing of terror, the wide-brimmed hat, a presence had appeared in the corner. Shimmering, it had moved to the wall. Something cold and accusing had brushed by his bedside, leaving Blumensteel blaming himself. What the hell? He hadn't done anything! A ghost? Just a phantom from the bottle, he concluded, and moving rapidly. Blumensteel's hand was shaking, he raked it through his hair.

Some sort of vibration...

She was waiting, her face pressed into one of the faces on the wallpaper. It was blue. *If you are not that animal here*, she was hearing, *you will not be that animal there.*

Who was she listening to?

Now, other noises. They had fallen back upon the sheets, exhausted of memories. Blumensteel was putting on his pants, his eyes bulging with fear. She was trying to remember and was finding herself naked. Her mind felt lost, empty, filled by the clicking of the latch.

Outside, wind was banging on the glass.

Sinclair sat up, and turned on the lamp. She listened: it was Friday morning traffic. Reality was rumbling in the distance. Her head banged with hangover and her throat felt like cement.

She groped for her clothes, strewn in odd places about the floor. The windowpanes rattled, assaulted by the slamming of a gate. Then, she heard the bus stop for him, change gears, and drive away.

Valerie got dressed.

To her left was a door, opening on a hallway. She turned off the light. There was a notice tacked to the wall next to it, something about cigarettes. Sinclair, wishing she had one, moved through the darkened house and out onto the street.

Taking her bearings, she saw The Red Lion in the distance. She went down the stone steps. Along the way, palm trees with green fronds reared like giant chickens against a sky still strewn with stars. Beyond the bushes, above dark wet grass, fireflies danced a litany to morning, their bodies emitting codes.

She reached the hotel and entered through the back door into silent corridors. At this hour, Security was not as sharp as it should have been. The hallways were empty. Had they made their rounds yet? No matter. With the approach of the mission, surveillance was certain to be tightened. Before Sunday, the screws would turn.

MI.5 would not permit laxity twice.

She went through the spectrum of events. Had she talked in her sleep, let the cat out of the bag? The American, captured in fleeting photos throughout the night, had certainly not been there to hear anything. A proper gent, he had merely looked in on her. Same side, weren't they? Just a few drinks too many, that was all. It happened. Ruddy nice of him to get her off the streets, where drunken men prowled, and into a safe house. He knew how to treat a lady, alright. She thought of Hamilton, who had ditched her early, who had dumped her on de Beck. The Commander's dark secrets, as far as she was concerned, were still in the dark; as safe as if they had never been uttered. Valerie jumped! She had heard something:

You will not remember this night...

"How's that?" Sinclair rasped. Voice in her head now, was it? She could taste the retch of the whisky—no wonder!

She walked into the bathroom and pulled off her clothes. She was looking a fright, she was. What a pot of porridge! Here she could have had her dibs at the Dance, and she had to take up with a Yank who was old enough to be her father! Was it *him* then, had protected her like a daughter? If it was protection she wanted, she wouldn't be looking to the Americans for it! No, what she had looked for was love. What she had hoped for, was his. A loud knocking came on the door. "Smythe! Up?" It was the morning Security round.

"Present, sir!" Valerie piped from the bathroom.

The Spy had saved her from guilt.

What had yet to be answered was why.

III

Winston Churchill from Chartwell Manor, near Westerham in Kent, was on his favorite telephone, the old-fashioned stand type, fire-engine red, and he was talking with Lord Louis Mountbatten, Supreme Commander, Asia. Theoretically equal in status to Eisenhower, though militarily one notch below, and affectionately nick-named "Supremo" by Churchill, Lord Louis, at the moment, seemed to be just the right man for the job. In England, where Friday's sun was breaking for the weekend, this last day of June could prove the first day of hope. Black onyx egg cup matching Malaysian serving plates of solid gold sat forgotten; both men had finished eating. But it was Mountbatten who'd been interrupted. The Prime Minister did not have a great deal of time. He was leaving on an American Dakota to fly to Cherbourg, where he planned to spend several days determining the delivery facilities of the Mulberry Harbor. Reports would have him there a month later as well. The public, of course, did not know of either schedule "—and how is Lady Edwina? Over the beastly grippe? Appetite, good?" Breakfast there was dinner here. Mountbatten checked his watch: Ceylon was eleven hours ahead of London.

"Completely recovered, thank you."

Lord Louis stared at the pouring rain battering the wooden trailings of his favorite pagoda across the courtyards. Beyond, fields of sweet bamboo rose in green tufts to the invisible ridge, fluted with rainbow and rich in the afternoon from beams of the equatorial sun. High in the mountains of Peredynia, newly headquartered in the King's Pavilion, Kandy was as good as it got. Convenient to Trincomalee, the Fleet's main base, Ceylon was Mountbatten's favorite place to be. The rain was to be expected, the humidity not all that bad, what with the prevailing winds. But did the Prime Minister really want to know?

British banter.

Churchill laughed, and lit a cigar. "Suppose we make it 'Weather Directive,'" the man wearing the tugboat captain's hat said, leading Mountbatten. "I've just been on the ringer to Eisenhower. The cat may be out of the bag. He tells me that GOLDILOCKS—he doesn't know the code name, of course—is not as popular with him these days as Creasy's *Fifteen Decisive Battles*. You see my meaning, I'm sure."

"He knows about the Waterfall mission?"

Mountbatten was good at putting things bluntly. MI.5, who was supposed to ensure that telephone calls like this didn't happen, had no compunction in having pulled a fast one on Eisenhower. Transferring the General's Weather Directive to the R.A.F. had been necessary to guarantee their part of the mission. Lord Louis, the fastest planes in the world at his disposal, personally planned to be in England before Sunday, Edwina and Bridley in tow. Having relaxed in the confidence that all was secured, here was his political boss calling him up to say that security had been breached.

"It's De Gaulle, I think," Lord Louis heard him say. "The girl herself seems to be clean. No way *she* can bolt, of course. She signed for it, under pain of death." True, the girl was a new experiment, but was she a link already locked? What about the other links? Inconsistency had been noted in the Baker Street Irregulars. Their action was in the back rooms, the most likely place for duplicity of loyalties. Mountbatten could sense it: in England, something had gone wrong.

"The best defense may be disclosure."

Had Mountbatten missed something?

Churchill continued. "Seems that someone may be mucking

about in our porridge. David reported an outside surveillance, fellow in a trench coat, following the girl. Herbert Marshall type, I'd say, from the Report." The Prime Minister had classified his own right hand man, Sir William Stephenson, that way. "Girl claims she couldn't see his face. Could be somebody who knows what he's doing. Since we got her in a deal, someone may be trying to extract extra credit before Sunday's launch makes it irrevocable. Can't think of who, though, except—?"

"Free French?" Lord Louis offered. "Could be LeClerc."

"Well, let's not point fingers," said the caller, who had just jabbed the air with his own. Mountbatten could sense it, the black Havana. "If we hope to lock in with the Underground, there are things we will just have to put up with."

"Yes? For example?"

"For one, to get her in, we will have to go with the Frenchman. The entire working information, intact in her *memory*, is what we'll need to look at. We *are* in accord there, are we not?"

"Absolutely."

"Splendid! Then she is still our best shot. Personal motivation is what we're gambling on this time. You might give some thought to having one of your people call her on the Code Override, just before the mission. Means a lot you see, to one of these shop girls, to hear from her government personally. Much like you or I getting a call from His Majesty, I would imagine."

"Yes," said Mountbatten, enjoying the dig, "I would certainly imagine that you would."

The Prime Minister grinned, he did it with his bottom lip. "Just so we understand each other, Louis."

"That we do," Mountbatten admitted. "Now, about the Code Override. Is that—?"

"Yes," said Winston Churchill.

The Code Override, the ultimate device for aborting this mission, was in four parts, arranged so that any caller holding one part, would have to disclose it to the officer he was calling, in exchange for disclosure of the next completing part. Each call following would be verified by the one preceding it. Thus, to override Hamilton's Security at The Red Lion, preset by MI.5, four keys would have to cojoin to fit one lock, forming the Overriding Code. Each of the four designees had been issued one of the four parts. The Royal Navy, however, controlled three of them, including the one for the turnkey. Able to block the sequence in either direction, they had made it mathematically impossible for anyone on Eisenhower's staff to obtain the completed Override. From the British view, the value of mathematical reality was the value of the men who could make it work. Accessed to MISSIONS, Ike had been excluded from this one.

Created for Churchill by Alan Turing, it was the ultimate insurance policy: serving to tighten the net around Sinclair while protecting the identity of the caller, and keeping the Americans at bay. With the Southampton office holding one of the parts, it would be Hamilton's job to make sure that she received the call and that she kept it confidential. At the same time, any knowledge of its source should be kept from his own Operatives. For the Commander's sake, Mountbatten suggested, Hamilton's Security Team should be apprised that she had been called, after the fact, of course; and that the call was unprecedented.

Credit to Churchill.

"David Hamilton has worked damned hard for us," Mountbatten said. "I should think it's the very least we could do for him."

"GOLDILOCKS is not just any mission," the Prime Minister reminded him. "Best that one hand not tell the other." If the girl were to hear from them, Mountbatten would decide.

"Anyone in mind?"

"Why, yes," Mountbatten said, "it's Bridley, I'm thinking of. He's about as personable as they come, and would leave just the right impression with the girl. He certainly has Edwina eating out of his hand. She insists on calling him James, you know."

"Yes, of course, one has to call them *something*," Churchill shot back. He was thinking of Turing. Sarah brought him small bits of gossip now and then, like unexpected lumps of sugar, dropped into his tea. Clementine, too, had taken an interest. Relegated increasingly alone by war and its demands upon their men, or busy knitting socks, the ladies wanted to talk, and were demanding someone to talk to.

"Bother and drat!" Churchill put it.

Mountbatten, half a world away, agreed. Bridley, The Boffin—

filling voids as mysterious as his own comings and goings, his Blackmail List, if not his heart, an open book for thirsty wives— proved an unexpected windfall for the husbands. Wives and daughters, when not in the services, in hospitals, or on bond-raising platforms, retreated into their own parlors, eager for news of the "child spy," being a female like themselves. Excluded from the purposes of the mission, they had become anxious in recent weeks to know if Valerie Sinclair were being well-treated. It was Bridley, of course, who assured them that she was.

"Listen to this," Churchill said. He had just finished reading Blackstone's Report containing David Hamilton's *Review of the Girl*, an assessment he was looking forward to sharing with Clementine. The fact that it was important to the Prime Minister brought Mountbatten's seasoned attention back to the specter of an outside interest. They discussed the press, centering on CBS and Paley. The American correspondents had treated Winston Churchill like royalty; Mountbatten, like a regular guy. Murrow and Seldes, for starters, might have a beef with Bletchley, or Blackstone perhaps; but their devotion to the British struggle was beyond dispute.

"I understand, Winnie, but where there is smoke—"

"—there is usually," Churchill chimed, "a really good cigar. No, Louis, put it out of mind. Otherwise, next thing thing you know, one of our more enterprising writers will be describing you as paranoid."

Mountbatten blinked.

Hanging onto a previous statement, and getting an unfamiliar picture, Lord Louis was thinking quickly. Of course, the Prime Minister didn't *say* that GOLDILOCKS was being monitored by an outside Operative, known to Churchill but not to himself, which would have been an affront to their relationship. He merely said that the mission wasn't as tight as it could be: it seemed to have widened. Their chances of pulling it off, for which he was sticking his neck out, were predicated on keeping it contained. Mountbatten would not relish any change in plan, were he not first consulted as to its direction. The inferred outside Operative, the fellow in the trench coat, didn't register as a Gestapo profile. Hamilton would have said so: Winston would have known. The fact that they did not was troubling. Mountbatten frowned. Ike had called Churchill, not the other way around. It was looking like a narrow field. Could it be somebody on the inside talking?

Bridley?

But Bridley was here. Here, in Kandy, was he not? Of course he was! Lord Louis liked having him around. He was such a comfort to Edwina, especially when they traveled. His thoughts darkened. Trench coat, be damned! If counterespionage, which Bridley should have foreseen, had arisen in his absence, then...?

It could be anyone!

Thunder boomed, shaking glass. The clouds opened, making a racket; it was on the palace roof. Something inexplicable had entered on their phone line. Not being tapped, were they? Wouldn't be Eisenhower, would it? Lord Louis listened.

Vibration of some sort...

Sounded like a ship's bell. Mountbatten banged his receiver. No problem. All was right on the line. Both men were back on it.

"You still there, are you?"

Mountbatten said that he was. *A weather phenomenon...* So! The P.M. had them protected.

"Work it out in England," its Prime Minister was saying. "You do your part, we will complete ours, the mission will go off as planned. I sense worry, try to relax. What time may we expect you?"

Lord Louis told him.

The rain was louder. "I suspect David may have had enormous problems with Blackstone over his choice, for the girl." Both men agreed. "He liked the other one, the Frenchman, though."

"Hamilton's department," pointed out the Navy man. He was thinking of Eisenhower...an unwelcome hand, tapping him on the shoulder. From the first mention of him, since that interruption, the clock seemed to have jumped. He would be anxious to get home, quartered at Beaulieu Abbey. "David Hamilton, you see, does what he does best. It's unfortunate though that Dwight..."

"Found out?"

About his Weather Directive?

Mountbatten said: "I don't see how he could. If you would like me to..."

Yes, he would like him to: That is why he'd called.

"Well, Supremo, what are you going to tell him?"

"That would depend on how nice he is, wouldn't you think?" Churchill hadn't missed a beat. Four hundred years of Windsors were in the tone.

Cigar smoke billowed, touching the thick leaves of books. "Precisely. Between us, and GOLDILOCKS, is where one finds the paradigm, the *conscience* of the war. I wouldn't call it negotiable, would you? Of course not! It is *our* neck, not De Gaulle's, not Eisenhower's!" Winston Churchill had no love for the French.

An American intrusion, either.

Mountbatten said it: one did not throw the Empire out, to throw an American in. De Gaulle's position, on the other hand, was that of the man in the dark. In the Royal Navy's production of Punch-and-Judy, the French clown entered last.

Churchill had made an exception: Hamilton's department, SOE. He might have to jiggle things a bit, rearrange their portmanteau, as it were, to insure a proper fit. Should it come to that, SOE's inflexibility, *fifteen previous failed missions*, could be traced directly to the Chief French Occupant of the green Rolls Royce. The Prime Minister, rummaging through his pantry of political savoir-faire, would come up with just the right bone to toss to the French.

"I understand," Lord Louis assured him, removing Hamilton from his Blackmail List. In times of crisis, there could be no Middle; the Middle, personified by Hamilton, had just disappeared into the Top.

As they talked, Mountbatten distant, Commodore Blackstone kept coming to mind. If Blackstone saw Mountbatten as competition, so much the better. For a man to serve as a goat, he should begin to smell like one. One mentioned it, the other answered. Churchill flicked his ash. "Aye?"

"Thinking," Mountbatten said.

Aware that Blackstone's office had conveniently, and stupidly, branded Eisenhower as England's Number One Security Threat, an attempt to make something of Ike's alleged affair with his personal driver, Kay Summersby, Mountbatten of Burma, sensing an alternative motive, was listening intently.

The insult to Eisenhower threatened like a parang.

Churchill was pressing. Whoever got nailed in the Middle,

it was not going to be Winston. The words from the Prime Minister were coming slowly, intentionally: an intermixture of courtly references with soft courtesies. *The velvet glove.* Behind the oatmeal words, stood a man of impenetrable steel.

"Are we in accord, Louis?"

"By God, yes," Mountbatten said.

Ike's Packard, the Irish girl installed at the wheel, could not be the issue now. Perhaps the Baker Street Irregulars, Bridley taking the heat, if necessary, could quite simply just back off. Meanwhile, the Prime Minister, one eye peeled for emergent justice, was having the entire mission closely monitored, including any sudden change in Valerie Sinclair. They would scrap her, if it came to that. It wouldn't, of course. Important Mountbatten fly back at once. "You have seen worse, Louis." Memories arose; he had put them away—explosions, the tilting deck of a destroyer.

Corsica. He had known fear.

Lord Louis agreed.

Churchill, making the point, made it without smiling. While they must have the atomic information, it simply could not be had by splitting the Allies. The Prime Minister was making it clear to Mountbatten that the wheels of the gods, grinding slowly, were running out of men to grind. Lord Louis, obligingly, was thinking of candidates. Presuming Whitehall would be able to position General De Gaulle, it would be Mountbatten's responsibility to find an honorable exoneration, after the mission of course, for key links in his chain-of-command. He remembered Grimes, easy that one, sought by Hamilton as a hedge against Parker. He was the one who'd had him transferred. Snatched from under Blackstone's nose, he would make sure that Hamilton's personal spy was quartered at Beaulieu. If Blackstone got wind, however, it would be Hamilton who would bite the bullet. "I will vouch for the integrity of my Staff," Mountbatten reminded his caller. As head of the Commandos, Royal Marines were for the using.

Quite dependable, actually: British, at least.

England's undisputed leader, who had called to determine the cast, was rising word by word above the cause of his own intrigue: as peachy clean, Lord Louis concluded, as a baby's bottom. The Prime Minister's exhortation of "blood, toil, tears and sweat," was either efficiently understated, or generously overwhelming, depending on whose blood he had in mind. His message to the Commodore was as logical as two Aces over a Jack: Eisenhower's oxfords were *not* the toes that they could afford to step on. Plenty of chaps yet, untapped for suspicion. There, but for the grace of God, would go somebody else. Accepting reality as a valid excuse, Churchill was writing their new axiom. It was life at the Bottom, at the Top.

Club talk: new cards, please.

"I cannot tell you how much I appreciate your making that clear," Lord Louis acknowledged, "you had me worried there for a moment."

"Understandable," said Churchill.

After due deliberation then, accomplished in a flash, the Prime Minister was prepared to hand mission responsibility back to Mountbatten: correct it, he was saying. When Mountbatten started to object, some matter about his word to Blackstone, the P.M. rose to the occasion. For such an early hour in the morning, it was his finest. "I do not ask of history that you will have justified your allegiance to England by discretion at the proper time—I *demand* it."

Lord Louis had heard clearly: *I do not ask of history...I demand it.* At least he knew to whom he was talking; he began to consider whom he would call.

Churchill again: "David is certain that she holds the key, and that she will surface satisfactorily from the mission. When she does, you won't be wanting any loose ends. Submarine's on Sunday, I understand. Hamilton has also assured me that she can't be made to talk—absolutely topping girl! Safe as the Bank of England!"

A shareholder, Mountbatten winced.

That was not the issue. Lord Louis knew that Eisenhower had his own counterintelligence sources. If smarting over criticism of Kay Summersby, the Supreme Commander would not hesitate to use them. "Well, we'll have to see what we can do about it, won't we?"

"Glad to hear it," announced Churchill.

"She drives for him." Mountbatten pointed out.

That Windsor voice again. "Morality and *bosh!*" boomed the Prime Minister. "Must this entire bloody war end up in the foul waters of rumor!" The rumors were true. It was what their American Commander might do, that bothered them.

Mountbatten put it flatly: "We have to launch GOLDI-LOCKS as scheduled." It was the opinion of his men. In the respect of those men, rested the honor of England. People like Eisenhower had come, but they would leave again. "Couldn't we just explain it to him later? Surely, the interest of the Commonwealth...!"

"No! You make your peace with Ike. You make that peace now. Grab it by the horns, sir! Decisions must not be set adrift." The caller slipped the cigar from his mouth, and snuffed it. "I do not consider it politic, with Bradley's present crisis, to have this come up later. With this new technology—pointing towards us out of hell!—it would be importune to extend an opportunity for others to level false charges against us, however ill-advised, that our interest in a major German breakthrough in physics is anything other than our own survival. Motives of self-aggrandisement, to the benefit of our Financial District, must never—never, sir!—find any safe harbor in our recorded histories, now being written!"

"But we're *paying* for it!" Mountbatten shot back.

"Exactly, sir! And should events prove that we are entitled to any rewards that may arise as the consequence of nuclear peacetime use, then that will be time enough to clearly state, and for others to understand, how very dear that price will have been!"

In the background, bankers reared like ghosts.

"Finders keepers?" Lord Louis coughed, so as not to grin.

"There, you see it? You have the picture faster than imagined. As you know, I was never in favor of this nuclear type of weaponry to begin with, but since we have had to attend to it or perish, we intend to *keep* what we buy—with our blood, on our beaches, and in the backwaters of Europe."

Heavy water, heavy price.

In the Lewis Carroll coloring book, Dunkirk would not be colored black. They both knew the mission to be a winner. It was the losers, still essential, who might have to be accommodated. Later, words would match print, called history. At the moment, they were editing.

"John Blackstone doing well, is he?" Mountbatten inquired.

"About as well as Gladstone," purred Churchill, speaking for Lord Randolph. The Prime Minister's American mother, fond of Victorian mansions, had never cared much for amber waves of grain. Though the Code Center's doors out at Bletchley had opened to American analysts six months ago, no Americans were currently in residence, nor any French either.

"This ultimate weapon then," said Mountbatten, "is destined for responsible hands?" It was not a question, it was a vote. Churchill nodded, he said, "yes," but he wasn't through. Mountbatten felt it, approaching yet invisible, the way he sensed ships on a shoal. At forty-four, his watch with the Prime Minister nearly ended, he had come to the dawn of his life. Over Peredynia, the rain had stopped and the sun was sinking. In England, it was just rising.

It was the future, shaped like a mushroom cloud.

"If, ultimately, our decision is to let the Americans have it—along with the advance judgment of the world—we will live with that also."

Lord Louis: "Are you saying then, you would have me steer Eisenhower left rudder? Sometime after Sunday, I presume."

"Too late for that. No, we need to attend to it now. I will be talking to Monty, later today. Bit of a strain between himself and Ike, you know." A gifted understatement, it would have been lost on Bradley. Mountbatten nodded. To preserve the contents of the German labs, a few British army movements, under the direction of Montgomery, might have to be changed. Whitehall, not to be caught napping, had quietly provided for it. "Nothing set in stone, you understand."

Mountbatten could see it. He said, "Of course."

"The Boffins are already on top of it. Little touchy for Monty, but I think he'll go along. Eisenhower's law office is where it may get sticky—" static on the line, "—bloke named Bernstein. I'll send you the whole report. Once we get her away from the possibility of Eisenhower's *lawyer*—" news, for Mountbatten, "—and safely en route, we should be able to put a whole new face on it."

"Matter of hours," Lord Louis pointed out.

The less spread, the better. Mountbatten's job, now defined, was to pull the string on Bull Durham—he had once seen Eisenhower in a pair of cowboy boots—and to close off criticism while insuring that Sunday night's launch proceeded smoothly. Lord Louis said, rather softly Churchill thought, "I will straighten it all out."

Mountbatten had a curious way of tacking—sometimes into trouble. This time, neither man could afford it. "Ike must not be compromised," the P.M. repeated. "Do you have that?"

"Certainly."

"Excellent! Well then! I expect you'll do your best, Louis," Churchill beamed. The red telephone was heading for its cradle. "That's what the Crown pays you to do."

Mountbatten took it on the chin.

The Prime Minister hung up.

Footsteps were approaching....

Commander Hamilton listened. It was through the spindle of rock. Crunching carefully on gravel, the footsteps stopped. The approacher was bending over, photographing a bug. The telephone number of Sergeant Blumensteel's barracks still written on the inside of her thigh, Valerie Sinclair appeared in the entrance to the cave. Above the wild cliffs, the morning sun had just broken through. De Beck, nursing a headache, showed up a few moments later.

"Now, the most important thing when you arrive in France," said Hamilton, having begun the briefing, "is to act completely natural." He looked at Sinclair, who was blinking at the walls. "Remember, the people you'll encounter will have no knowledge of why you are there. You will be issued French identification cards, identical to those approved by the Gestapo, and French francs, most of them to Pierre. As a student, Valerie, you would not be carrying much money, you see."

"Cameras...no?" Pierre was scraping guano off his boots.

"No. No minicameras or microfilm." Any mechanical aids would be carried by the child, hidden in child things. "And no guns. The plans are simple. Their very simplicity, we feel, is your safeguard. In the unlikely event that you are suspected and searched—"

She was staring at the walls. They were wet, and oozing dark liquids. Blinking her eyelids, she took a picture of them.

"—just act French." She hadn't missed a beat.

He waited. Neither of the spies reacted.

"Right. Well now, Pierre, any information you feel *you* may have difficulty in remembering must be written in code, and placed in the heels of your boots...your French boots, you see? The code will be based on your directives issued at Castor. You've already received the ciphers."

Valerie raised an eyebrow.

Pierre yawned.

"You see, Sinclair, Pierre does not have your advantage, your photographic memory—"

"That's not *his* fault, Commander." She was trying to make up, for last night. "I'm sure he has other abilities that are just as important."

Photographic memory?

Pierre snapped awake! He had not known that about her! It would be covered at his final briefing.

"Your knowledge of yourselves is knowledge of each other," Hamilton continued, throwing the Frenchman a glance. "I won't be there to help you. That's why we're having this little get-together. Come over here, the two of you." The Commander got up.

They approached, and stood together.

"Pierre has persistence, and fluency in languages. As I told you, Lieutenant, we were both on the Dieppe raid in 1942, although with different units, and he was at Dunkirk. Before that, in France, he fought for his life against German oppression. He is well able to defend himself and you too, Valerie, I assure you. Most importantly, he has had experience in killing."

"Thank you, sir."

"Sinclair, you received your Operative's training when you joined Naval Intelligence, and you were the best in your class." That was for Pierre. "Enemy lines, however, are quite another matter. If you have to kill, you will have to kill with what you have. As for your remarkable memory—no thanks to the Navy, what?—well, sir, you were born with it."

"Sir? thank you, sir."

"Yes, well...Pierre? Your memory, old chap, is of a different order: Dunkirk and Dieppe. We expect this partnership to be formidable. Singly and together, you should both present a decent accounting of yourselves. Are there any questions?"

"I..."

"Yes, Valerie?"

"Suppose neither of us makes it. What would happen to..."

England?

Hamilton interrupted. De Beck present, her question was inappropriate.

"Good thinking, Sinclair." It was as if he could feel chains. "Remember Achnacarry: 'Selfconfidence is the backbone of courage!' Well then, that covers it, I would think, but there may yet be something."

Seymour was right, she could be unpredictable.

In MI.5's plan to shape Sinclair into the persona which had survived the French girl's corpse, Blackstone was leaving the enforcement to Hamilton. Pierre was French as was Valerie Marchaud. Stripped of their military skins, in France there should be nothing for the Germans to spot. The British had come up with a weapon for which the Nazis could not possibly have imagined a defense: a French girl who was a dead girl who was a camera that didn't exist. Her partner was Pierre de Beck. Running a tight ship, David Hamilton would steer them through the shoals, each with separate instructions.

He would have to talk with her privately.

"The plan seems very straightforward, Commander," said the girl. "The fact that Pierre's parents live near where we're going ashore is a great point in our favor. Supposing we had to try to find out where the French Underground was operating, with no help at all once we were there?"

Pierre finished it for her. "We would find ourselves in a cauldron of stew." He turned to the Commander. "Dieppe, sir."

It was on his agenda.

"Thank you, Pierre. Listen up, Sinclair. At our last briefing prior to the Dieppe raid—remember? I told you at Achnacarry—the entire operation was thoroughly explained: where we would land, our objectives, how we would return, et cetera. The raid was rehearsed eight times and yet, it was a bloody holocaust. It is obvious, you see, that our security was penetrated," he paused, "by a German Operative. A bit too coincidental, don't you know, that maximal forces should have been waiting for us. We do not want that to happen this time."

"Not a chance," murmured the Frenchman.

"Now I cannot impress this on you enough: do *not* be overconfident. Make your moves with extreme caution and do not, whatever you do, cause any suspicion. Consider what I have said carefully, and ask whatever questions you think necessary." Valerie could sense it; her question had breached security. The Commander had cut her off. "Pierre, are you sure you have nothing to add?"

"I do not think you have overlooked anything, sir," replied the Frenchman.

"Very well then," said Hamilton. "Tomorrow we will go to the motion picture studios at Elstree. They have French people there who are experts on clothes and cosmetics. They are also members of British Intelligence." This wasn't quite true: MI.5 insured their jobs. "Take the early train, Sinclair. I want you at Waterloo Station by 1200 hours. Pierre, see to the Rolls, will you, and you'll join us for Elstree."

De Beck nodded.

"Good. I can now tell you when. On Sunday night, you will meet me at the Polperro marina at 2100 hours. You should have no difficulty in locating me. Look for the motor launch." Anxious to leave, the Frenchman was dusting off his trousers. "Clothes, shoes, and supplies will be issued aboard the submarine, along with the necessary identification papers. As for the remaining part of today, you may spend it at leisure—"

Valerie smiled.

"—other than code and rowing practice for you, Pierre."

De Beck's own smile fell, then brightened. There would be parties in London. Saturday evening, too.

"Lieutenant Sinclair?"

"Sir?"

"I want you to write two letters—to your family and your son—which you must hand to me tomorrow. They are just for the record, to be posted if you do not return."

Valerie longed for fresh air: the bird-reek was getting to her.

"Tell them you have arrived in Southampton, and that you are finding the new training...interesting, just as you would, you see, had this been the case." The Commander studied the shadowy walls of the cave, then brushed a tiny white feather from his sleeve. "'A feather found is like Cupid's compass, pointing ever to love,'" Hamilton revealed abruptly. "That, gentlemen, for whatever it is worth, comes straight from Emily

Blackstone, your Commodore's wife." She had slipped him wise sayings, from time to time, to use with his agents. A postscript from the gods, the Commander hoped it would give them something to think about. The tiny feather fluttered to the floor. "Hmmm. Birds made quite a mess in here."

"Sorry, sir!"

"It's nothing, Sinclair. So, there you have it! Stay sober"— he raised an eyebrow—"and stay alert." They would return separately to the hotel. "And not a word of this to anyone, Lieutenant. Do you understand?"

"Yes, sir. I do now, sir."

"Good show." The Commander checked his watch. "Let's pack it in then, shall we?" The two men walked out into the sunshine. Valerie watched them leave.

Pierre stopped, he examined his boots. He did not like birds, knowing they carried lice. "Commander, back there" he jerked his thumb, "what kind of birds?"

"What kind?"

Valerie came dashing out of the cave, she was holding a feather. The Navy man placed his hand affectionately on the French Captain's shoulder. He winked.

"Shitty ones, old boy."

"Go ahead," said Eisenhower.

Lord Louis Mountbatten grabbed Bull Durham by the horns. "Delighted, yes...well! Indeed a pleasure to speak with you. It's about this morning's call from our *Boss*, you see—"

"Yours, or mine?"

"—asked me to clear up a few things for you. Seems there may have been some misunderstanding."

Eisenhower waited. "I don't think so," he said. "It's about the Weather Secretive, isn't it?" Churchill had filled him in, his phone was still warm. "Care to tell me the *real* reason...for conning me out of it?"

The Con, steerage of a ship.

"Come now! A bit harsh on each other, aren't we?" A Royal Navy man, Lord Louis disliked the American usage. "The entire matter can be explained, I assure you. You know about the mission, then, I presume?"

"I know about *a* mission, if that's what you mean. I also

know you needed our Weather Command to pull it off, and it looks to me like you really didn't care how you got it."

"I see...."

In previous meetings, and in friendlier days, he had noted Ike's voice to be similar to that of Clark Gable. When it came to brawls in a Klondike saloon, Englishmen usually didn't fare too well.

"That your view, is it?" Mountbatten loosened his tie. He could hear it, thunder was rumbling. "Would you feel better if I disclosed the entire matter to you, after the fact?"

"After *what* fact?"

Mountbatten, smiling through it, said: "I have an idea. Let's start at the beginning, shall we?"

Two days ago, Eisenhower, quartered at Southwick, had turned the Allied Weather Command back over to the British. The meeting, in secret and curiously called, had been with Air Marshal Tedder, a close advisor, valuable to him in his difficult dealings with Montgomery. Ike recalled it; something odd in his manner—too much urgency when Whitehall's man had handed him the pen. Still, Art Tedder's logic had made sense: the R.A.F. would work better with its own suppliers.

By the next night, doubt had entered.

Ike had called Churchill. At Churchill's request, Ike had just agreed to meet with Tedder again, this afternoon at Portsmouth. "Teddy will work it out," the P.M. had suggested. Now, here was Mountbatten, all smiles and a mile wide, live on the line and trying to hogwash him.

"Okay," Ike said. "Let's take it from the top. What's the code name of the mission?"

"I can't tell you that."

Ike, in England, raised an eyebrow: "Wait a minute, what are you telling me? Something special?"

"Special? To British interests, yes." The American Command was not in position to have MI.5's access to the facts.

From Ike's perspective, the cards on the other end did not appear to be the regular ones; more, Lord Louis seemed bothered by them. If a weak hand, he should try to get it on the table.

Mountbatten had called....

"Well, as far as *I* know," Dwight Eisenhower said, "I'm supposed to be in charge here. Since you're using the Armed Forces

Weather Command to cover up the mission you don't want to talk about, why don't we start by your telling me exactly what kind of mission it *is*, that's so god-awful important?"

"I would if I could, old boy, but I can't, you see? It's...something different, is all I can tell you."

"'Something different'? Look, I think it might be a good idea if you simply leveled with me. If you're counting on me to go along with somebody's colossal screw-up—" what else *could* it be? "—that *is* what you're counting on, isn't it? For me to understand your position, to work with you to straighten it out. That right?"

"Not right." How much did he know? "The Prime Minister, indeed, is very concerned about all this—" Did he know about the girl? "—but I'm afraid it's too late now for us to do much about it."

"Meaning, I take it, that you think it's none of my business." After the signing on Wednesday, Tedder had met with Montgomery. "Tell me," Ike said, "is this some deal between you and Montgomery?"

"Monty?"

"Monty. Because, if it is and I can find out"—this afternoon's meeting—"you can kiss it good-bye!"

"Here now, Dwight, don't be ridiculous!" Manners, man! "You know bloody well that we wouldn't..."

"...wouldn't what?"

Ordered to nudge Eisenhower into safe harbor, the Commodore was finding the decks awash; he had tacked into rough seas. "As I was saying"—veering into the American wind—"or rather, *trying* to say, right?" Mountbatten laughed; he was good-natured about it.

Ike could have liked him; there had been times. That all-night party last year with "Pug" Ismay, before the Roosevelt–Churchill meeting at Casablanca...

"Go on."

"Fifteen previous missions," Mountbatten said, "all with SOE, all with female agents, and you were the very first, outside of ourselves, to get a full report—"

In a lesser man, the voice would have carried censure.

"Yep. Thanks a million."

"And?"

"I read them. I also know you stopped sending them after what happened to the Gladstone girl—" He had the dossiers in front of him. Bernstein had got them. "—six months ago, wasn't it? And now you've got a new one?"

"Well, perhaps." Lord Louis, at any cost, intended to protect her. His voice, coming through loud, now fading, *vibration on the line.* "You've brought in an outside Operative. Civilian, isn't he? Your man in the trench coat? I can't very well see how you could know about her, though—"

Ike grinned. "You'd be surprised what I know."

What the hell was he talking about?

Both men stopped; they were listening.

A third ear...it had taken over the phones, working faster than the eye could follow...pulling wires and rearranging circuits: magnetic current breathing curious from where another's interest was running parallel—each man thinking it the other.

Something had entered...

Ike was hearing it—against a Kansas skyline, the creaking of the wagons. Mountbatten pausing, didn't Ike hear it?—spilling over into the sea swell...the ghostly sound of a Corsican bell...trailing away now...into the wake of remembered time.

"You there?" Ike said.

Mountbatten stared at the phone: it was in his ears, the cloy of accusation. Ike tapped his receiver a few times, it seemed to have passed. Couldn't possibly have been a tap, could it? *No.* Locked and secured downline, that possibility didn't exist. Weather condition, from Ceylon probably. "Anybody on the damn line?"

"Hope so," Mountbatten said, both voices clear. He had seen a picture, or thought he had, during the static. It was the man in the trench coat; face not remembered, in the black sky below marble stairwells; the day of blue rain streaming across Peredynia. He had sensed it, during the lull.

Eisenhower knew about the girl!

"Getting back," voice in England was saying, "I think I would like some answers."

Looking in on GOLDILOCKS, and searching for bears, what else had the faceless Informant told him? Could The Spy not be leading both sides into a goose chase?

"Yes, I suppose that you would. It isn't as though we've been going ahead, you see, trying to hide something from you. Were that the case, it should have been clear to you that—"

"Bullshit!"

That was clear enough.

Mountbatten said: "I am not at all sure this is getting us anywhere, so why not have a go at it this way...?" Ike listened. "To begin with, I must say that I can vouch personally for the morality of this mission. Since it is my mission, you see, I stand personally responsible for it. Now, I readily admit that you were excluded. Moreover, I think it fair to tell you that you can probably count on that continuing to be the case, at least until after Sunday night."

Ike made a note. He would be in Normandy. Mountbatten must have known. British Commanders had petitioned to change Army movements. Review had become necessary to reinstate American policy. Leaving tomorrow, spending the fourth with Bradley's First Army, Ike would return on Tuesday night.

"For the moment," Lord Louis said, "all I can say is that the real reason for this mission, to use your words, exists precisely in the fact that it *is* based in national self interest, the autonomous self interest of the Commonwealth, and that I cannot, and will not, divulge anything more than you already know, because you see, to *do* so would be to betray my own principles, as a man."

"I understand that."

"Well then! I cannot tell you how pleased I am to hear it!" Mountbatten could relax. Churchill congratulated him; it was over his shoulder. He was smiling:

Buddha's voice, in the rain.

"—should this prove to be the breach of trust it *appears* to be," he was suddenly hearing, Bull Durham rearing from the ring, "then I think your 'national self-interest' may have to go by the board. Anything this important that's done behind our back, my friend, does *not* support its own morality!"

Mountbatten switched on his desk fan: he needed air.

The Waterfall project was not being mentioned. Tightly protected in the most inaccessible reaches of British Naval Intelligence, it could not even be imagined. From Mountbatten's point of view, indeed, from Churchill's, the logic was simple....

It did not exist.

"See here," Lord Louis said, "I have told you all I can."

"Which is *zilch*." Eyes sweeping the desk, Ike spotted the pack of Raleighs. Left by his Orderly, Colonel Tex Lee, he felt like smoking one. Tapping it out, he coughed: it was the weather. Wiping his mouth, the General continued, "Something's fishier than *hell*."

"Oh? Really?"

Lighter clicked. "Yes. *Really*. While I do not purport to speak for Tom, Dick, and Harry, I *do* speak for Kilroy"—G.I. Joe, soon to be on half the walls in France—"for Bradley, for Collins, and for the policies of President Roosevelt, who—"

"Good luck to him."

"*Listen!*" Ike was pissed. "I think I've lived long enough to know that nondisclosure by one of our Allies"—De Gaulle, for one, to whom FDR was allergic; Mountbatten, not much higher on the list—"could certainly be viewed by our government as a cause for real alarm." His hands, scarred forever from his boyhood, from pulling Kansas wheat, were full with the war. Against its callousness, he saw the specter of the military-industrial complex, curling into his future like a snake, turning to confront him. In the race for post-war positions, the Soviets up shit creek, the American thought he might know: a grab for power, suddenly explaining the parts. And what Ike was hearing, he didn't like.

"That's right. I don't like it."

Mountbatten looked at his cards, his hand had not changed. He wouldn't mind: Ike could like it less. Whitehall, barred by FDR from the Manhattan Project, had not forgiven him for the slight. Now, to complete their project, the Oppenheimer Group had begun to voice their need for more reliable data. From any source, at any price.

Meaning Germany.

If the American investigation, which this call was meant to contain, could be kept in the dark for a few more days, presuming the mission would launch on Sunday night, deliverance would come from the information relayed by Valerie Sinclair; revealing the locations of all the German nuclear projects in Occupied territory. Montgomery's armies would take care of the rest of it, reaching the secrets first, especially, the Waterfall. World parity for the British Empire was certain to follow from Whitehall's seventeen Merchant Bankers, nucleus of the London Financial District; from its Royal Navy scenario; and from its MI.5 cover.

Except—!

It would not be the Oppenheimer Group who would get it!

Mountbatten, returning to brass tacks, got down to them. "—strictly an in house struggle between us and Special Operations Executive. You know how SOE is. Worse than a bloody woman! Sore, wouldn't you know, because they feel they have not been properly acknowledged. See now, last month, that mess we had with De Gaulle. A few weeks, that's all. We'll get the entire matter straightened out with him, and have it Johnny on your desk. We seem to have had a bit of a misunderstanding, you see."

Kay, he meant. Telegraph Cottage, was where.

"Nice try. Is that how you cooked it up, out at MI.5?"

Bloody Blackstone!

Sighing deeply, Mountbatten pushed it forward: it was a gambling chip. "About the mission, Dwight, be a good chap with me now and let's put it to rest, shall we? The Prime Minister, himself, is of the opinion—"

Ike looked on his console. "Who do you think you are talking to?" He pressed a button.

So much for the Prime Minister.

With Eisenhower collecting, he would have to buy time. Mountbatten's best credit was himself. A frustrated Windsor, he answered as one: "This mission, not launched, yet one in which we seem to find ourselves being judged, as though after the fact, is not the issue. There is just the one issue, you see: whatever brings the war to a close. I therefore ask that you give serious consideration, as we have, to the possibility that such a decision on our part, admittedly at risk, be looked at in the light of responsible motivation, and by that I mean, in our hopes for an early peace!"

"What *is* this…a private war?" An orderly entered, Ike motioned for coffee.

"Come, man! We are not talking breach of faith here. Merely a few weeks, as I have told you—" Logic of the Realm, often that of the Allies themselves, this cousin of the King had made it his own. "You see now how that is, don't you?"

"Hell no, I don't," Ike snapped, uncomfortable with this one-on-one. The Supreme Commander's job was victory, not peace. Mountbatten, an intellectual, had just tried to outflank him. Without the facts, it was not Ike's habit to pick up the phone to the Potomac; but one thing had emerged as clear as China. In Mountbatten's argument those facts were hiding as surely as if they had been admitted. "I don't see the point of spending any more time on this," Eisenhower said, "unless it's—hold on, will you?" An Aide had entered, bearing papers. He put them on the desk. "Hold a minute, Louis." They were stats for the Portsmouth meeting, more for Tedder than himself. "Thanks, Major." He pushed them aside; the door closed. "Louis? Stay on the line, will you? About a minute…thanks."

"Right-o."

Ike needed this minute, to think.

Lord Louis had pointed a finger. During the electrical storm, materializing between lines, news of an outside Operative had emerged: Mountbatten seemed to have been accusing Ike of sending him. As a golfer, in a game he was still learning, it was as though Eisenhower had suddenly seen an invisible man enter, moving his ball in the rough with black-gloved hands. Mountbatten's allegations, real enough, were not those of a man who didn't believe them. Louis, mentioning a civilian, the man in the trench coat, had seemed resentful about it. Ike shook his head, he reached for the phone. Wasn't *theirs*, that was damned sure!

"Lord Louis, please"

On the Fairway, dark clouds had appeared. Wind was rising, blowing across the grass. Something was forming…it was in his mind. *Familiar noises on the line…a clicking.* Ike held his wrist up, he looked at his watch. The players were moving up. Following behind them, hidden by the trees, and closing like a cloud, The Spy was watching. On the Greens, birds fluttered down.

They didn't know why.

"—amazing," Lord Louis was saying, "how clear the connection is. Envy you, old boy, being in England."

Bull Durham was thundering towards him.

"As far as I'm concerned, so let me just say it now, and be

done with it—friends who are friends, do not *do* this to friends. Suppose you think about it." Both men knew if the war were over tomorrow, each would relish nothing better than to tell the other to go to hell.

"Through, are we?"

"Let me put it this way, Commodore," said General Eisenhower, whose voice had a fluted rasp to it, as though he had a cold, "this isn't over by a long shot!"

Mountbatten coughed, it was on a golfer's backswing.

"Ho! Just like in polo, what?"

Eisenhower listened, it was in disbelief. All the way from Peredynia, a wooden ball had landed on his fairway. Like polo, golf had its own rules, and men who played fair and square didn't cut across the 18th hole, into another man's play, with a wooden mallet.

Eisenhower hung up.

The man on the horse, he considered, had just made an unfortunate swing. Not an American problem? He had been keeping his next card palmed, for a rainy day. Beyond the high windows, humid as hell, the early-morning sun was blaring. It being a Friday, the General started to ring for Tex. Instead, Ike pressed a button and spoke into a speaker. "You there?" He lit a cigarette.

"Yes, sir!" The voice was young. It was his private switchboard.

"Round up Captain Bernstein for me. Tell him he's got some calls to make."

"Captain Bernstein. Yes, sir!" At the Command Relay Board, the older WAC looked up. "Something good?"

The breakfast bell rang.

In Southwick, in the classiest part of the war, hallways echoed to the sharp click of footsteps. The senior WAC, who looked like Betty Grable, got up and closed the door.

"Well?"

"Chief wants his lawyer."

The call went through. Doors opened. Coffee came. Ike felt better: he was talking, between swallows.

After listening, Captain Bernstein said, "Right. You got it." Morris Bernstein made a few notes, they were on a legal pad. Lighting a cigarette, he reached for the phone. One of his calls, to Martin Seymour, was interrupted: trouble on that line. Seymour called him back. *Parker?* When Bernstein hung up, he kicked in his scrambler, and called Ike.

"Looks like you're right. Whatever it is, it's *big* and they're after it. I'd say the Germans have it—*technology*, it looks complex as hell. What?... No. No, they don't want us to know about it!... That's right. Their British girl is specially trained...has a photographic memory. No, a *photographic* memory! Looks like...sir? Yes, sir! That's why they're sending her." Ike asked him something and Bernstein laughed. "Well, you could call it an SOE mission if you *want* to...yes, sir, I agree with you." The lawyer was sketching in his case:

Kick some ass.

"Yes, sir, we will want to talk to her."

"Take care of it."

"And if they won't?"

"Then that's their decision, isn't it?"

"On my way."

In the fanged and viperous world of the truly old, Ike's young heart beat with hope. His Jew, in this hot summer of 1944, did not pretend to worship a bank that called itself a church. Using his lawyer as a hammer, Ike would pull the British nail that had him pinned.

Within the hour, Bernstein's briefcase would contain a letter to a man whose face he had never seen. Just returned from the can, he was stubbing out his cigarette when the phone rang.

Betty Grable answered it. Whoever it was, knew the right words. "Why, thank you! It's so sweet of you, to say that." She looked up, impressed: "It's a Mister Bridley."

Bernstein grabbed it.

In the background, outside the King's Pavilion built for Victoria, warm rain was falling. "Morris?" came the familiar, deal-making voice, on the other end.

"Jimmy, *baby!*"

It was a Sidney Greenstreet kind of day with a Casablanca fan droning dully overhead and tessellated shadows from the French windows forming pools of reminiscence from beams of the late afternoon sun. It reminded her of Malta, and the hot winds of the sirocco. Rose-colored trees of Sliema, dripping with water...

Life without a heat wave, she concluded, was like David Hamilton without a secret. The Commander, who appeared to have an inside track with the weather, must be getting it from *somebody*—and very high up! Could that somebody be the someone? Hamilton, of course, would be hiding his weather secrets behind the clouds of security.

Were those same clouds hiding The Spy?

Following the briefing in the cave, she had spent the afternoon strolling about the peaceful seaside town staring into the shop windows and wondering about boats, knowing she was a part of something, yet feeling on her own. It was difficult to realize that just fifty miles across the Channel, Englishmen were fighting; and that many of them, at this very moment, were fighting for their lives. She had returned to the hotel along the beach, ducking flying things buzzing up from steaming mounds of seaweed and trudging ankle deep through dunes as white as salt.

Arriving back at her room, she washed her hands and emptied her shoes off the veranda. The stream of sand brought an indignant shout from a fat man in a chaise lounge one floor below who was staring with horror at his drink.

Sinclair looked down.

She went back inside. Throwing her shoes in the corner, she pulled off her stockings and returned with a chair. Propping her feet up, she assembled paper and envelopes, along with a pen she had swiped from Carrington's office. He wouldn't miss it. She began to write:

Dear Brian...

She finished the two letters as Hamilton had instructed. Her family would believe her because they believed anything. The one for her son, she addressed to the Commander. Checking the letters and tossing them on the dresser, she hauled the chair back inside, placing it under the Casablanca fan. Wanting it to go faster, she got up on the chair and stretched but she couldn't reach the cord. Belly-flopping on the bed, Valerie flipped the pillow to its cool side, and closed her eyes. No matter how dark it got, inside it was darker: the curtains that were drawn in her head. Iotas were dancing back of her eyelids, squiggled geometries that floated slowly away across the dark blue concaves of space, jumping up again, veering off to the side, clottings of spiderweb. Her breathing became still.

Distant, a clock chimed.

It must have been a troubled dream. When she awoke that evening she discovered that the chenille, upon which she had slept, was soaked in sweat. She got up, pulling the curtains and clicking on the lights. Stripped to her panties, she hit the floor for push-ups. Hedging at the forty-first, she faked her way to fifty, her boobs banging on the rug. She straightened up and went into the bathroom and brushed her teeth. Flashing through a bath, she toweled off, taking care to protect the love note on her thigh: her Sergeant's name and phone number.

What if they canceled the mission?

She stared at it like some mysterious hieroglyphic, it was upside down. She walked back to the mirror, and looked closer. She would have the devil of a time trying to decipher it.

It was a two-man job.

Valerie put on her face, got dressed, and went downstairs — into the mauve world of night. The lobby hummed with war's sweet urgency, muffled in the thick carpets of other years. Black curtains draped the front glass. Cigar smoke drifted about the desk. The dining room was packed; she would wait for it to clear. Sitting in an overstuffed chair, her feet barely clearing the floor and leafing through a magazine, she gave the appearance of waiting for her mother. From the mezzanine, low laughter and the velvet thrumming of music: a private party.

Not invited, she would seek her own.

Entering the dining room, she ordered a proper supper on Hamilton's credit: sipping demurely on soup before wolfing down roast beef and strawberries, topped with apple pie and American coffee conned from the waiter; and a cigarette from his private pack.

"Name's Clive," he said. As part of the deal, signified by fluttering eyelids on her part, he would be expecting a date with her, on Tuesday.

It was just ten o'clock.

Stubbing the cigarette, Sinclair went to the bar and ordered a double Scotch, her favorite! She sat off by herself, drinking it and wishing for Sergeant Blumensteel; but the Americans who had come to the dance were not in tonight. Their barracks were distant, and they had come by bus. She didn't know how the Sergeant got back.

She hoped he got back happy.

Sitting quietly, she fingered her glass. Neither Pierre nor the Commander were on hand. Perhaps Hamilton had dined earlier. Pierre, no doubt, was already on his way to London: which seemed to be his favorite hangout.

As though peering into a crystal ball, she stared into her drink. The future lay in France…a tall-dark-handsome stranger. Pierre? Why were they always tall-dark-and-handsome? Why not fair, broad-shouldered, and free? She could see it: she would hand her lover the letters. She thought of the vicarage and of her father's cruel joke, paraphrased from sailors, comparing her mother to Australia: *We all know where it is, but nobody wants to go there.*

She glanced up.

The kitchen was closing, and the music had stopped. She was relieved then when the barman called time. "Time, Gentlemen, Time!" There was a rush of orders for doubles. Valerie read her watch. She would have an early train to catch. She thought of Basil. *"Ge' on with it,"* her dead husband chided gently, *"n'stop muckin about."*

Stay out of it, Basil.

No wonder she couldn't get a date! Sinclair slugged her drink, pushed up from the table, and hurried out of the bar. At the rail, heads had turned. One of the locals, who had been sitting there rehearsing what he would say to her, nudged the fellow next to him.

"How'd you like t'take 'er 'ome tonight, mate?"

Valerie Sinclair, in panties and bra, having hung up her uniform and brushed her hair, was just climbing into bed when the knock came. Two knocks, to be precise. Turning on the light and struggling into her robe, she opened the door a crack, leaving the chain on. Seeing it was Hamilton, she let him in immediately.

"Ah, there you are! I am so sorry to disturb you, and I hope you will not get the wrong impression, but I felt it best to come at once." The Commander was looking worried. "Important to go over a few things with you privately, as it were." He surveyed the room, then found a chair. "May I? Thank you." He glanced up at the fan. "We covered most of it this morning, cave and all that, but there are still certain personal matters that we need to address."

She was tying her robe.

"Just a little review, you see? I think I know what's important about you, from the files when you joined Intelligence." He ticked the list off on his fingers. "Born in South Wales, lived in Malta, Dorset, and Devon. Your father, vicar of a small village church, was born in Cairo; your mother, part Maltese, in Devonshire. Both are British citizens. Your late husband came from the North of England, family scattered. Both of his brothers, one from Wales, are serving in the Navy. We have also received an excellent report on you from the First Officer of the Ferry Pilots. You've been with us—what, two years now?—and your performance record has been outstanding. To sum it up then"—with these last words, he got up and paced the floor. He came back to the chair to make his point. The chair was gone. Sinclair had placed it next to the bed for his convenience.

She waited for him to continue, wondering what he was going to say, but when he still stood frowning, she asked, "What is the problem?"

"The problem?" After spending the first part of the afternoon with de Beck, Hamilton had spent the remainder of it at Bletchley Park. "Well, let us not call it a problem. There *are* these last minute evaluations, you see. Actually, things are where they should be, except—well, you are so very *young*, so very—" He groped for the word.

Expendable?

"—so very new to this business with no experience of espionage, and here I am sending you on a mission with de Beck, a...Frenchman."

The problem, then, was Hamilton's.

"Perhaps I am being overprotective"—the Commander stood before her, made of iron. Sinclair was attracted to him immediately. Her sex pulled him closer, like a magnet.

"Won't you have a chair, sir?"

"Why yes, thank you. Here, is it?" He glanced at the bed, and sat down. "You see, Sinclair, we just don't want anything to go wrong. We have to be absolutely certain, as it were, that our selectees are ...compatible."

She had moved behind him.

"As for de Beck"—Hamilton was forced to turn, to see her "the Commander of the Free French has vouched for him"—he stared—"so I should really...have no doubts." The chenille had caught in the bedspring, she was trying to pull it loose. "Here now, let me give you a hand." He jumped up and knelt down, freeing it. She flapped out the bedspread, obscuring his view. Hamilton ducked; he decided he was safer standing. "Now, about the French, you see? I have just been in touch with Commodore Blackstone, our Chief of Intelligence."

"Oh, yes?" There!

He waited. "Have it together, do we?"

"Sorry, sir." She sat down in the chair. Unless the Commander kept standing, the next place for him was the bed. She was so proud, it was shipshape. She wanted him to feel at home.

"You were saying, sir?" She reached down and retrieved the last pillow. She clutched it in her lap.

"As I was saying, Sinclair"—she tossed it on the bed—"the Chief made it clear that my uneasiness about de Beck is quite unfounded."

Was it her question, in the cave?

"It's just that certain sensitive matters are better served if we keep them between us, you see?" Blackstone had made it quite clear that it was he, Hamilton, who had selected him. "There is no time to find a replacement. The mission must go on as scheduled, otherwise—"

Valerie looked up at the Commander with troubled brown eyes.

"Relax, my dear. In such a dangerous undertaking, one must be absolutely certain about relationships. My concern is for your safety, a fact which may have nothing at all to do with de Beck. However, the Chief did add that if I still felt doubtful, to give you a word of warning."

But that wasn't it at all, she realized. Yet Hamilton did not tell Valerie Sinclair exactly what Commodore Blackstone, O.B.E., V.C., and Chief of Combined Intelligence Services, had said.

It had gone like this:

"Hamilton, old chap, why are you so concerned for the safety of this particular girl? She has volunteered. She must know she is expendable."

"Each officer assigned to missions is my concern, sir."

"It was at your *insistence*, David, that we made her an officer." For this, Hamilton owed him. "She's the first woman ever, you know. My God, man! It just wouldn't do for this to get out. There's a certain long, and if I may say so, very proud tradition involved here. The Royal Navy is the Royal Navy, Commander! A man's navy, sir! Why, this Sinclair is barely a third officer, and a *female* at that. Bloody cheek, I'd say!" Churchill himself, calling them the "backbone of the navy," had refused to allow Chief Petty officers, including Valerie's rate, to be promoted to officer rank. Flag officers considered women incompetent, inferior, actually: an embarrassing political assumption. *Abwehr*, dispatching all comers, had just sent fifteen traditionally trained female agents to their deaths. Going by the book, if not by the board, SOE was going down the drain. Blackstone was on his guard, De Gaulle was on his case, and Hamilton was on the carpet.

Sinclair was in his hair.

"She could at least have been a *man*," the Commodore had fumed. The girl from Newton Swyre, condemned by opportunity and swallowed whole by the Royal Navy, had lodged in his throat like a bone.

"She's a full Lieutenant now, sir."

"*Oh*? Oh, yes, well, embarrassingly so, I suppose."

Hamilton had fought like hell for it. The Prime Minister, to whom John Blackstone had immediately appealed, remained neutral. The Commander, holding his ground, concluded that Churchill, aside from causing it, had finally nudged Blackstone to agree. In the higher offices, the commission of Valerie Sinclair had been viewed with something akin to apoplexy.

"It's just that I feel she's the most qualified, sir."

"Rot!"

The Welsh Commander had stuck to his guns.

"This is not like you a'tall, David," the Chief had retorted. "I can never remember you having a feeling like this for any of the girls you've sent on a mission, and up to a few hours ago, you, above all, felt de Beck was exactly the right man for the job. An impeccable background, sir, connections in France, and all that. See here, I'm beginning to wonder if you have more than a military interest in the girl. Come, David! I thought you were a confirmed bachelor."

Hamilton hadn't answered.

The Commodore had looked at his Commander intently. "Isn't she a widow with a small boy?"

"Yes, sir," Hamilton replied.

"Well, then, I can see your concern," the Chief muttered. "Ah, you been dating lately, have you, David?"

"Sir?"

"See here, old boy, it happens to the best of us, you know," Commodore Blackstone glanced at the silver-framed photograph of the woman on his desk. It was a snapshot of his wife, Emily, who was full of wise sayings.

"'Straightening out a relationship,'" the Commodore informed him, "as Emily says, 'is like ironing a wrinkled shirt: it flattens out the stress.'"

"The stress? Are you saying—?"

"I am saying, take care of it, David! But not—how shall we say?—at company expense? Try the theater district...a few days at Brighton, um?" Hamilton's cool side was showing signs of heat. "Meanwhile, I assure you, there is nothing worth stewing about with this de Beck matter. The man is absolutely top grade!"

Blackstone had cut the deal with LeClerc.

"I feel certain Sinclair will come through for us, sir!"

Smooth as an owl, Blackstone answered: "One of them, yes, most certainly, I should think..." The Commodore, heavy with the burdens of office, sighed wearily and looked favorably at his favorite genius, whose expression had fallen several fathoms.

"Come, David! Look at life as life is. She's a pretty little ratchet-wrench, it's true," he had seen Crichton's film on her, "but it's her photographic memory that makes her valuable to us. The camera, you see, doesn't have to have a brain—it just has to have a shutter. Be a good fellow now and listen to the voice of experience." He remembered his Hannibal. "She's a military mouse, a stratagem, like poison gas. A trump card, I'll admit, but certainly, old chap, nothing to get excited about. See here, David! Need I remind you? A woman—on a man-o-war?" The Commodore, whom three wars had failed to ruffle, leaned back in his chair. "As for your Frenchman, if you still have doubts, perhaps you could try de Beck on her for size."

"I may do that, sir." Hamilton felt his jaws clench.

"Some loose activity, was there, at the dance?"

Blackstone knew better. The Commodore, who had pulled Hamilton away early, allowing the Frenchman a clear shot, was now ordering the Commander to test her. Informed of the Frenchman's womanizing, he had turned it to his advantage. Should the girl prove to be sexually vulnerable, they would need to know before Sunday. To back it up, Blackstone showed him the first part of a TOP SECRET directive: decoded by Parker, and just in. This latest coda, sniffing out guilt, had come in during their conversation. While finding it personally distasteful and without disclosing its source, except to say that it was civilian, Blackstone didn't mind passing it on to Hamilton. Meeting adjourned. The Commander was almost to the door when the Chief hit him with his broadside. "This girl has a whiff of the *sleazy* about her, if you know what I mean, sir?"

That meeting had left Hamilton angry and adrift in a sea of words too painful to express, too formidable to challenge. The dark inferences of the German super weapon, the Waterfall, known to both as the real reason for the mission, had not been mentioned.

It was the droning of the Casablanca fan that brought him back to The Spy: that Blackstone had shown him *part* of a secret order had not been lost on him. *Civilian!* That man without a face again, was it? Following their mission from London? In with Blackstone, was he? What kind of fool did they take him for? Attempting to answer his own questions, the Commander suddenly put on brakes. The man without a face, transferring guilt in a steady line, had come to mind again simply because Hamilton didn't know. Now, he remembered he had turned the girl's report of The Spy over to Mountbatten.

Smiling, not too broadly, but enough to feel better, David Hamilton was aware that he was holding Valerie Sinclair's hand. He was also aware that she was doing the squeezing. Lamplight was buzzing in the corner, flaring shadowy figures against the wall. It was nearly midnight. The Commander stood up, and touched her shoulder. He felt warmth there, and trust. There was still so much unattended. Blackstone's suspicions, the point of his visit, were now interfering with it. Rising up in front of him, it was a nightmare worse than any dance floor.

Seducing a child! How could he live with it!

Sinclair, hot as a light bulb, wasn't helping any.

"I have just forty-eight hours," Hamilton began, clearing his throat, "to, er, save your life."

That sounded good!

Sinclair listened, trying to get ready.

"Very good." On safer ground, he had decided to wait. "Now, should you become separated from Pierre, and yet reach Allied lines, I would advise you that you make yourself known immediately, and ask to be taken to the highest-ranking British Officer. As for the *Americans*, you will so conduct yourself as to have as little as possible to do with them. We wouldn't be wanting them to know about you, of course."

"Of course."

Wasn't he going to do anything?

"There are certain things that you will be taking with you—writing devices, invisible ink, that sort of thing. However, it is highly unlikely that you yourself will be using them."

"Yes, sir. May I ask why?"

She guessed he wasn't.

"With your photographic memory, you won't need them. De Beck, on the other hand, will need to have your data committed to *writing*, you see. The articles will be for him." Pierre had her out-ranked as far as France. She mentioned it. "That's true," Hamilton admitted, "but if you get in a hole, the best thing to do would be to ask Captain de Beck."

"But suppose he can't answer? I mean, supposing the Germans are looking at him, or something?"

"And you're on hand?"

"Yes, sir."

"Well then," said Hamilton, "in that case, you would watch." She untangled her legs.

"—cautiously, of course. For example, let's say you're walking behind him, and he does something that's a custom of France. You just do the same. In a French setting, with the possibility of Germans, whatever de Beck would do, you would do."

"Like 'Follow the Leader', sir?"

Hamilton considered this.

"Well, *yes*! I suppose one could put it that way," which is not the way he wanted to leave it. De Beck was picking him up tomorrow night. He had planned to talk briefly with her, Saturday evening at the hotel, some last-minute items, that sort of thing.

Now, he must.

"Even so, something may arise, you see, for which you are not prepared. How shall we handle such an event?"

Valerie shrugged.

He was thinking ahead. This time next weekend, where would she be? The Germans had beds; they had other rooms, as well. He got up and walked to the window. Female agents appeared in his mind. They had been waiting there, throughout the summer. "I realize it's against orders," he heard himself saying, "but I have decided to send a cyanide capsule with you." He turned back around. "Pierre, of course, is not to know. I will see to it that it is in your purse, aboard the submarine."

"Will it get us into trouble, sir?"

"No no, child, it's the 'L-Pill'. You're familiar?"

Valerie coughed. "Yes, sir." The poison, contained in a glass capsule, would pass through her body if swallowed. Death would occur if it were crunched by her teeth. She searched his face. "Do you think we're going to die, sir?"

Blackstone had said, *one of them.*

"No, I don't," Hamilton answered, his jaws tightening. "We're just betting on the safe side, that's all. Unfortunately, not all of our agents come back. In the present case, however, I am fully expecting that you both will. Still, one must sometimes take these risks, no matter how deeply it may affect one personally."

Valerie looked at him.

Hamilton blushed.

"I understand, sir. That information we're after—?"

"Yes?"

"—it's as good as in the bag, sir!"

"Good show!" The Commander expected as much. "Now, where will you hide the pill? Once you have obtained it, of course."

Valerie began to think.

Hamilton moved from one spot to another, then back to the chair. "There are other hiding places, naturally, used by women of British Intelligence—but not for you, my dear."

"Why not, sir?" Would it melt? If they could do it, so could she!

"Because it's—*confidential*, you see."

"Consider it forgotten."

Hamilton beamed, he was feeling tired; this SEX thing, Blackstone's insistence. Or maybe it was the cyanide. From somewhere, he seemed to have a memory of a bad dream, turning itself off.

"I know where!" Sinclair cried, turning it on. "See?...right here. If I tuck it into my bra, next to my skin, I am sure the pill will be safe."

"Ummm...?"

She offered to demonstrate it for him. He handed her a coin. It fell out, rolling under the bed. In retrieving it, the front of her gown dropped.

Hamilton looked.

Her breasts were driving him crazy. He couldn't bear the thought of it, those Everest breasts in enemy hands, that would be the first thing the Germans would grab for. The brassiere was out, at least the one she was trying to get back into.

Sinclair faced the mirror. She smiled at the glass, for identity. Hamilton had her blocked. He stepped aside, his feet were killing him. He yearned for a place of tranquility and peace. Also, he could use a drink. "Now then!" said Hamilton politely. "Where was I?"

"The pill, sir!"

"Oh, yes."

"What about the inside of my thigh, Commander? Some tape? Surely the Germans would not look there. If they captured me—" If they did, the phone would ring down the road.

An American sergeant would answer it.

The Commander stared at her, then shook his head, as if to clear it. "With the Germans, Sinclair, nothing is sacred. How could you possibly have thought of your thigh?"

She didn't know.

"Your shoe might be a better idea," he offered, casually. He moved to the foot of the bed. His own feet hurt. The chair was empty. Gratefully, he sat down. She kicked off a slipper. Hamilton, lunging, saw it sailing past him. It whanged into the fan, which threw it into the blackout curtain. "What *is* this?" croaked the Commander, walking over to get it, "a bloody cricket match?"

Sinclair, who had grabbed the chair, was looking at her other foot. Perplexed, he looked at what he was holding.

"My *fuzzy*, sir?"

Hamilton returned to the center of the room, the place where it all started. He was holding the... 'fuzzy.' "Here you are, Sinclair." He leaned over, and placed it in front of her chair. Her face was in her feet.

All he could see was hair.

"Well now! We seem to have had a most instructive go at it!" He would have *words*, for Seymour. As for the mission: "All hands on deck, ship ready for sailing, would you say?"

Sinclair looked up. "Yes, sir. I couldn't have said it better myself, sir. Speaking for my own person, sir, if I may be so bold—"

"Get to it, Sinclair!"

"Yes, sir! Things may turn out ruddy well, sir!"

"Right-o. Well then, let us surely hope so," said Hamilton, glad to be leaving, "in this line of work, one can never be too cautious."

"Got it, sir."

"Tomorrow, the studios at Elstree, hmmm? Fitting you out as a student, sort of thing. The latest French fashions, Sinclair! Even your bra, although no doubt, we have found a better hiding place."

"We have?"

He clasped her hand tightly. Then he was gone.

She took off her robe, looking into the long mirror, on the front of the wardrobe. The turquoise gown, thin-woven, Egyptian, was certainly flattering. A better hiding place? She stepped forward, and opened the front.

"Oh my!" she said.

Rigid as bullets, they stood at attention. If she glued the pill to one of them, would they notice?

Another Friday night, and no date!

Her simple needs, so long repressed, so long imprisoned at

the bottom of a class society, now rose to the surface, bobbing along on secret currents of desire, trapped in a too-small room, beneath soft cotton:

Keen for love.

She stood and looked, transposed on a sea of glass. She knew he would have liked to see her without her robe — she wished that he had. The best hiding place of all was her heart.

Nobody ever went there.

She sighed, uneasy at the ending of Hamilton's visit. She turned off the lights, opened the blackout curtains, and climbed into bed. The night was hot and her body pulled at her. She threw off the covers, kept the sheet, and fixed her pillows. Hamilton, inseparable from British interests, lingered for a moment in the middle of her thoughts. He had seemed so worried about de Beck. Not a word about *Marchaud*. Why was it she felt the girl was still alive? She did so wish to help her. To return her safely to France. There seemed no one else to protect her. She wanted to see her before Hamilton did.

What was the weather like in France?

Her eyes had closed.

Beyond the harbor, across the breakwater where it joined the Channel, iron buoys tugged tautly on streaming chains. Below the surface, falling away into the open sea, the muffled creaking of metal and the rubbing of sounds wailed like a gnashing of bones.

On the sea road, at the outskirts of town, covert as the cat who listened to it, the motor of a limousine was idling. "*Sunday*," she heard him say, and she knew it was him. Late from his travels, gaze directed to the wall of the hotel, he stood alone atop the high dune, driver waiting.

Sunday...

Lights in her bedroom suddenly went out! She arose from her bed, and she was in the Camera Shop. All around her, pitiless and unretouched, were the pictures of her life. She was at the vicarage. *Inhabitants* pulled at her, but they wouldn't listen. Trying to talk to her, they were causing the night to cry. Sinclair looked up, and into the eyes of time. Staring back at her from across the bridge of life, they revealed the new voice rising. Stamped on her brain, like a schema, it was hers:

She was screaming!

The Camera was useless, ringing metal split...it was because of the missing face. Terror clawed like a wingless bird, flopping helplessly at his feet. Peering up, a dreamer's glimpse of his wide-brimmed hat. Now, too late, his cold eye counting, she felt herself rising and standing straight at the tunnel's mouth where the trapdoor yawned. There, coming to claim her, and extending a black glove—The Spy was standing!

She backed away. He raised his hand...

The wind was blowing.

It was increasing.

Sinclair was running!

She tripped, sought desperately for balance, and found herself staring into the face of Marchaud, coming back the other way and who was fighting to arrive. The Spy flew at their heels! Into the entrance of the cave, through the trapdoor and down. Hurry! We must get there before the mission!

Turn loose! I'll catch you!

We can't take any cameras. No, not even reminders. You must leave all your memory in your body. Yes, leave it there, with the night that will have passed without us. This way, quickly, we have to go back:

Back.

All the way back, to when time was, before dreams. Arranged by The Spy, an evolutional duplication of the accelerated regression of her life, and of all the lives before her, Valerie Sinclair had just been swept away on a tide of terror; and whether she dreamt it, or would even be able to convince herself later that it actually happened, for this moment, for the longest moment of her life, she would not be able to say. Chased by the man without a face, the wall of what she had been taught to believe was reality, had cracked. Spilling through it, already spinning through her past, she had slammed into the surprised Marchaud along the way; and had grabbed the girl, to keep from falling herself.

"Est ce L'Espion!"

"Oui! Allons-y!"

Black is the air that claws about them in the physical tunnel of time. They move, and are moved, as if swallowed by a snake, whose bones are made of rock and timbers, worming under the sea-drowned land somewhere above them. Half-crouching and resting on knuckles, not knowing or seeing—departing from human, before there was human, before language; now limping and feeling, and before love:

Velocity was coming...

They had changed their hides and burned their hair with fire; and their weapons were metal, found, no one knew where, from the gods in their passing, for caves came before the world was, from the shattered plantations of stars. It would be a hundred million years before time would hint that they might count; up from the round bore hollowed for living food, rearing and reaching, deserted by rats that were yet to evolve.

Distance claimed, devouring, runic litter...

Past the passageways of graves where no one dies and no one lives, stooped loping on haunches, and cringing and waiting, because the floor made their muscles for growing but their bones were compressed from the crouching, and they ascended.

They were not supposed to be here...

The magnets of their bodies pulled them forward, and faster, and up to the Top, where the flatlands were; for in the timeless gulches that had cleaved around them, the Bipedal Block had formed; leaving ruts behind where life could crawl; and stand, at last, to seek among the killer stars the greater prey of war.

Two girls came bursting through.

A nightbird shrilled across the flats, an eerie coda to their skills, and spilling from the tunnel's mouth, their clothing scorched, suspicions born, the earth released them from its grip. Tourists from the dark terrain, they stood on the shores of Brittany. They were in the future. Cones of light shone down upon them, aligned with the horizon, compressed below a distant river of stars.

Sunday, he'd said.

Had they landed undetected?

"Over here!" It is Pierre's voice, uncertain. Something shimmers, moving through the trees. Framed as children, shadows emerge from the hedgerow. Whispers come, friends are parting, trading girl-things; and de Beck does not hear it. Nor does he know: *Marchaud, escaped from the Gestapo, has been hiding in its future. But The Spy has known, that is why she is here.*

The girl approaches. De Beck, her partner, thinking her Sinclair, motions her over.

The French girl listens, she gathers close.

Pierre will leave for the farm. She is to stay, and hide. First contact, behind enemy lines, is a man's job. Intending to kiss her, instead he grins. *"Bonne chance, cherie."* He turns, and disappears into the darkness.

The French girl was home, in France. Could her English other find her way back?

Marchaud was twelve—*n'est-ce-pas?*—and she hoped to graduate. It was all right to travel—wasn't it—she had all her papers.

A cloud scurried across the moon. The moonlight paled, and was gone. A darkness had come over the girl, and fear. The white cross with the gold chain, given her by Hamilton, was missing from her neck. Had he not given it to her yet? Was it not yesterday evening, on Saturday? Was it not the Cross of Lorraine?

She would put it on, and feel safe.

Dreaming...

Would the cross given her by Hamilton prove enough to protect her from the Bram Stokers of Hitler? Spawn of ghost and goblin, iron ghouls who tramped by night: *Les Nazis*, bobbing like Jack-o'-lanterns, across the graveyards of France.

Soldiers, smelling of rotted kelp.

Fiddler crabs were marching in blue moonlight, gliding in crackling swells of bone and claw over rocks as sharp as razors. They'd come pouring out of their holes, alerted by, and running from, the dark-eyed creature's smell. It was the smell of bath powder, ferociousness, and sex: menacing spoor of the she-killer, who'd invaded their territory.

In the high reeds, Marchaud closed her eyes.

Valerie's dream, her fevered sleep, was preceding against the background of what it would become. She stared at the Casablanca fan, and wet her lips.

Sinclair went back to sleep and had a second dream.

There were bluebells in Brittany, but they were brown.

France, she remembered, had changed.

She, too, was a part of that change, some insignificant mote of its memory. She looked up at the stars. Before, missing wonder, had she taken the world for granted? She loved it so. She looked about, evaluating, tongue wetting dry lips. Her hand flexed. She wished for a gun.

She had been following Pierre.

Dreaming, frightened, she thought of Hamilton. His words, like those of an owl, cut through the beams of sleep, bringing wisdom: *to do what Pierre did*. What he had told her, less than moments ago.

Pierre stopped!

Valerie did the same. Had something made him suspicious? She jumped behind a tree. Pierre listened. Protected, biting pillows, she watched him. What was he doing? Weren't they partners? *Anything he could do, she would do! If he turned, she would turn. If he ran, she would—*

He was shaking the leg of his pants.

—run.

Valerie did the same. De Beck had turned, he glanced over his shoulder. *Something?* A face, he thought, back there on the shore. *Shimmering.* Just a tree, with a low limb. Valerie had stopped in midair when she saw him. He moved on, footsteps crunching into the sand. Dropping the leg that looked like a limb, she stepped from behind the tree. She followed, in step with his movements, arriving at the place where he had stopped. She looked down.

She could tell it was him, from the initials.

In the training film for the cross-country, the narrator had compared soldiers blazing trails to cats marking their territory. Seymour had borrowed this rare footage, she'd learned, from his own instructor, chap named Bridley. She bent down, like the soldier in the film, rolling sand between her forefinger and thumb. She sniffed, cataloguing the smell. Pierre, on his home ground, was obviously leaving a trail for her to follow: *good to know, in case he got lost.* She straightened up.

De Beck had disappeared!

A dark form was cutting across the field.

She distinguished the outline of a hedge, and a shadow, fast disappearing through it. On either side, blackened by war, lay the ruined ruts of wheat: *the road to the farm.* Damp red poppies bent low to the earth. In the dim light, they looked like drops of blood.

They were moving as a team...

Out of darkness, a VOICE that turns her heart to ice!

"Wer geht da?"

Still running, she skidded to her knees and froze! Through the branches, she could see it: the back of the Frenchman, his hands raised.

"Ami," she heard him say.

A rifle bolt opened, it slammed shut.

"Freund. Ein Freund!" Pierre amended, seconds from death. The shot was held.

Lucky Pierre. Not to die at dawn. When to die then? Was she next? Did they know she was here? How could they know! Her heart pounded wildly, like the heart of a bird.

Sinclair groaned, she kicked off the sheet. She was ripping at her gown.

Crouched, trembling, Marchaud became the grass.

She wished herself a shadow, she dreamt herself a tree. Something was at her window. She remembered she'd been playing with dolls. Dolls, without heads.

A twig snapped.

She opened her eyes.

"Vorwärts und weisen sie sich AUS!" barked the Bogeyman. She closed them.

A pillow slid from the bed. Valerie felt herself falling. She fell into a ditch. De Beck was being arrested! Two men were talking: they were German. One of them was Pierre, he had an American accent. The second man, older, a Commandant, he was...?

Von Schroeder. He is a Banker...

A Banker?

The Commandant peered at the prisoner, studying the Frenchman's countenance. A broad grin spread across his face. *"Horst Liebeck! Wo warst Du! Willkommen zu hause!"*

She grabbed for her camera! Where was it?

"—Horst Liebeck? The Commandant waved the guns aside. Gratefully, Pierre lowered his arms. "So, Liebeck! How is London? Still standing? Tell me about Marley Square!" For the past four years, it has been Pierre's favorite place to go.

He has been expected...

Von Schroeder was showing Pierre a photograph. They were

looking down, staring at the corpse of a British spy. Her face of white is wet with blood. Black tears, forming ruts, drip down onto the road.

Marchaud gasps, places her hand to her mouth. Sinclair, her *other*, will be shot by the Gestapo after extraction of the information in her memory: photographs arranged by von Schroeder. He will give them to de Beck. *But what are they looking at?* In darkness, she listens:

Rain is falling.

Beyond its echo in the summer night, comes a voice, frightening and faceless, yet clear, like stars and wind, and whispering.

Her name is Mary Gladstone...

"Wer ist Frau Mary Gladstone?"

She is you, unless you remember...

Her eyelids seemed glued together, bonded, as if from dead streams of tears. She tried to focus and found the bedclothes disarrayed. Why wouldn't she remember? Because of her camera? Had she taken it? Dawn spread its thin film across her field of vision. *Had she opened the curtains?* Daylight came, the sun slipping through, hot on her cheeks.

Sinclair yawned...

She was awake.

IV

Saturday's sun was hitting them hard.

Through the left rear window a corner chop of light flashed on braided felt, touching the unyielding shoulder of blue broadcloth, just under the epaulet. The driver lowered the visor. Commodore Blackstone, O.B.E., V.C., was sitting stiffly in the back of his personal car, as he had for some thirty years, eyes straight ahead, for all appearances cut from the same marble as Nelson. His driver, maneuvering the black Bentley through the Buckinghamshire traffic, shot past raised beds of blue and yellow flowers down early-morning lanes of red mercury gravel.

Once past the sentries, and into the welcome brick of Bletchley Park, Commodore Blackstone found solace. Equal to Mountbatten in pay, if not in public relations, Blackstone's hatred of Lord Louis, the sponsor of Valerie Sinclair, engulfed him as he walked down corridors that smelled of cleansing solvents and into the large office where his Adjutant, Lieutenant Conrad Parker, had already arranged the morning's dossiers. Fluent in German, familiar with Berlin, Parker had been recruited from the London School of Economics. Having personally seen to his Clearance, the Commodore considered the future banker, who was dark of thought and insidiously silent, a particularly valuable asset in the ongoing business with his European partners.

"By Jove! 'Pronto,' as they say, ah?"

Following their journey through the labyrinths of history, the thick stack of files had reached their final destination and were now awaiting one of the two hand stamps that would determine their fate:

KEEP, or DESTROY.

The decision was Blackstone's.

In looking back over his life, he knew that people in high places were afraid of him. Yet he had come too far to let this influence his judgment. Controlling the ticket office on MI.5's midway of recent attractions, a hot cup of tea at hand, the Commodore opened the first of the folders, turned it sideways and read the name: *Erich von Schroeder*. Their positions analogous, von Schroeder orchestrated Intelligence for Germany.

They had met, before the war.

He looked inside: *J. Henry Schroeder Co., Schroeder Bankers, Hamburg. Present Rank: Commandant, Abwehr. Present location unknown: presumed France.* Without glancing up, he said, "Good work, Parker." He flicked through the rest of the tabs. "By the way, have Bridley call me, will you?" Not gone five seconds, there was a tap at the door. "Now what?" The Commodore looked up.

It was his Adjutant.

"Sorry, sir. I just remembered. About Bridley—?"

"Bridley, yes? What about him?"

"There was a cable early this morning, sir. I didn't want to bother you."

"Ay? Nonsense, Parker! Out with it!"

"Bridley is out of the country, sir. No one quite knows where, but the cable did state that he would be sending a message—to Commander Hamilton, sir."

"Intercept it, Parker."

"Yes, sir!"

So! David Hamilton, sucking up to Mountbatten, thought he had Bridley in his pocket, did he? That torpedo who worked for him, too! Lieutenant Seymour, wasn't he? Marty Seymour's kid. Why, the bounders were as clear as a spyglass! There was a new breed of blackmailer these days—but he still had a trick or two. Blackstone scribbled a note. Alone with his thoughts, Parker gone, he read:

Von Schroeder. Pre-military: Goethe University, London School of Economics. Present at meeting with Adolf Hitler, 4 January, 1933, Berlin. Schroeder Banks financed the debt incurred by Hitler's private army. Represented by the London office of Sullivan and Cromwell (J.F. Rulles) rep. V.S. Bank.

Schroeder is listed among 17 Merchant Bankers who make up the Financial District of London. With Belgium Banker Franqui, #8 of the consortium, the Schroeder family financed the American President Hoover. Hoover, a mining engineer, serving Franqui's copper interests in Singapore.

There was more, the print being small; and he finally reached the bottom of the page: *In 1936, Schroeder merged with Rockefeller, #3, re-forming, in 1937, the Canadian Cartel of Bechtel-McCone International: Ottawa and London. Bechtel, accessed to Washington, is responsible for the favored selections of Chairmen of the Federal Reserve; and, often, other Government Posts. In 1938, the London Schroeder (Bank) became Germany's Agent in Great Britain. In 1939 Schroeder Bros. Erich and Bruno, #5 and #6 respectively, arranged with Lord Docker exchange of Shares, Bank of England.*

See Bechtel Construction.

"That would be *Boer's* Bank," the Commodore concluded, and jotted the note on a separate pad. All Rothschild Associates, himself included, owned Shares there—until Emily convinced him to go with *National Westminster*. Thinking of their future, she had started handling more of their affairs lately, what with the war.

Bloody nuisance, sometimes, these dossiers.

He tore the note from the top of the pad, folded it carefully, and placed it in the side pocket of his blouse. A shareholder in what he was investigating, Blackstone's own motives were above reproach. "Conflict-of-interest" was one of those American phrases. Among International Bankers, trained and recruited at the London School of Economics, the first secret was that there weren't any.

The American Fed was a hoax. Had been, since 1913.

Purchased by Germany's Paul Warburg—spelled Rothschild—with Congressman Carter Glass doing the selling.

Name changed, from the Owen-Glass Act. Lights out, in Congress. The Bill's sponsor, Senator Robert L. Owen, waiting in the wings. No further mention of Owen. Hmmm. Politics, that: somebody had to throw *somebody* a bone.

Pensioned quite well, was he?

Leave it to the bloody Yanks!

Cleaned up, as it were, and under its final name, the American Federal Reserve Act of 1913 had actually been authored and successfully lobbied by one Paul Warburg. Nice touch, that "Federal". In the consortium, Warburg was listed as *#4. Neither an American Agency nor the 'Central Bank' of the United States Government,* the London officer had underlined, *but a foreign-owned private credit monopoly.* When Roosevelt was elected, he appointed James Paul Warburg, the son, as his Budget Director. Nephew of Max Warburg, Paul's brother, and Germany's top spy. Both brothers had attended the Paris Peace Conference: Paul Warburg as President Wilson's Chief Financial Advisor; Max, #7, heading up the German delegation. John Maynard Keynes, the economist, representing *England*? Opposing German reparations? Had someone taken leave of their senses! Hmmm...let's see, who were OUR chaps? Ah, yes! Lord Balfour and Baron Edmund D. Rothschild. Good thing the *Bankers* were there!

League of Nations? Ridiculous!

In his final reference to the Federal Reserve Act, having already appointed Paul Warburg its first Chairman, Woodrow Wilson confessed on his death bed, *"I have betrayed my country."* The President's funeral, in the rain, in 1924, had included the attendance of two men, one of them Warburg.

The other, an outside Operative.

The Commodore glanced over his shoulder. Seems he'd heard something...a vibratory *clicking* of some sort...there, amid darting shadows! An invisible presence, it had moved faster than his eye could follow. Blackstone blinked. Air currents, Victorian plumbing. It was forever drafty at Bletchley. He turned back around...was he being monitored?

Who would dare!

The strange sound lingered in his mind for a moment, like the closing of iron doors. Adjusting his glasses, the Commodore flipped quickly through the rest of the file. Attached by metal to the back of the folder, a yellowed document revealed itself to be the U.S. Naval Secret Service Report, dated December 12, 1919:

> *"Warburg, Paul Moritz. New York City, German-born naturalized citizen. Was Vice-Chairman Federal Reserve Board. In this capacity, arranged twenty million dollars converted to pounds, transhipped in gold, furnished by Germany for Lenin and Trotsky. Has a brother who is leader of the espionage system of Germany."*
> Note: *With Rockefeller interests, family controlling stock in German rail industry.*

Twenty million in gold, for the Bolsheviks. A sealed train, by night, transversing Germany. An insignificant amount of money, internationally; but to *whom* had it gone, unbeknownst to the rest? Traveling on Rockerfeller's rails...

Had the American Navy tried to prove something?

Blackstone knew, and had known all of his life, that the London Financial District, made up in the majority of Seventeen Merchant Bankers, controlled the monetary policy of the United States. The conversion had taken place in London. The goal of international banking was a stable price label. The Czar had threatened stability. Lenin, his adversary, had thus served international banking far better than anything drummed up by the Radicals.

Trotsky entered, spokesman for the Left.

Blackstone admired Hegel, as had Lenin; but he hated Frank Harris, who honored sexual license. Harris, later backed by Victoria and supported by writers Jack London and Rudyard Kipling—odd union, that—would ultimately appraise Marxism in its own right, calling its philosophy a fraud. Trotsky, ignoring reality, tried to get rid of money. Lenin, ultimately, got rid of Trotsky. Roosevelt got rid of the gold standard. Rothschild and Associates would get rid of the gold:

Leaving a string, too short on one end.

Paul Warburg, who had paid cash, and who had stolen the produced wealth of millions of Americans, condemning generations to massive debt and reverting their nation to a colony, had conveniently died and gone to heaven, leaving the location of *the Receipt* as the greatest unanswered question of the century.

So, where was it?

Blackstone chuckled.

He didn't know...

The final notation, dated and initialed 24 March 1943, and on whiter bond, was from Bletchley Park.

P. Warburg, immortalized as Daddy Warbucks in the comic strip "Little Orphan Annie."

The verifying officer, unable to resist black humor, had scribbled on the side in India ink, *"Sandy, no doubt, was wired for sound."* It was Blackstone's favorite. In any event, a proper gentleman read *The Times*. The lower classes, shopgirls and that sort, read *The Daily Telegraph*.

Mayor La Guardia, in New York, read the funny papers.

Which brought him to bibliography, *Bechtel Construction Corporation*, filed under ATLAS.

Warburg, Paul Moritz. Born 8/10/1868. Married Nina J. Loeb 1894. Kuhn, Loeb & Co. Dir. B & O R.R. First Chairman, Federal Reserve Board 1914•18. Appointed by Pres. Wilson. Died 1/24/32.

Blackstone, turned the page, he wet his lips.

...the Council on Foreign Relations...Bildiburgers ...the Royal Economic Institute, and with Bruno von Schroeder is a Trustee of the Rockefeller Foundation.

"*Was*, you mean," the Commodore corrected. But the dead were not there to bear witness. Behind him, salient as a dream, a shadow moved across the sun-drenched walls. In spite of the day, he was feeling cold. Perhaps he should take Emily up on it. A few weeks in Bermuda. Blackstone adjusted the lamp, turning the pages. Outside, the first day of July rose hot.

"Hello?"

Secret profiles on American war correspondents: George Seldes, marked ITALY, and Edward R. Murrow, tagged MINISTRY OF INFORMATION, apparently out of place. A Note stamped by the Admiralty read "bears watching." Seldes, turning his back on the British Official Secrets Act, had nearly let the cat out of the bag: Four years ago during *Götterdammerung*, the final moments of the Blitzkrieg, the injuries to England were so massive that Churchill, unknown to the public, had been within eleven hours of surrendering. Seldes, who had the story but didn't file it, had been nipped by the War Office. What bothered Blackstone, was that he wrote it.

If that blighter Hearst got wind of it...

Blackstone pulled the files of the two reporters loose, scribbled the correct routing, and placed both in the OUT file. The rest of the data was tediously written, unusually thick, and already bracketed....

ULTRA SECRET.

The Commodore lay the cumbersome dossier aside, and turned to the one it had been hiding. American stock brokers had lobbied Roosevelt not to bomb the Krupp watch factories in Germany. Roosevelt had said *no*. Deal struck with R.A.F. concurred; protesting Air Marshal replaced...

"Bloody dark business, I'd say," the Commodore said. He finished the page. The name of the officer, his late friend, had been mercifully removed. The initials confirming this were unclear, but it looked as though the ax had come from Tedder. Advising Eisenhower these days, ay? About what? Weather reports? *That bloody Irish mistress?* The file on her was growing thick. No! To put the proper face on it, Parker should let slip to Bridley that Tedder's advice to Eisenhower was actually about Mountbatten! Cousin of the King, was he? What Lord Louis got first hand from Bletchley Park, via Bridley, wouldn't hurt his betters. Mountbatten was a fish, he'd swallow anything. Blackstone rang for his Adjutant.

He returned to his files.

Historically, the protesting Air Marshal no longer existed. Secretly, Blackstone wished the same for that blasted girl, their new Lieutenant, with "the Big Ones," that agent who wore panties!

Lieutenant, indeed!

As though before a slow mirror, uncomfortably and with distress, the Commodore's thoughts turned to Sinclair. In forty-eight hours, she would be ashore. The same sun that was rising on Occupied France was glaring through his window. The knock at the door was Parker. Blackstone instructed him to pull the blinds. He did so. The Commodore had other instructions: "leaks" to Bridley, for Mountbatten. He spoke in a low voice, and the Adjutant listened intently. "Take care of it then," Blackstone said. The younger man nodded and left. The Commodore, starting to call after him, watched the door close. He had meant to ask him about the vibration. Some problem with the pipes, probably. He returned to the folders, his attention disturbed, reading the same page twice. That damned girl! Telling Hamilton she'd been followed by a man without a face! What nonsense! She had them wrapped around her little finger. Churchill's conception, granted; but it was his, Blackstone's brains that were making it work. It had been *his* idea to paint over *HM Tuna*, to send an unmarked sub; his idea that the records would show her in port tomorrow night; his idea that...

He looked at the doleful photograph of his wife, Emily, and wondered uneasily if this Sinclair had ever seen, or had access to, the files on his desk.

But how could she?

Of course not! Not even Hamilton had seen them, nor did he know of them! Certainly, his own office was safe! Still, one should never take these things for granted. With that *photographic memory*... He stared at them, bibles of strangers, and reviewed the security measures taken to protect them: no duplicates, no tapes, and the Southampton office outside their wire. Nothing to worry about then.

Just himself, and Whitehall.

He gave each of the remaining half dozen or so little more than a cursory glance, familiar with their secret histories, assigning them to judgment. Now, there were just the three. The first was the dossier on de Beck, painstakingly added to by Hamilton; and which bore, on the opening page, the current list of the Frenchman's Medals and Commendations. He would serve them well. Blackstone thumped it with pride, threw it on the stack, then sat staring for a long time at the folder in front of him.

Sinclair, Valerie.

His smile faded.

Jaws clenching, he shoved it to one side, attending first to the buckram, coded with a red stripe. Here, the subject matter, unshared with the Yanks, was more cryptic and to the point: ROTHSCHILD.

Blackstone read.

Not much there. The usual list of charities. Helping in the war effort and all that. Internal data. The Warburgs again. Felix M. Warburg—that would be Max. D.O.D. 10/20/37. Left a daughter: Mrs. Carola Rothschild.

In Diplomacy, all the right people were connected.

The Commodore wet his thumb, and turned the page.

A block history, and all old hat. Meyer Bauer, forming banks, had changed his name to "Red Shield" or Rothschild; and, in 1846, gained control of the Bank of England. *Certain about that date, were they? Waterloo, wasn't it?*

Rothschild was #1.

Taking his time, he went over the last few pages.

Kuhn Loeb...ah, *Schroeder!* The connection? Brown Bros. Harriman, New York. Yes, of course. That would be #2. But where was he? Where was #2? Stephenson's file? Sir William Stephenson, a Canadian, was rumored to be Churchill's personal spy. Seems Parker had mentioned that. The Commodore double-checked...no file on him? Hmmm, curious that, he should have been listed. The others seemed to be there. To a man, all good men, and true.

Blackstone closed the files.

Compared to *them*, what was one officer—and a *woman*, at that! If forced he would discredit her, and remove her from honor! *That wouldn't look very good for Mountbatten.* Blackstone, smiling thinly, scratched his nose and placed Sinclair's folder on top. Satisfied, he opened the desk drawer, took out the ink pad and the large hand-sized stamp. *All Files*, the wife had written, *pass beneath the eyes of the Sphinx.*

He acknowledged the wise saying.

As for this other, this Interloper—this Sinclair-Marchaud thing—chances were the Jerries would kill her straightaway: they had, the others. But if she prevailed? Suppose she talked? Correspondents were getting sharper, and nastier, these days.

That Murrow fellow, for instance. Hadn't his car recently exploded? Certainly it had! Few weeks ago, wasn't it? Protest by CBS? Fire in the Hotel Ritz, big row with Paley?

Britain couldn't police the whole bloody world.

Then there was de Beck. Someone dependable, that. Understandable, that he had been off his stride at the dance. One then, is all it would take. David Hamilton had his orders: if the girl failed to show, *and on time*, he and de Beck were to leave without her. Even the Almighty could hope. De Beck, certainly, could bring him what he wanted; delivering what partners needed to know. "Photographic memories," indeed! No point to keep sending these bloody women. Besides, surely Churchill was ahead of it. Insurance was his field—that business of his Code Override, absolutely smashing—provided Hamilton wasn't rash enough to bag the credit. Rumor had it that Winston had already started his Memoirs. Naturally, the name of John Blackstone, otherwise known as #11, would be prominently featured. Meanwhile, with the Commander moving up in the Firm; the Commodore was concerned that he not move too quickly. In the Royal Navy, in its history books, one had to earn one's place! Well, he would handle it. Hamilton worked for him. He must remember to tell the P.M. that...the next time he was invited over.

Blackstone pulled in the files. He raised the stamp. It was the DESTROY stamp. Hitler was a threat to business! But that girl, a threat to—and he slammed the stamp home, remembering his first piece at Dartmouth underneath the midnight limbs with that working girl who needed the money and whose tears had mixed with the blood on his trousers, there on the grass, before his wars, and before Emily.

Breathing slightly heavily, barely noticeable, really, John Blackstone stared uneasily at his wife's photograph. When was their club date? Emily had looked forward to it for months. He glanced at the calendar: *Saturday, 1 July 1944.* Next week? He remembered: *Wednesday, July 5th, 1900 hours.* And who was that, the guest artist? Alec Templeton, the blind British pianist. Back from America? *Chesterfield Supper Club* sort of thing, was it? Tux, and all that? There could be no question about it.

Britannia ruled the waves:

Fragile to her enemies, yet concealing a barnacled fist, enduring, endearing, the Little Orphan Annie of nations. And it was he, John Blackstone, who would save her—her Empire, her Eminence, her grandeur and her glory, the glory of the Royal Navy itself—from this...hybrid exigency, these *females* that Whitehall had so painfully thrust upon him. In the arcane orifice of a Victorian mansion, in the rarefied world of the mega-bankers, the Commodore stood tall upon the crest of their finest hour, the Union Jack thrust forward into History, gripped firmly in his authoritative hand. A hand, that would never change...

Just like Daddy Warbucks.

Orphan in a foreign-owned hotel, Sinclair scratched her head. To travel through time, one must start in one's bed. Too bad she had slept through it. How could one recall such things, if one's eyes were crossed? Splitting a beam of light, she brought her own back into balance. Maybe she would meet him at Elstree. It was certainly something to think about, the man of her dreams. After Hamilton departed, she had not remembered the night. Her camera without film, it had vanished.

Gown gone, naked...pillows on the floor.

Maybe it wasn't a dream. On the one hand: falling asleep, the last thing she remembered was sex. But with whom? How would Hamilton, who hadn't put it, put it?

Arrived, had she?

Tortured by vague recollections, Sinclair had turned and was noting, in the cool shadows of the room, provocative sculpturing, body parts, appearing in ravaged sheets and gathering in the crumpled chenille: faces of gargoyles, tongues hanging out; elongated legs and pieces of torso; triangular eyes staring up at her from the black sockets of the quilt. The air crawled with invitation, and the walls thumped.

Party time.

The couple in the next room, not caring who knew, yet hoping that somebody would, had been transmitting their lovemaking in *voice prints*; and these wishes, as it were, forming faces in the fabrics all around her, had taken over her room, the one she was suffering in, without a partner. Hamilton, stickler for privacy, had taken charge of her dating schedule, which was void of dates.

Such a sport.

Splashing about in the bathtub, and examining herself with alarm, Sinclair was thinking of love. Where was it? Sergeant Blumensteel, the daddy type, drinking double whiskies in which she had allegedly joined; and whose out-of-town affair, with somebody else, that same night and the next morning, she had not been able to remember; it was seeming to her now that she had not experienced anything approximate to last night's—?

Coming together of parts?

—in more than a year, if then. She wet her lips: they were slightly parted. She got dressed. Glancing at her watch, she recalled she had to be on a train. She sighed, gathered up her gear, and limped from the room.

Along the route, a rough ride, she thought of Hamilton, comparing him to his descriptions of Blackstone. One seemed so different from the other. Commodore Blackstone, emanating suspicion, hid in her mind like a black shadow. Was that why her film darkened, each time she focused on him? Sinclair stared moodily out the window, searching for happier subjects.

Face to the sun, she found them.

Bouncing along, she took a few pictures, mostly nature studies: gulls gathering, clouds flying, thatched roofs. Birds were moving, the way they did in early motion-pictures, sweeping across the platforms in a tide. *A feather found is like Cupid's compass,* Emily Blackstone had confided hopefully to Hamilton, *pointing ever to love.* So, the cameras had come out of their cases; parts in good working order. Cutting fast on a curve, she snapped one of a huge billboard, rearing above a trestle. An advert for the R.A.F., the chap in the sign was pointing to heaven, and asking the world:

"Is there an Aeroplane in your future?"

With things nearly normal then, and having escaped, as it were, on the first day of July and late on Saturday morning, Valerie Sinclair stepped down from her train at Waterloo Station. Giving up her ticket at the barrier, she immediately ran smack into half a dozen American servicemen wearing Special Forces insignia, who had also disembarked, and who were lining up in front of a Red Cross jitney. A panel had been opened on the side of the van, forming a counter, behind which stood a proper English matron, handing out hot coffee and sandwiches.

Valerie got in line.

The wonderful smell of ham and cheese and the aroma of freshly brewed coffee—Maxwell House?—drifted back to her. The woman in the van was effusive, personally thanking each of the soldiers in turn and dispensing food from home as though from a bottomless pit, eager to express her gratitude for all the help America was giving. One of the soldiers told the matron he thought the war would be over any day now; and the woman repeated this to the man sitting at the wheel, who was anxious to leave. The matron, who was patting her enormous bosom, was shedding a tear in her heart, as she put it, for all the brave young men. Sinclair, knowing the war could easily turn the other way, sniffed and moved up. When the soldier in front of her got his, she would be next. She peered around him; the woman was loading him with sandwiches.

Sinclair licked her lips.

Balancing his food, he joined his companions. Valerie stepped forward. As she did so, the panel slammed shut and the jitney drove away, revealing Commander Hamilton standing on the other side and looking about. Spotting her, he walked up.

"Ah! There you are! Had a good trip, did we?"

"Yes, sir," She was watching the soldiers. One of them was flicking his tongue rapidly over the top of his coffee cup, inviting her to look.

Sinclair gulped.

"Wonderful show, the Red Cross, what? There when you need them. Nothing too good for our boys, as they say."

"Yes, sir." The one she was staring at was really in need! Hamilton turned. The Americans smiled, the sex fiend saluted. Hamilton felt gratified. Respect, that's what made the services tick. "Special Branch...they entertain the troops, you know. Probably heading out to the studios, where we're going, to make one of their marvelous films. Ready, are we?"

"Yes, sir." She hoisted her purse.

"Charming chaps," Hamilton purred, "absolutely top of the line."

Valerie looked back. The soldier had emptied his cup, and was jerking it back and forth in front of himself. She paused, to read his lips. *"You're the cream in my coffee,"* he was singing. His tongue was going sideways, making love to her. He was sliding into a dance routine, and pointing to the cup. Valerie turned her own head sideways. *Click!* A tough shot, but she got him! From out of nowhere, an iron hand clamped on her shoulder.

Sinclair jumped!

It was Hamilton. "Come, come, my dear. You mustn't take what I say so literally." He'd had to come back, to get her.

"I'm sorry, sir, I thought it was someone I knew."

"Ay?" His eyes watched the departing soldiers. "Feeling all right, are we?"

"Yes, sir. It's just that I didn't sleep very well last night, sir." The voices of Brittany had spun away, into the air. She had slept like a rock.

He hoped it wasn't anything he'd said. "Have to keep a stiff upper lip, Sinclair. Nothing but the *best*, you know."

"The best? Yes, sir! I see what you mean, sir."

Outside the station, the Rolls Royce was waiting.

They walked over. It had been freshly washed and waxed. De Beck, taking the credit, also took the wheel. Once again, Valerie found herself in the back seat with Hamilton. Patting her on her hand and expressing a vague apology for having frightened her, he was thinking of last night's admonitions. Underneath, she was still a young girl from the country, and he had probably kept her up too late. Sinclair closed her eyes, imagining him the soldier:

Special Forces, Hamilton.

Her chin dropped to her blouse. In the bedroom of the car, time flew like a dream. Eyelids fluttering, they were floating …floating away, on a China sea of coffee cups. The limousine slowed. Pierre hit a pothole, and her dream popped! Sinclair opened her eyes. Hamilton threw her a glance, he nodded. She looked about and yawned.

"I think we had best have a good lunch here at the studios," announced Hamilton. They had arrived at Elstree. The blazing green Rolls, their car of state, breezed through the front gates, and parked. "After, we'll fix you up in your French clothes."

For a Saturday, the lunch hour was scattered, the lot being mostly empty. Hamilton ate quickly, and excused himself. Ignoring her, Pierre moved over and chatted with one of the actors. Valerie looked. She had seen him in the movies, playing German villains.

Sinclair ate like a star.

A buffet, they had lots of ices, and she went back twice for dessert. She turned in her tray and walked out into the hall lined with publicity stills and posters.

It was Orson Welles!

Holding a cigar, he peered down at her, like God.

She moved along: Boris Karloff, ladies man, was sporting a purple tie. Bela Lugosi, in gleaming tuxedo, was set to bite. To her left, a frightening sight! Lightning, crackling from the coils of some evil laboratory, was making the lady's hair stand up: it was Elsa Lanchester. Across the hall, a new one: Stewart Granger, who looked like Lord Louis Mountbatten.

Even in wartime, with most of the performers in uniform, movies were still being made. A number of the stars had enlisted early; many of them had given up their lives. She paused before a poster, and studied it. It was Leslie Howard, who had been shot down on his last mission for British Intelligence. She would never forget him as Ashley Wilkes in *Gone with the Wind*. Now, he was simply gone. Valerie knew Hamilton would consider it an honor. She considered Hamilton. Where was he, by the way? From the other hallway, she could hear footsteps. Was he coming? She glanced over her shoulder, and checked the light. Lining it up, she blinked her eyes, photographing the poster in its entirety....

A souvenir, she would take it with her.

A large portrait, in shadow, caught her attention. She went up to it. Set in a gold frame, it was a painting of Gale Sondergaard, dressed in black. A monster moon was over her shoulder, threatening the ivy-brick wall of a London mansion, lighted gable window high above the fog-drenched grounds. The air looked colder; she thought of trench coats. Turned sideways to stare, and next to it, a poster of Simone Simone:

The Cat Woman.

The girl returned to Sondergaard. The portrait stirred in her heart, like worship. Inside, of course, there would be stairs, and wouldn't The Spy himself live in a house like this? Sinclair was peering into the window, when Hamilton walked up. Seeing no magic, he invisioned no dreams. A couple of quick blinks, and she joined him. "By the way," the Commander remarked casually, "Charles Laughton, the husband of that actress over there, Elsa Lanchester, is a friend of a friend of our Lieutenant Seymour—chap named James Bridley." Sinclair recognized the name.

Seymour had dropped it, trying to get a date.

Baker Street Irregular, wasn't he?

Having made all arrangements, the Commander now led her down empty corridors, across silent stages, and into an undisclosed area in the back. He knocked three times on the door, waited, then knocked twice. Someone opened it. It looked to be a large fitting room, reeking of paints and body smells, and attended by screens.

The door closed behind them.

A pleasant, mannish-looking Frenchwoman came forward, taking Sinclair under her wing. Valerie noted her hair was rubbish-red—or was it strawberry? Hamilton introduced her to Madame Roc. She spelled it for them: "ayr-r-r, oh, si—Roak! We mak' you look lak' leetle baby, no?" Her voice was deep, nearly guttural. Her body was as thick as her accent. Without taking her eyes from the girl, the woman shouted instructions to her English assistant, "You there! Get clos' from boxes closest me! Hurry up bras, n' underwears. Stockin' too, ask Frieda where." Her mind, quick and sharp as a sewing needle, drank in Valerie's figure and personality. "Yes…is special girl, this. Hey! Bring eberzing uh?" She turned to Hamilton. "How *ol'* you wan', Comman-dair?"

"Try a teenager," Hamilton said, inspired, "a very *young* teenager."

"Ah! We call *gosse,* you call 'keed'. *Ecole,* eh?"

"A kid, yes." That sounded about right. Hire an expert, he had told Seymour, and pay her what she's worth. In the matching of perceived ages to current modes, Roc was the best in her field. If you *had* to turn a sow's ear into a silk purse, you would leave it with Madame Roc.

"Is too young for college, no, Marie?"

The assistant nodded vigorously, throwing a quick glance at Hamilton. Expecting a call from Seymour, he was headed out the door.

The Frenchwoman knew her job. Her hands were fast, her mouth was full of pins. Between selections and fittings, she and Sinclair began to converse in French. In telling her about the posters, Valerie discovered Elsa Lanchester was Madame Roc's closest friend; and that her assistant, Marie, was hoping to get a job as an actress. In English, "Eef play cards right," Roc confided darkly, "who knows?"

Typically, Valerie was less concerned with how the clothes looked than with how she looked in the clothes. Each bit of apparel bore a French label. She stepped behind the screen and tried on several brassieres, left over from a previous fitting. They were too flimsy. A week ago, she would have loved them. Still, as Hamilton had reminded her, a brassiere was much too obvious a place of concealment. Besides, it was her boobs, not the brassieres, that were causing her this problem. One did not fit two silk purses, of this caliber, into a single sow's ear.

The door burst open.

"Something a bit more sturdy?" Valerie asked, her words lost in the flurry of activity on the other side of the screen.

"Give her this one," she heard Hamilton say. He had re-entered the room with a package. Something flew over the top and she put it on. "Fits!" she said.

Immediately, she took it off and looked.

The bra was constructed around a two-way, contoured elastic board. The inside pushed her in, and strapped her flat, without a doubt. The outer, stitched with cheap lace and concealing false shells, appeared to pull her out—but not very much. It was exactly what a French Catholic schoolgirl would wear under her blouse: a brassiere, for appearance's sake, concealing breasts not yet mature enough to fill it.

Hamilton grinned. He could hear the awe.

Designed by Helena Rubinstein, close friend to Emily Blackstone, the brassiere had arrived by morning courier from Bletchley Park.

"Compliments of the Royal Navy!"

"Yes, sir! Thank you, sir!" sang her voice, from the other side. "Dammit!" She had it on backwards, stuck on a clasp.

"How's that?" Hamilton perked.

"Nothing, sir!" In the steamed room, her voice rang like a bell. "Ready when you are, sir!"

Hamilton looked to Madame Roc, and nodded.

Clothes landed! She prepared them fast, dressing quickly. She stepped out.

"No, no," objected Hamilton, whose experience in fashion was limited to black neckties, "dress her down again—younger!"

Madame Roc raked a thick hand through Sinclair's hair.

" 'Youn-gurh,' m'sieur? If she is any youn-gurh, she will be an *egg!*"

"Do it," Hamilton said. He studied Valerie's face. "And when you come to the makeup, make that face no less than twelve." He would settle for fifteen. "I shall be back." He spun on his heel and walked out of the fitting room. Madame Roc strode over, slamming the door behind him and sticking out her tongue.

"*Que fait-il? Rien!*"

Marie raised an eyebrow.

The Frenchwoman sighed heavily, and set to work again. When she was satisfied, she took Valerie over to makeup, which also served as the operating room. There, the French woman and her helper put on white frocks and masks. Valerie got up into a barber's chair. They tucked a sheet around her, cranking her back. From above, Madame Roc leaned down.

"*N'est-ce pas que c'est beau?*"

Someone was taping her arm.

"Well, she's certainly different," the voice of Marie said.

Flat, with eye pads, the thrust of a needle: three sharp punctures, painful as a hook, tiny drops of blood…her eyes were watering. Her lip felt crooked. The anesthesia had come, cloying in her throat, like sweet chocolate.

"*Elle est sortie, eh?*"

The world blacked out.

"*Bon!*"

The surgery was subtle: the young girl's face stung terribly in the darkness—occasionally, the snipping of an instrument. An hour passed. Voices faded, and there was very little talking …distant, salve and wet-packed gauze, cool on her raw skin. The pads came off. They raised her up and she felt dizzy. Hamilton had not told her about the surgery. A little nip and tuck, he'd said.

Sheets were flapped.

Roc was radiant.

The conversion of her hair was next.

"First, cham-poo," instructed the Madame, "then cut heem,

n'treem." The hands of the assistant flew through Valerie's hair like birds. The hair was cleansed. Again, into the barber's chair for the flashings of razor and scissors. From the laboratories at Bletchley Park, a secret rinse was applied which turned the coarser hair of the adult into the softer sheen of childhood. Following closely on the heels of staccato instructions, Marie deftly completed the first part of MI.5's latest stratagem: *The Construction, and Care, of the Military Creature.*

"It's nice baby, no?" Madame Roc smiled broadly, and patted Sinclair rapidly on the cheek, which stung. She then had her undress and lie flat on a brown massage table draped with an enormous towel. 'Allo? Madame Roc had come to the phone number, written on the girl's leg. She bent her head, to read it. Hmmm. Had the Commander already wired her? She poked. "Theese 'phon nombre, what ees?"

"Oh, *that?*" Valerie raised up. "Just a phone number...from a friend."

"Get reed of this nombre," Roc said to Marie.

Valerie panicked! She had not yet recorded it.

"Lay down, you!" Marie poured some liquid on it, then dabbed it with a cloth. Roc directed. Sergeant Blumensteel was gone! The French Resistance had rubbed him out. "Ees from boyfren', no?" These two were not interested in boys. Both women now worked fiercely. From foul-smelling pots, Valerie's body was quickly covered with the waterproof makeup. The eyes of the assistant shone like a blackbird. The girl was then hoisted upright, and great attention was given to her hands and face. Because of Roc's genius, it was already in the process of accelerated healing. The Intelligence community, sequestered in their windowless rooms, had first dibs on advanced procedures and medicines. Outside these secret enclaves, the public might get them later. "The smell and the itch, she will go. Get op!"

"Get dressed!" said Marie.

"He wan' child," the older woman observed, hard voice soft, "he *get* child."

They had laid out the French clothes, she would wear them in France. Sinclair put them on. Marie picked up the telephone and Madame Roc walked the girl, whose face was throbbing, over to the full-length mirror. *"Nous nous regardons,"* she clucked. Valerie peered into the glass:

"Oh my *god!*"

She wasn't in the room; she was in the mirror. What she was staring at, lips slightly parted, was the likeness of another. The face, trapped in time, aflame from surgery, was colored like oils, running in a fire. Her hair, dyed black, had been cut into a pageboy bob, shaved high at the nape, Catholic convent style. Her eyebrows were thickened; and her brown eyes seemed ten years in the past. The darker skin, accompanying, had taken her just this side of puberty. This is what she was seeing, but it was not what others would see. As the mirror obverses, so would the woman: for no spy has ever seen her own face. Framed in the glass, a part of the living picture, was a door like the ones in the movie posters. As though from another time, it burst open; and Hamilton and Pierre walked quickly into the room.

She turned around…

There, where the woman had stood, now stood THE WEA-PON, as child; a very dangerous child. Petite, clownlike, a child of the trapeze, Churchill's answer to Werner von Braun had tears in its eyes.

Valerie Sinclair had utterly vanished!

Valerie Marchaud had taken her place.

Roc handed her a handkerchief and slapped her on the butt. "What you think, Com-man-dair?"

It was the opinion of MI.5 that mattered.

Hamilton did not immediately answer. *Bruises covered, were they?* Hands behind his back, he walked around his protégée observing her from various angles. With a mused look, her tears stopped, Valerie's eyes followed him. At last, his face lit in a broad grin of recognition: "I do believe, gentlemen, we are looking at what the Americans call 'jailbait.' " He turned to Madame Roc. "Well, done, sir!"

Madame Roc beamed: it was high praise.

As for the glasses, de Beck was trying to make up his mind. An ass-bandit, staring at her bodice, his assessment was direct: he liked them young, not flat.

Seeing the Frenchman perplexed, Hamilton said, "I thought glasses would make her look more ordinary, more studious. Doesn't it fit the picture? She can discard them if you think…"

Pierre shook his head.

Valerie walked over to the mirror. She fussed with her blouse. "I look the blimey kid I did in Malta," she told them, her voice sounding a little cracked. Reacting like a father, Hamilton cleared his throat. He threw her a glance: that British attitude would have to go.

Hers, not his.

Pierre perked up. "You lived in Malta?"

"Why yes, my mother is part Maltese."

"Mine's French," Pierre said. He was having trouble in appearing not to notice. Damned if hers wasn't, too! "You're gorgeous, Marchaud."

Valerie blinked.

"Excellent!" said Hamilton. "Well now, Lieutenant, if you will, they have some clothes for you...girl clothes, you know. Leave what you're wearing with Madame. Bring your uniform along. Pierre? Why don't we wait outside?"

The men left.

They gave her some odds and ends to wear, befitting her age. She stripped, and got into them, wearing the new bra. Following Hamilton's instructions, Marie packed up her uniform. Sinclair was looking about for a cigarette. Roc told her to help herself. The half-empty pack was there on the counter, tangled in ribbons and scissors. Valerie pulled one out. It was French, black tobacco, a Gauloise. She sniffed it, putting it in her pocket. The assistant was tossing in some belts into a bag; a pillbox hat, light blue; junk jewelry. Madame Roc looked up. She was at the sink, drying her hands. *"T'en fais pas!"* The Frenchwoman shouted. "Com' back, eh?" They had other clients, waiting.

"Si tout va bien..."

The assistant handed her the bag, opened the door.

"See you," chirped Marie.

Dusk was falling and de Beck drove them back to Waterloo Station. The Commander and the girl would train to Polperro. Commissary had packed them a box lunch, for supper. It rode on top of the bag. Stashed up front, Pierre had his own.

Along the way, Hamilton gave him instructions.

Pierre would meet him at the The Red Lion later tonight, at 2400 hours, and drive him to Portsmouth. Hamilton had a full day tomorrow scheduled with Seymour. De Beck would drop the car off at Free French Headquarters, Castor, making his own way back on Sunday.

They would not see him again, until the marina.

The Commander also had instructions for Valerie but felt it prudent to wait until they were alone. His first opportunity came after Pierre dropped them at the terminal, before they boarded for Falmouth. "Now, I realize, my dear, that while looking like a child is one thing, *being* one may prove quite a different matter. The older, the more experienced the adults you encounter, the greater their likelihood of spotting you. Believe me, the Germans *know* the difference, and we're calling upon you to outsmart them. You can best do this by doing what you do best. Do what a child would do. Do it the way that a child would do it. Be the child, in their eyes, that they want you to be."

The girl with the scalded face looked up.

"What's important is that no one suspect you. You may count it as a certainty, they will try to entrap you. If you can, divert their attention. If they offer to bribe you—with food, for example—shake your head. If you must, *put the guilt on somebody else*." He stressed this. "After all, who is the finger going to point to, you—or him? Adults will also be looking for good manners, you see, upbringing, that sort of thing." He patted her head. "Got it?"

"Got it."

Rushing through the busy terminal Hamilton and the girl ran the last few yards, jumping aboard the Falmouth Express with seconds to spare.

Unfortunately, the train was crowded and they had to share the compartment with an older couple. The husband was snoozing, but the wife kept peering over her magazine:

Something odd about that child…

With the rails clacking beneath them, the Commander sat as quiet as the summer wind, browsing through *The Times*, clearing his throat occasionally, and helping the girl sort through some item or other in her bag. The woman across from him could not help but notice, he had caught her look. She was thinking he was traveling with his daughter.

Something the matter with her face?

Hamilton wet his thumb, and turned the page.

Valerie, scattering things in her bag, smiled up at her: *she healed quickly from cuts.* Alarmed, the woman looked. Valerie was clutching the box lunch, staring at it mournfully, as though it were not for her.

"Hungry, are we?" Hamilton noted, intent upon his article.

"No, sir." Valerie said quietly. She dabbed at her eyes.

"Would you like a biscuit, dear?" the woman asked, concerned.

Valerie shook her head. When Hamilton wasn't looking, she touched gingerly at her face. Getting the woman's eye, the sweet little girl jerked her head to the child-beater sitting next to her, who, as the woman could plainly see, was hiding his guilt behind his newspaper. The eyes of the woman narrowed. She nodded slowly, letting the desperate girl know that she understood.

The Commander sat sternly.

When the train pulled into Falmouth, the woman woke up her husband, pulling him quickly to the door. There, she turned to the Commander, who was looking about for the box lunch. He was unprepared then, when the woman screamed at him:

"Beast!"

"I beg your pardon?" Sinclair handed him the lunch, afraid to hold it.

So!

Valerie, having moved to sit behind him, out of danger as it were, tapped her temple and made a spiraling motion with her finger: *it's his brain injury,* she informed the woman, who was reading her lips; and who had become so flushed with outrage, she could hardly contain herself.

Hamilton jumped up.

"The fact that you have a brain injury, sir, is no excuse to visit its horrid consequences upon this Innocent!"

Her husband grabbed her. The door slammed. The train had stopped. "What in the *hell* is going on?" Hamilton demanded. Valerie shrugged. "Let's get out of here," and he picked up the sack into which she was still stuffing the rest of her things.

Valerie followed the sack.

"That's what I mean," he explained over his shoulder, as he hurried them down the aisle. "This war makes people crazy."

153

"Mum's the word, sir."

"Necessary to stay ahead of it, you see, constantly alert."

"You can count on me, sir."

Disembarking, they connected to the local for Polperro where the Commander immediately secured them an empty compartment. Unnerved by the deranged passenger, he tested the lock on the door. Valerie wished their schedule had allowed time for a few rounds at Trelissick House, famous for its bar. She sat down, sighed, and crossed her legs. Settled in, and with the train moving, the Commander doused the lights and raised the blackout shade.

They had dinner, the miles slipping past them.

Hamilton wasn't hungry and the girl ate most of it.

It was a clear horizon, soft with moonlight and sharp with stars, and with the River Fal behind them, flowing to the sea. Trees were bending in the wind. Finished with eating, she was stowing the garbage.

Hamilton, who had been observing the onrushing scenery, handed her his newspaper and leaned back, comparing their present location to his home in Northern Wales. As in a background, she could hear the great Welsh voices; see, in eyrie green-veined sunlight, the mouldering dark-eyed castles. Cardiff reared in her mind, and cities of pain, where blood turned to coal and where the salt-brined sea made prisoners of those who joined it.

They had been on the train for some time now. It had not seemed that long coming in. Maybe it was because of what had happened today and because it was Saturday. To the Commander, picturing the child Marchaud across from him, the flashing night in this setting of sea and sand was as pretty as a postcard. To Valerie, his voice seemed trapped in time, cloaked with curtains, somewhere in a darkroom.

Prints were emerging: the family album in her head.

As he talked, her photographic memory took her back to the days before the war. Her hair was long. Her parents had brought her here, to Falmouth, for a holiday; with some Egyptian friends of her father's. They had attended a concert together in the second-story hall of the old Conservatory. It was ten years ago, and the temperature was 79°. She knew, because one of the Egyptians, who was five feet seven and a half inches tall, asked her why she had blinked her eyes. The vicar, not wishing to hear his daughter described as *a camera,* explained it as a nervous twitch.

She had been looking into the sun.

The Programme that Tuesday night was Dvorak's String Quartet in F-major, *The American.* She recalled the composer had also written *Humoresque,* one of her favorites; that the boy next to her had a gold tooth; that his mother, wearing fuchsia lipstick, had also worn a dead corsage and that she had reeked of *Lady Esther,* splashed on a lavender dress.

"Beautiful night," Hamilton noted.

She mentioned the Conservatory. Did he know it? He did. For security reasons, it was closed for the duration. Enemy agents, posing as patrons, might use it to signal. Situated on a hill, the cobalt-blue windows stared darkened at the sea:

Sunglasses worn by The Spy...

In her mind, a periscope had surfaced:

Lights blinking in the night...

She stared out at what was passing—bushes and blazoned buildings—bone-white houses of sleep. In Europe, rain would be drilling into the mud; men shivering in ditches without warmth. Had spies, sent by Hamilton, not prayed to the same God as the Germans, until captured and shot, they had died with their mouths full of the same earth? Would they be alive now if they had asked questions—staring at these blue-white stars holding high above the window of this speeding train? What *were* the nights like in France? She leaned forward and touched his knee.

"Yes, my dear?" The Commander looked at her curiously.

Valerie chewed her lip. "Sir? What happens to us if I get killed? Or if Pierre...?" The question was important to her. They were not in the cave now.

The train turned, its darker shadows sweeping across the landscape. "My dear—Lieutenant—you must try not to concern yourself with such *dreadful* questions." She sat cross-legged on the seat. "We will face that if the time comes—"

Wind was batting at the windows of the train. Polperro was coming up. The air seemed colder, pressing into her body. She wished she had something warmer to wear. She definitely missed her uniform. Riding along, they looked at each other. The Commander was neither anxious, nor was he not anxious.

The question nagged her, though he had answered part of it. She had been thinking of France. She felt Roc's cigarette in her pocket. "May I ask you," Valerie Sinclair said, "are you yourself afraid to die?" The train was slowing.

Hamilton smiled.

"Well now, I wouldn't *welcome* it. You don't welcome it, do you, Sinclair?"

"Never!"

"You see, we're cut from the same cloth." Hers was tacky cotton, he was wearing his. They felt the screech of brakes. She jumped up and pulled the shades, plunging them into utter blackness. *Death*, he had told her at Achnacarry, *is an unfathomable darkness*. From its eerie silence had come a voice:

"Got a light, sir?"

Telegraph lines were jumping, chattering like clowns. Disembarking, the man and the girl walked the short distance to The Red Lion. It was after eleven and the streets were deserted. Bags, leaves, and discarded newspapers scudded across the cobbles, plastering themselves against curbs and at the bases of trembling lamps. The wind, stronger now, had followed them up the coast.

She accepted his arm, and burrowed into it.

The wireless that day had hinted at foul weather, but the details were vague. As usual these days, shipping was being warned in a roundabout way. Polperro felt sucked dry, as if by a giant vacuum, common before a larger storm.

The Commander tested the air. By tomorrow night, all hell would be breaking loose. Hamilton was no stranger to it. Often, prestorm weather at sea had left him eager and apprehensive, on the keen edge of coiled and explosive excitement. Sinclair could feel it, in his grip. Entering the hotel, she could hear the raging of the wild air, high above them and along the abutments of the cliffs.

The lobby was deserted, fronted by a single clerk. As they passed him, Hamilton nodded. They hurried up the stairs, the Commander silencing her with a look.

Arriving at Valerie's room, he took the key from her hand and unlocked the door. Checking the hallways, he motioned her inside. They must not be seen together. "Why is that, sir?"

the girl whispered. The Commander did not answer. He would not acknowledge it. Closing the door behind them, he remembered why:

If you still have doubts, said Blackstone, *perhaps you could try de Beck on her for size.* Intended to assess the Frenchman's weakness, it was actually to determine the girl's. Once on the mission, each spy's vulnerability would affect the other spy's life. No British officer worthy of the name would leave that determination to a Frenchman.

Hamilton had decided.

After weeks of delays, and days of duty, after briefings and bullets, Achnacarry and caves, after Bridley and Farvillant, Elstree and LeClerc, and underneath the Casablanca fan, Commander David Hamilton officially kissed Valerie Sinclair. In the history of the Royal Navy, no Lieutenant ever surrendered faster.

Valerie tasted him; it wasn't right.

"Sinclair, how can I ever let you go?"

She heard his voice coming back to her, mechanically and distant, as if from the soundtrack of a foreign film. She had heard such arrogance before. This officer, for all of his pride and honor, was no better than the gate guards at Weymouth. At least they were honest about it. Hamilton, on the other hand, was acting as though bestowing a blessing.

Sinclair opened her eyes.

She kissed him quickly. "Think of the waterproof makeup!" A line reserved for the Frenchman, she had just thrown it away on a fish. Having offered himself as bait, he was now swimming away.

Hamilton wasn't worth a damn at these things!

It was embarrassing. The man was inept. Sinclair was off the hook. If he hadn't planned to fuck, he should have said so! A breach of promise, she shook off her shoe.

He threw up his arm, but not in time — his cap deflected the blow. Hamilton stared in alarm, at the bent insignia. "My god!" he muttered. "What strength!" With fingers of steel, he pulled it right.

"I am so sorry!" she cried. She was wiping her nose on the chenille. "I didn't mean to throw it at you!" Feeling safer, he popped on his hat.

"Bloody thoughtless of me."

Blackstone sighed, it was in disgust.

"More 'tests,' sir?"

"Come now, Sinclair! You know better than that!" It was easier, when they cried. "But we had to be *sure*, you see. Whatever I do, whatever we've planned—the shit, as you would put it—is all geared to keep you alive."

"That's *not* how I would put it!"

"Of course not," he fended, "of course you wouldn't, but you understand. We must probe their armor, their weaknesses, you see." Valerie had moved to the wardrobe, she was hanging up her clothes.

Drat!

"Sinclair?" Feelings hurt, she was jabbing in her bag. Commander Hamilton walked over to her, he touched her arm.

"Sir?"

"Sit down." Unhappy, she would get over it. "Now listen to me..."

He knelt, gripping the chair. A military professional, his voice was sincere. "If Pierre de Beck leaves you alone at any time—for anything other than a reasonable time"—and he emphasized the words—*"be on your guard."*

Her lips parted slightly, her eyes were puzzled.

"Yes, you see, unknown to you, the Germans could have captured him or shot him. Do you understand?"

She studied his face. "Of course," she said, "but couldn't the same thing happen to me?" She jumped up. "Surely, if Pierre could be shot or captured, I could. What's important, I would think, is to get the information."

Otherwise—!

The question eluded her, it was something he said on the train. "Even together, Commander, we may have but a fifty-fifty chance."

"My dear Sinclair, it is not a matter of *statistics*; the information we're after is far more complex...."

"But if we're equal in our purposes—?"

"But you *aren't*." His voice had metal in it. Hamilton then made a strange admission: "You're a daughter of the Commonwealth. You are a part of England, and England is a part of you. You represent her, but Pierre does not."

"He *doesn't?*"

"No, he represents the Allies."

"The *Allies?* but aren't we—?"

"How can I put it?" The Commander's hand went to his forehead, as though to alleviate unseen pain. "It is *England*, you see, who stands to be destroyed."

She was stunned. Hamilton spoke for Churchill.

"That other weapon, you mean?" Her eyes widened. "The one you spoke about at Grasshopper Bay?"

"The Waterfall, yes. Actually..." He hesitated, then decided. "*Waterfall* is the German Code inversion for 'Heavy Water.'"

Did he mean rocket fuel?

Without knowing why, she suddenly felt uncomfortable. "I'm not sure I understand—"

"Of course you do!" But she didn't. Hamilton now made a second decision: to withdraw the option of disclosure. He would not return to it. One did not share physics with one who did not already know. "—far too technical, really. Suppose we leave it for the experts, shall we?"

She could see it: *the world in flames.*

"It is England's problem, you see, and it is for the *English* to solve it."

"It is not an Allied problem?"

"No...not exactly?"

"Then whose?"

Hamilton looked deep into her eyes. Finally, he said: "It is mine."

Valerie was aghast. She turned and walked to the curtains. She peeked through them and out over the town, which was sleeping. Churchill, she now realized, was not without a certain lack of trust in his friends. Hamilton had as much as said so. It was as if the Prime Minister, after Coventry—perhaps as a consequence of it—had grown ever more secretive, ever more paranoid, as the war thundered to its conclusion. As to *whose* conclusion, delivery in Brittany would tell. That was their position, was it not? As the Commander had made clear to her at Weymouth, without this information—vital to national survival—England would lose.

But what was "heavy water"?

She remembered that afternoon, when he had first told her;

and she remembered his words: *Waterfall…a weapon, which if deployed, will render us absolutely defenseless against it.* What kind of weapon? Hamilton had mentioned Einstein. She recalled from files since destroyed—one of her first jobs following her Clearance—that Einstein and a man named Szilard had written a letter to Roosevelt…that a copy of it was in a folder called the *Manhattan Engineering District*, intended for Bletchley Park; but that it had been routed to Weymouth instead; because of the mistake of an officer who was no longer there. A man in civilian clothes had come—just as Hamilton had—asking her if she remembered anything. She had lied, and told him *no*.

"How do you spell Oppenheimer?" he had asked.

Photographing his motives, they spoke to her a picture:

The London Financial District had not forgiven Washington for excluding them, and making them wait in line. And what they were concealing: was *a tool of power*. War or no, there were men willing to steal these tools of power from other men in order to use them for themselves. Later, looking at her prints, photographs of this picture had not developed. Something had happened in the dark room. It had to do with guilt. Beyond the limits set by MI.5, she was forbidden to see: truth was for experts. It was all very much an ULTRA secret, heavily censored, and far too dreadful for her to know. Whatever it was, whoever was after it, whatever the cost, MI.5 was counting on her to photograph it.

That's why there was a mission.

"I understand," the girl said. But what was it she understood? She was staring at men without faces; at pictures without parts. This *weapon*…could that explain the presence of The Spy? Was that why he had followed her? Dark pathways into the truth ended before steel doors; and people like her were not supposed to go there.

She sat down on the edge of the bed.

Hamilton took his turn in the chair. "There are still a few loose ends…" She looked up. "Now, for one thing, you'll want to wear your street clothes to the marina…"

"Security reasons?"

Hamilton nodded.

"But what do I do with my uniform?" She was so proud of it.

"My dear Valerie..." his voice was strong, "a uniform is forever. Just leave your things in the room, as is. We will take care of it."

"Yes, sir."

He smiled at her and she recalled his remark, following Achnacarry, the afternoon they'd arrived in Polperro: that it was too dangerous to discuss plans in their rooms. She understood now, that had been meant for de Beck. But her partner was someone that Hamilton hadn't talked much about. "—your uniform, I dare say, will be waiting here for you when you get back."

"It will?"

"Of course. And who knows? Perhaps another ring...hmmm?" An upgrade in rank, he meant. She looked across at him and knew, in the way she knew things, that a further promotion for her was not his to give. More, that her commission must have cost him dearly. Somewhere, in plush offices and iron-clad security mansions, forbidden to her, David Hamilton hung on a cross. Dispensation would come from there, from his superiors, depending on whether she lived—and delivered.

For the Commander, she was the ultimate bet.

He asked her for the two letters.

She walked to the bureau, licked and sealed the envelopes, and handed them over. They would go as they were.

"What about Pierre?"

"What about him?" *Bloody damn!* Hamilton pocketed the letters; he could see she was wrought. He must repair any doubt—he had caused it. "Pierre is at fever pitch for the mission, and at top form. You are, as I have told you, a formidable match." He motioned her aside. He needed the bed for a table.

Produced from an inside pocket, the Commander unrolled an oilskin packet with stitched compartments. "Now then," he said, "—your battered glasses. The left-hand temple is removed and becomes a pen. The writing, of course, will be on your body and will be invisible." He had not mentioned the cyanide. It would be in her purse. They had already gone over it. The items would be given to her aboard the submarine.

Sunday...

"This perpendicular bar, you see, also contains the ink." The Commander had extracted a gold chain, with a white cross attached. "The point pops out on the verticle." The sight of the cross made her uneasy. She thought of Marchaud. *Hadn't she seen it before?* He showed her: how all the things would work. Tucking them back into their compartments, he rolled up the packet, and returned it to his coat. "When you wear the cross, wear it well, and may God go with you."

God was important to her. Hamilton worked for him.

"I do not feel afraid now," Valerie said, "I know I'm going to come back safely." Commander Hamilton stood up. "What you told me last night, about de Beck—?"

"De Beck, yes..."

"—to do what he does?" The Commander smiled. "Captain de Beck and I will get along just fine, sir." She got up from the bed, and walked over to the mirror.

"Lieutenant," he said, "I would appreciate it if you would forget this 'Commander' business when we are alone." Sinclair looked at her own watch. Anything personal was generally offered, and withdrawn, in less than a minute. From the table of high romance, Hamilton was careful not to pick up too many tabs.

"Sir?"

"My friends, you see, call me David."

Until now, she wasn't aware that he had any.

"Yes, sir, David!" Sinclair's salute plummeted past his composure like a can of paint from a bos'un's chair.

Hamilton forced a smile.

"What would happen, Commander, if I were prevented from going?"

"Ah!" Predictably, like those before her, Sinclair had found the courage to put her greatest anxiety into words. Hamilton said: "In that eventuality, we would promptly leave without you."

It was a standing order, from Blackstone.

"I'll be there, sir!"

"Yes," he answered wryly, "we all rather thought that you would." For each espionage, planned or unplanned, there was a counterespionage; but bigger fish than Blackstone were circling. Still at attention, she was looking up at him. "At ease," Hamilton said. The cards could not have fallen better to his advantage. He had saved the best for last.

"The Prime Minister sends you his best," Hamilton lied.
It was coming, she could feel it, momentous.
"Did he call you?" the Commander asked.
"*Me?*"
"Why, yes, he does that sometimes," the Commander admitted, voice of Cheshire cat. Dark winds tugged at the blackout curtains. Commodore Blackstone had ascended from the lower depths. The Mission-Commander's grey eyes held steady, bathing the girl with honor. In the distance, a clock struck the hour.
Her minute was up.

"Your training is now completed," Commander Hamilton said, "and you are at Liberty. Normally, our 'Jack-dusty,' the Supply Officer, would have issued you grey strides and a blazer—or in your case, grey skirt and a blue blazer. But since you will not be wearing your uniform on the mission, we saw no need to attend to it."

They had neglected to tell her that.

"Oh well, it's just one day, isn't it?"

"Exactly. I knew you would see it our way. At the dance you were officially on duty, you see."

"I understand," she said.

"Good show! Well then, I'll expect you at the marina at 2100 hours." His hand was on the knob. "Sorry we didn't have more time to enjoy the weekend. If it were any other night—"

He wouldn't be here.

"Oh, that's all right," Valerie sang out. She was peering into the closet, to see what she would wear. It was mostly coat-hangers. She stood there, her back turned. Their time together was ending. For the girl risking her life, and who had less than a day to enjoy it, opportunity had never been withdrawn. To the Commander, it had never existed. It wasn't that Hamilton hadn't wanted to make love; he had simply wanted to make sure—for the Commonwealth, you see?—for MI.5. The child, Valerie Marchaud, was their invention. Sinclair, the woman, was the price.

What survived, would be the Bomb.

He looked at her, the way a man does. Blackstone was right: it had been a while. The Commander cleared his throat, resuming authority. Like the makeup, it was waterproof and it would not wash off in the rain.

Valerie turned around, she smiled at him.

Hamilton opened the door: a job well done. He could feel Commodore Blackstone's reassuring hand on his shoulder. "I have thrown caution to the winds for the past hour," he confessed, shooting himself in the other foot, "but they have been the most wonderful minutes of my life."

Before she could answer, he was gone.

Valerie Sinclair stood still in the room that had died and stared at the walls that were loveless and cold. At the moment, she did not feel like going to bed. She turned. Where Hamilton had made his exit, the door stood ajar. She walked over, closed it, and tested the latch.

"Good-bye, David."

She sighed then, and reassumed the room.

She finished unpacking, hanging her uniform matter-of-factly in the wardrobe. As she undressed, she cast a curious look at the strange and forbidding bra, also Navy-issued. Tucking it into the top shelf of the wardrobe, and fishing out her gown, Valerie began to sing. She sang it to her little boy, Brian, or to her Daddy; either of them could hear it, if they wanted:

> Go to sleep my baby
> Close your pretty eyes
> Angels up above you
> Peeping at you dearie
> From the skies.

Slamming the panel:

> Great big moon is shining
> Stars begin to peep...
> Time for little piccaninnies
> To go to sleep.

The new brassiere, and the entire day, took her back to the boardwalks at Blackpool, where the flim-flam men, dark forearms curling with green Indian snakes, churned calliopes into mechanical tin-songs on the afternoon air of long-ago summers. No one had asked her, and perhaps no one ever would; but that was *not* where she wanted to be. Oh, they wouldn't mind reaching out to her—coaxing her from behind the tent-walls with their ruddy gifts!—and she saw herself running from them, chaps who could never help her.

When this mission was over, she knew exactly where she was headed: knocking at the great doorways of the world to enter sweet-smelling and voluptuous salons in Lisbon, London, and New York where rich and important women with dark tans and mirrored sloe eyes creamed with mascara held court for their buyers on pink brocade couches; and whose tiny feet, shewn with silk, had sunk deep into dreams on their Persian lamb rugs, coming closer and ever closer to her ideal...wearing slippers. From there, she knew, the brassiere had come. This mission then, might represent a real chance for her.

Doubts had arisen, like fog under streetlights, but they had failed to frighten her, for her ambition was strong and true. Nor was she plagued by possibilities that it would be Blackpool and not Elstree, Newton Swyre and not London, that she would be forced to return to.

She put on her dressing gown.

The lovely Egyptian garment, shimmering with the deep shades of the sea, seemed shorn of its allure. Now it was just something to wear. Her father had sent it. She rearranged her street clothes. A vicar's daughter, she didn't own anything, and there was nothing to pack. There had been little time to shop.

Perhaps Sunday.

She moved from the chair onto the bed. The day had been terribly long. She yawned, the overhead fan humming a dreamless song. When she looked up again, the lights were still burning:

It was dawn.

Valerie got up and turned off the lamp and opened the curtains. The sea was up and threatening. On the horizon, morning ascended like a spirit.

She shook herself out, exercised, and turned on the taps. Her training was over; Hamilton had said so. Splashing *Evening in Paris* under the running faucets, Sinclair thoroughly enjoyed the luxury of an early morning bath. She stared at the tiny bottle on the shelf. Personal cosmetics, taken-for-granted things, she would miss. She checked the makeup on her body. One would have thought she'd been three months at Blackpool, or a lifetime on the Riviera. She would put sunglasses on her shopping list. She lathered, scrubbing gingerly at her cheeks. Her scalded face was feeling better.

Waterproof, it was.

Her brown eyes were drawn to the perfume again...to the label. Her feet pressed against the iron of the tub and she thought of the coast of France. There, the iron was lethal, and a thousand miles deep. She reached for it, but it was gone, a missing memory. *Danger that awaited her, speaking German in the night, and murdering things that landed.* Hitler must be defeated, or love could not breathe.

Then, she could get on with her plans.

What was it the Commander had said? If she were to be killed, and not Pierre? His words hung like motes of dust in the still air; like negatives without a darkroom: they were there, and yet they weren't.

Steam now erased their passage. Colorless vapors misted the bathroom window, camouflaging the black dawn beyond, where the foul clouds of war had been rising and gathering for four long and terrible years, and where SURVIVAL had proved to be the one headline that mattered, until now. She was going to be famous! She could see it: on the front page of *The Daily Telegraph*:

VALERIE VICTORIOUS! FUEHRER FUCKED!

Armed with a foreign name, and with another's history, they were sending her backwards, into time. Well, she had lived in stranger places: she thought of the vicarage.

Her father again...his face.

Why didn't you love me!

She pulled the plug. Her eyes widened, because her mind knew: he had turned a deaf ear. He had taken her share, without her permission, and given it all to God. The wind wailed. She listened. There was no answer. He would be too busy, praying for her soul.

Good-bye, Daddy.

The new brassiere was too tight. *Blame somebody else*, Hamilton had advised.

Valerie kicked off her fuzzies.

Employing *dynamic tension*, accomplished at considerable

risk to her jaw—that is, by hooking her toes into one end of the bra while pulling up mightily with both arms on the other—Sinclair had been able to stretch it enough for a comfortable fit. She snapped into her underwear, turning sideways to the mirror.

The Cat Woman!

Her eyes narrowed, hissing sparks. She checked her makeup, and looked up. The Casablanca fan was wobbling. The curtains flapped. She walked to the window. The pale orb of the sun had disappeared, dark clouds rolling in from the sea. Turning to the glass, she put on her pillbox hat; fluffing up her hair, and feeling like a silent movie star.

After lunch, she would explore the town.

The hotel boutique was open, dedicated to Ladies Wear; and manned this Sunday by an Arab, whose relatives worked in the beachfront hotels. Upon seeing the strange-looking girl approach—blue dress, hem too long—he smiled broadly and slammed his cash register shut.

Sinclair walked through the door.

"How do you do?" she said. "My name is Smythe."

"Of the Bristol Smythes?" They were his favorite customers: he didn't owe them. Sunday business was at an all time low and the Arab was anxious to make a sale. She wanted sunglasses. He was out. "Something for your mother?" He was trying to place her. "Big postcards, with belly-dancers—" No..? Rugs, a *choice*: belly-dancers, or camels! No? "Leather goods, perhaps?" His handbags were wrinkled and pink, sand-dune thin, and raspy as paper. *"No?"* With secret eyes, he glanced at her purse. The businessman scrutinized her carefully, seeking where to bite. This Smythe was a hard sell, the intellectual type!

Something warm, for her shoulders, at lectures...

"What a coincidence," he confided, "this is your lucky day! These Moroccan shawls are *just* in, absolutely the latest thing!" He flapped one out, holding it high in front of him, for her inspection. Valerie walked around behind him, to study the counter. When he lowered the shawl, no one was there. Puzzled, he stepped out into the lobby, looking to the right and left. Sinclair appeared at his side. She felt safer in the lobby. She tapped him on the shoulder.

The Arab jumped!

He'd thought it was his cousin, to whom he owed three quid. "You! I thought you had left. Did we decide on the shawl?" He glanced over his shoulder, escorting the girl back into the shop.

"My mother would like this hat pin," Valerie said. "How much?" It was pearl-headed, long, and very sharp.

"How much? For a *Smythe*?" crooned the Arab, plucking the pin from her hand, and assessing it with reverence. "For your mother, special price. Nine shillings."

"I'll take it." He beamed, and handed it to her. "Oh dear," she observed, "look at this blemish."

After getting him to toss in a genuine Japanese silk handkerchief with a picture of a fan on it, merchandise difficult to move these days, he settled at three and sixpence.

"Thank you so veddy, veddy much." Thinking her a Bristol Smythe, she wouldn't want him to get the wrong idea.

"My *pleasure*, Miss Smythe."

As soon as she left, hat pin bobbing happily in her pillbox hat, the Arab locked his door. Business had been bad lately, but never *this* bad. Crossing the lobby, Sinclair entered the dining room. The waitress greeted her cheerfully, "Disgusting day, isn't it?" She had seen the Arab, taking advantage of her.

"Yes, quite," replied Valerie, in her best grown-up voice. She had no problem with it since it was hers. "Tea first, please." The server, who was a hard thirty with sallow skin, dropped a menu and returned to the kitchen. She had been trying to call her husband, who was off work today. "Clive still running around on you, is he, Gladys?" taunted the cook, grilling chops.

It was the talk of the kitchen.

"When I catch that bitch she'll need a doctor," vowed Valerie's waitress, talking over her shoulder and arriving back at the table.

Sinclair, alarmed, looked up. "Oh, I am so terribly sorry. Is your dog sick?"

"Nothin' to concern *you*, love. Parents stayin' at the 'otel, are they?" Such a *pathetic*-looking child! She picked up the menu, which seemed to have hat pin holes in it. "What'll it be, dearie?"

Touching gingerly at her hat, which was barely holding, Valerie placed an extensive order. When it arrived, she enjoyed it with gusto. The cook stuck his head out the door to see who was eating so much. Single, he was glad he didn't have kids. Making quick work of a chop, Sinclair kept glancing at the service door. Where was that waitress, had she gone to the bathroom? Sinclair didn't feel like eating alone. She wished for a gentleman to share her lunch. Perhaps that nice waiter from Friday.

When her tea arrived, it was cold: children got ignored in restaurants. She lifted the cup distractedly, and stared through the glass: the sky was like soup. Towards the east, black clouds towered.

"Fancy more tea, Miss?" It was the waitress. Valerie asked her where the waiter was, the one who had served her two nights ago. "—we have an appointment to have a date on Tuesday."

The pot crashed to the floor!

Sinclair had wanted to tell him she would be out of town.

"Do ye now?" the waitress snapped, sidestepping the carnage. "I'll be sure 'n tell 'im—" A man came running out of the kitchen with a mop. "—'e's me 'usband!"

"Your husband?" Valerie turned to the man with a mop. *Poor bloke.* "How do you do, sir? The name is Smythe." Valerie laid some money on the table. She hesitated, trying to figure, then added to it. She turned to the waitress. "Please do be so kind as to give this to your waiter. Tell him, if you will please"— she lowered her voice—"that it's for the other night."

"Anything else?"

"Got a cigarette?"

The waitress leaned down so that Valerie could hear, "A cigarette, is it? Where would you like it, ya little brat, up yer ass?"

Valerie shook her head.

As she did so, her hat fell off. Trying to keep it from hitting the floor, the man with the mop batted at it desperately, and slipped on the tea. In falling, he grabbed the waitress for support, taking her with him. As she fell she kicked at the hat, which soared over the heads of the guests, who followed it with interest.

The hat rolled out the door.

"Excuse me," said Valerie, over her shoulder, running after it. "Good luck with your cigarette!"

What a peculiar custom!

The Arab, who'd had a terrible day and who was just leaving, saw a blue pillbox hat rolling his way, being frantically pursued by his customer. In bending gallantly to retrieve it, he stabbed himself with the hat pin. The end of his finger was turning red. Valerie handed him the handkerchief with the picture of the fan on it. Gratefully, he wrapped it around his bleeding finger, just as the Manager walked up. Guests were listening; he would have to settle it. The Arab, who was holding the handkerchief up with both hands, was trying to explain what had happened. The Manager, staring in horror at the red circle in the middle, a miniature Japanese flag, grabbed the Arab by his elbow and steered him over to the front desk where he called Security. Within seconds, one of Hamilton's Operatives showed up, taking the Arab into custody in front of some women with flowered hats, late arrivals, who were demanding to know when his boutique would open. Peering around them, and spotting the girl, the Arab threatened to kill her. Hearing this, the Operative produced his weapon, and marched the Arab into a back room at gunpoint.

"Anything I can do for you?" the Manager purred, to Valerie. The ultimate diplomat, he didn't have a name.

"Yes," said Valerie. "Would you be so kind as to send somebody up to my room to adjust my Casablanca fan?"

"I *quite* understand," apologized the Manager, glancing at the door where they had just taken the Arab. "One never knows these days where the enemy is going to surface." Renting floor space to collaborators, could be a serious offense. He had come so highly recommended, too!

Valerie headed for the stairwell, the Manager following. Noting this, she stopped, and pulled him close. *She knew something!* The girl glanced over his shoulder and he lowered his ear. "The name is Smythe."

"Smythe?"

Sinclair nodded, she narrowed her eyes: it was a clip, from *The Cat Woman*.

Instantly, the Manager was back on the phone to Security. "That's right. That Japanese collaborator you just arrested? His name is Smythe."

"But isn't that who—?"

Smythe?

Up the coast, Martin Seymour's phone was ringing.

Hamilton was still on hold.

A major security effort, Whitehall had a month to blow the *Waterfall* to hell, or die. The exact date would come in the course of the day.

In the parlance of the back-room boys, the Three Bears were defined by their place in history, and they were all men. Mama Bear was Lord Louis Mountbatten, Chief of Combined Operations, on secret recall from Ceylon. Baby Bear was Commodore John Blackstone, Royal Navy, Bletchley, who worked for Mama Bear; and Hamilton, whom MI.5 had solemnly cryptogrammed as the Big Bad Wolf.

Papa Bear would be disclosed at the last moment.

Hamilton, who had a sure instinct for covers, took one whiff and detected cigar smoke. Though not present at the meeting, he concluded that inspiration for the atomic mission, GOLDI-LOCKS, had come from a writer named Winston. From long association, he knew that Churchill's fables were invariably Grimm; and that this one, his favorite, had started two days following a chance meeting at the Royal.

To Hamilton, in charge of the nuts and bolts, was left the honor of the password, by which Operatives from MI.5 would identify their counterparts in MI.6. For this Sunday's use, the Commander had selected SAINT IVES. There was no particular reason for it. It just seemed a good place to go. By Sunday nightfall, his itinerary would take him to others.

After leaving Valerie, who wasn't privy to the planning, he had slept in the back seat of the Rolls that had carried him from Polperro to Southampton and up to the dockyard gates. Behind him, in the chopped waters of the harbor, iron-grey ships were riding at anchor, their stacks yawing skyward against the approaching sun.

Hamilton got out of the car and walked up to the driver. "Don't dally too long on Liberty," he warned the Frenchman. He held his hat against the wind. "We meet promptly at 2100 hours. The marina—you have the slip number."

"No problem, Commander."

Hamilton knew damn well that de Beck would be dropping

off in London, saying good-bye to one of his whores, and grabbing a few hours sleep. "See to it then," the Commander concluded. "Easy on that car, what?" The last thing he needed was flack from General LeClerc. De Beck nodded, and backed the Rolls out of the gate. The Commander, braced against the wind, headed for the door.

Lights were beaming from the corner office.

Lieutenant Seymour was sorting through his mail: bills; a letter from a girl he'd danced with, drunk, scribbling out an address; and a postcard from Delhi, via Trincomalee. The cover showed a pale pink flamingo, card filched from Key West; message reading, "Mother eating porridge." It was signed, "Sister."

Bridley—wearing pith helmet and white suit, and whose mysterious trip had revealed itself in the stamp, post-forwarded—had been covering for Lord Louis and would accompany him to England.

Hamilton handed Seymour the cable. It had Parker written all over it. Seymour stuck with the card. "Lord Louis is back!" he announced. "Ceylon, is it, or—?"

"I know," the Commander said, opening and slamming drawers. "Where did you hide the sugar?" The teapot was already singing. Seymour walked over to the gun drawer, reached under the irons, and produced a box of American cubes. Intended for Conrad Parker from Captain Bernstein, Legal Department of Ike, and relevant to the release of data in Kay Summersby's file, the consignment had been intercepted by Bridley. Parlaying his heist, the Boffin had sent the sugar to Martin Seymour for his birthday. Bernstein, who had called Seymour several days ago from Southwick, an off-hand query seeking Bridley's whereabouts, was delighted to hear that his payoff to Parker had landed in Commander Hamilton's cup.

Connected to Mountbatten, wasn't he?

Bernstein, fishing for the code name, had pumped Seymour about their latest mission. The Lieutenant had covered: Bridley must have let it slip. But no, seems Bridley was being sought elsewhere as a material witness in a divorce matter. *Mrs. Loot?* Lieutenant Seymour and Captain Bernstein had talked before; they got along all right. Seymour, while bragging on their latest girl, hadn't told him anything of course; but had thanked him for the sugar. Which reminded him: he had promised it to Farvillant. A personal matter, Seymour thought it best not to enter it on his Blackmail List. Called to Hamilton's attention, the Commander had confronted his Lieutenant with a what-did-you-expect? Bridley was forever getting them into *something*. Two boxes, Hamilton noted.

"Include candles, did he?"

"No, sir. Just burning them at both ends."

By breakfast, consisting of yesterday's crumpets, Hamilton in his shirt sleeves, collar open and tie loose, was having an exceedingly busy day. This activity was flowing into Bletchley Park, where the otherwise calm of Sunday was being interrupted by the ringing of many phones. Part of this was caused by the O.S.G., the Overseas Security Group, Operatives who were coordinating GOLDILOCKS from the township of Truro. This group of men, assigned by Lord Louis, were responsible for the nationwide clamp on this most secretive of operations. Like minnows among the trout, they could operate with greater secrecy in the backwaters of Britain.

Their source to and from Mama Bear was a mild-mannered man with steel-rimmed glasses named Grimes, soon to be Hamilton's new Security Adjutant—as yet unknown to most of his superiors. On this strange morning, Grimes was quartered at Beaulieu Abbey, secret headquarters of Lord Louis Mountbatten. To secure this choice spot, Hamilton had petitioned Lord Louis himself. Grimes, then, Hamilton's spy-in-residence, was so placed as to function as catalyst between Lord Louis, the crew at Truro, and Baby Bear, who was connected to the other part of Grimes' line—where Hamilton could listen. By such an arrangement, it was Hamilton then, and not Commodore Blackstone, who had first access to the total flow of information.

Blackstone, an old hand, knew immediately that he was being tapped. From Parker, and an obscure folder, he got the name: *Grimes, Arnold E., Royal Marines: Captain, Communications. Transferred to Southampton office 23 June, 1944, by special order Chief of Combined Operations...*

Mountbatten!

Hamilton had used Mountbatten!

From Blackstone's point-of-view, this act was an unspeakable breach of military form. It was also damned bloody bold and he knew it. By placing Grimes in the middle, a ploy that would be perceived by Whitehall as removing weight from Mountbatten's shoulders, Hamilton had removed himself...leaving Blackstone with the credit, and looking good.

"—that damned elusive Pimpernel!"

Sinclair was not alone in catching the resemblance.

Blackstone's phone rang. It was Mountbatten, from Beaulieu. The conversation, via Grimes, was about two items of concern: Hamilton's choice of the woman, and the weather.

The forecast, first.

Weather Command was now firmly in British hands. Churchill, partnered to SOE, and observing from the sidelines, was there to catch the ball should it sail out of the American court, not considered a problem: as of yesterday, gone to Normandy, Ike was out of the country.

Mountbatten was waving him good-bye.

"Yes, I quite agree," purred Blackstone, "a bloody fine job." He nestled his receiver, and looked up. The blinds in his windows were swelling in Sunday's cloudy air, as if to the winds of another time. Recalling Saturday's curious intrusion, the Commodore cocked his head.

He was listening.

"The gale should be in full force by then," Lord Louis was saying. The storm was tacking in north, from the Channel. "You feel the craft sturdy enough, do you?"

John Blackstone, from Bletchley, informed him that Hamilton himself had selected the launch for the rendezvous. He'd be damned if he'd be blamed, if it sank!

"Yes, well, it's *his* mission, isn't it?" Lord Louis had still not cast his vote. "You're personally satisfied, are you?"

Blackstone said that he was. He waited for Lord Louis to ask his opinion of the girl: he didn't. Employing intuition, the Commodore decided not to press it. "*Marchaud*," Blackstone told him. "Yes, that's right. We did her up as a child, at Elstree ...yesterday, yes. How's that?"

There was something on the line: an unearthly, high-pitched vibration...*that damned bloody Grimes*! "Yes...I'm sorry, Louis, I didn't catch that." The two Commodores had to wait until the phones cleared. "Hello? Yes, I can hear you now. He's to what—?"

"—to contact Papa Bear himself. You'll be a good fellow and let him know about it, won't you?"

Blackstone assured him that he would.

"If they throw it back to me, I'll decide." In his offices at Beaulieu, an orderly had entered with late breakfast. "Thank you. On the table, please. Well then, Commodore, should it prove a go, we'll make sure our sub is where it's supposed to be. In that eventuality, see that David and his GOLDILOCKS team are on time. I believe he's on my call today...yes." Mountbatten, phone to his chin, spread marmalade on his muffin. "Understand there's been an outside surveillance, hmmm?" The Spy could be anywhere, Blackstone couldn't say he didn't know. "—after the girl, yes." Could be hiding in his files. "Civilian, apparently." He stirred his tea. "Yes, I would think so, too. Hamilton filled you in then, did he?"

Bletchley was working on it.

Mountbatten made a note. Blackstone might be dancing to a different tune. Could it be the song of The Spy? The tune of men without faces? Multi-lingual? Reports had it that he could be Egyptian. *Spanish*? Or had he dreamt that? No, the girl was the key! "You've met the lady, have you?"

Blackstone hemmed and hawed.

"—yes, well, she sounds like a charming girl." To Blackstone's ear, the voices of Hamilton and Mountbatten sounded alarmingly alike. "Give her my best, will you—?"

Blackstone stared hard at the picture of his wife: he was without a wise saying. "Yes, sir. I most certainly will...yes sir, thank you." He hung up and dialed Hamilton. From his basement at Beaulieu, Grimes lit another cigarette—three ashtrays were overflowing—and picked up his earphones.

"Southampton. Lieutenant Seymour here."

"This is SAINT IVES, Bletchley. Hamilton there, is he?"

The Lieutenant recognized the Commodore's voice. He put his hand over the receiver as Hamilton looked up. "Blackstone?" Seymour nodded. "I'll take it," Hamilton said. He waited a moment, then snapped in the line.

"Commodore?"

"Hamilton! I've just finished speaking with Beaulieu."

"The Three Bears matter, sir?"

"Quite so, David. Mama Bear wishes the very best for this

SAINT IVES thing." He'd be *damned* if he'd acknowledge that woman!

"Very good," Hamilton said. "What do you hear from Truro?" Truro, in the county of Cornwall. Grimes punched a button.

"They're right on top of it," the Commodore replied, "waiting for Papa Bear to come downstairs." The mission then was still pending. Hamilton frowned. His information wasn't good enough: Grimes should have let him know.

"Things clear at Beaulieu, sir? They're keeping in touch with you, are they?"

" 'In touch,' old boy?" Blackstone's voice had dropped to the level of an offended father. "Is that how you choose to put it, David?"

Hamilton placed his hand over the receiver. "He's found out about Grimes," he said, softly. Seymour's eyes implored heaven.

"Why do you think I spent half the bloody morning on the ringer to Beaulieu?" Blackstone was at his acerbic best. "I shall speak to you about this matter privately, David." Grimes lit another cigarette, followed by static on the line.

"How's that, sir? We seem to have a bad connection." Hamilton clicked his shutoff several times, to make the point.

"Dammit, David! Are you there! Hello?"

"Yes, sir. I'm here, sir."

"See here, David…oh, *rot*! Never mind."

"Sir?"

"—privately, David. Do you understand?"

"Yes, sir." Hamilton understood.

The Commodore had caught him. For the moment, that was moment enough. "So tell me, David. How do things look? How do we stand with the storm?"

Hamilton glanced at his watch: he had appointments.

"I expect it will be on time, sir."

"Um, yes. One would certainly think so. Mama Bear holds that view. All our people, of course, are in touch with Weather Division." Blackstone, redefining blackmail, had taken advantage of the widening gulf between Ike and Monty. Propelling GOLDILOCKS through the middle, obliterating motives, he had clouded their waters like a giant squid. When the ink cleared, the mission papers on her would be missing.

"Weather Reports look good—"

"Can't hear you, sir!"

Again, there were background noises on the line, as if from invisible men swimming. It was a transmission problem, originating from Truro: Grimes corrected it. "—how's the weather there in Southampton? And what's that bloody racket—?"

Hamilton glanced out the window. Southampton was normal—dreary, but normal. "About right for a Sunday, sir."

"And Polperro?"

"Bad weather for bears, sir."

"Excellent! Will you be at Beaulieu this afternoon, David?"

Hamilton thought that he would.

"Well then, that's your ticket, old boy. Incidentally, I've a message for you to deliver. You can take care of it there—can you? That's a good chap..." Hamilton waited. Blackstone, a Master at Bridge, thoroughly enjoyed taking the final Rubber. "Give my 'best' to this *Grimes* fellow you ran in on me."

Hamilton winced.

Southampton had just been added to Conrad Parker's Blackmail List. "Oh yes, one more thing. Papa Bear is waiting to hear from you. And David—?"

"Sir?"

"Best of luck today...at Beaulieu."

"Thank you, sir."

"Baby Bear out."

Hamilton hung up. His emotions were mixed. "Lieutenant, get me His Nibs."

Seymour opened the secret compartment in his desk, and glanced at a taped card. At the same time, he picked up the special phone residing there. "SAINT IVES calling Papa Bear." A Colonel, voice known to Seymour, came on the line.

"Come in SAINT IVES. Who's your animal?"

"This is Big Bad Wolf," Lieutenant Seymour said.

"Right-o, Wolf. This is Bear Country. Hold, please."

Seymour punched in a sequence on the decoder and nodded to Hamilton. The Commander picked up his phone.

"Oh, David. There you are at last." It was the Prime Minister. "So good of you to call."

"Yes, well..."

"Be patient, dear man. I know how you feel. Our sea voyage tonight is still on hold...there's good reason for it."

Hamilton put it flat on the line. "Sir, is there a mission tonight—or is there not?"

"I see no reason to give you bad news. You certainly have my blessing. I think you know that."

"Sir, what I need to know is—"

"It's because of this Commando thing of last week, David." Seymour lit a cigarette. "No one is saying that the party is not on"—Captain Bernstein loomed, an uninvited guest—"as you may know, the entire decision now is with Mountbatten. He *is* Chief of Combined Operations, Supreme Commander, Asia—"

Why the sop? Hamilton knew all that. He would have to go to Beaulieu.

"I don't understand," the Commander said, simply. "Is there some fault with the concept, some reason that—?"

"Of course not, David. It's a very bold and courageous idea...very bold." The knowledge of the awesome threat to England hung in the still air of Sunday. Churchill was glad to have the Mission-Commander on the line. It *should* come from the Top. Hamilton would need to review the Code Override. Lord Louis had enough to do out at Beaulieu. They were both thinking of the Waterfall. "Hold on, David..." The Prime Minister, with a flick of his freckled hand, motioned to an Aide to illuminate the large wall calendar, where his protruding look zeroed in on August. "If they launch, it will be by August 6th. You have that? Yes, *August 6th*." In Holland, German physicists were working feverishly, they didn't want to disappoint him. "How's that? Yes. That's her maximal time. You get that information for us, Commander, and we shall hurl a rod of steel down their throats!"

Hamilton felt better.

"Personally"—he had paused to light his cigar—"I think that women *should* go on missions...gives them a good gallop. That's what *I* do. I'll see you at Hyde. Good-bye, David." The Prime Minister handed the phone to an Aide, who asked the Commander if he had any questions.

Hamilton said that he didn't and hung up.

August 6th!

"Any problem, sir?" Seymour was closing his desk.

"Not really." *Five weeks!* "Lord Louis hasn't decided yet."

Hamilton handed Seymour his personal address book. "I'll be off to Beaulieu, let's get to work."

For the next hour, from Southampton, the lines turned hot:

"This is Red Code Zero, come in please..."

"SAINT IVES calling?"

"Hang on."

SAINT IVES calling...

"You'd better wait..."

"—thank you, Major Farvillant. Yes, thank you very much. I appreciate your doing this for me on a Sunday." The relay of details went down the line. The answers came back. Seymour checked them off.

They called the harbor master at Polperro, who would be honored to keep small craft away from the quay. Seymour hung up the phone and it rang again. It was The Red Lion. Something about Smythe. The Lieutenant listened. "Oh, *shit*—!" Seymour said. "So? What's his problem? No, let him go. Don't be ridiculous! Certainly, I'll vouch for him...yes, of course. Fine. Same to you!" Seymour tossed the phone back on the hook.

The Commander threw him a look.

"—Security, Polperro. Case of mistaken identity—"

"Keep on it," Hamilton said.

They called the Commander of the Free French...yes, Farvillant has it...*nothing new on de Beck*...make sure he's on time. "—yes, attend to it personally, will you?...yes, if you don't mind...thanks ever so much."

They called London.

They called Weather down coast.

"They're on, sir."

Hamilton picked up the phone to his Security Team at The Red Lion. Something about an Arab. "Settled, is it? How's that? Yes. All right. Let me have the rest of it later, will you? That's a good fellow." Of the two officers assigned to street watch, one of them had noticed a silver and black limousine, in town since mid-morning, but had not thought it important enough to say so. It was raining there, people did wear trench coats. It would come up at the review meeting, on Tuesday, when Hamilton would fasten on it.

They couldn't raise Transport on the phone, so Hamilton sent Seymour to get the driver and bring the car around. While waiting, he called Weather again, the submarine slip, and Grimes at Beaulieu, who told him he was expected. Finally, he got through to Transport. Seymour, with driver, had just left and they were on their way. *About bloody time...* Hamilton glanced impatiently at his watch. He lit a cigarette. Had he forgotten anything?

Yes, he had forgotten to have lunch.

Lieutenant Seymour appeared in the doorway. The Commander was stuffing final papers into his case. "Put my address book in the safe, will you?" He accepted his hat and Seymour helped him on with his coat. He turned. "So then! I'll ring you, if we're scrubbed. Otherwise, expect me Tuesday—"

Hamilton moved through the door, and was gone.

Within twenty minutes, his driver had him out of the Yards and through the suburbs, onto the Bournemouth Road. From there, it was a straight shot. Hamilton, as was his custom, retreated into himself and took a catnap. They reached the Abbey in late-afternoon, the dark windy air portending rain.

Lord Louis, dear to the hearts of all Commandos, received him personally in one of the large upper chambers he was using for an office. They shook hands energetically, Mountbatten breaking into a broad grin. Invited for tea, Hamilton got straight to the point.

"Is it a go? That's all I want to know."

"Sit down, Commander, and let's talk about it."

The question predominant in Lord Louis's mind was the reliability of the girl, Sinclair. Hamilton immediately suspected Blackstone. But it was Mountbatten's right. This remarkable man had spent all of his active life in the Royal Navy. There was a seriousness of purpose about him, an attention to detail, which Hamilton had observed before, and which he respected. In a very profound way, it was a hallmark of both their characters. Hamilton reiterated his case in his usual blunt and straightforward way, emphasizing Valerie's ingenuity and photographic memory:

The man without a face came up.

The Commander fielded it.

The girl's insistence that he didn't have one, Hamilton thought best to keep to himself. Credibility was delicate enough. There was nothing new to add to the girl's first report, but they were working on it.

"Let us hope so," Lord Louis pointed out. "One has to stay on top of these things, if they're not to get out of hand. You will keep me apprised directly, won't you?"

Hamilton said that he would.

"Well then!" There was really no battle, and the Commander could have relaxed. Mountbatten, enjoying this younger version of himself, had already decided. He reached over, clasping Hamilton warmly by the shoulder.

"Let's go for it."

"The mission is on then?"

The gracious man handed the Commander a sealed envelope. Hamilton, as Mission-Commander, knew it contained the rendezvous coordinates for the submarine. Lieutenant Pryor, the pilot, would have the other copy. If there were any last-minute changes, they could be radioed aboard ship. By this time tomorrow, de Beck would be behind enemy lines, in charge of disposable cameras. Sinclair, instructed to entrust the resultant prints to Pierre, would do so. The Frenchman, approved by John Blackstone, would then carry them back to England using the special codes arranged by Parker. That Blackstone's future was veering away from that of Lord Louis had become obvious to the Commander. But it was the future of Valerie Sinclair, once emptied of data, that now worried him. Surgically altered to fit Farvillant's *Biographie*, the biological profile of the French child reputedly killed, what were her own chances of survival? Rather poor, actually. It was not that Hamilton *wanted* this to happen; his own position on the Blackmail List made it expedient for him not to know:

He accepted death in war.

Lord Louis was wanting to wrap it up. The younger man rose to thank him, but Mountbatten waved him aside. "You have it, old boy. Get to work. However"—he pointed to the large clock on the wall,—"if I were you, I'd hurry. Your Captain Grimes is waiting downstairs...the basement. Lift's to your right."

"By the way, sir," Hamilton thought to ask, picking up his case. "I understand that Bridley came in with you. Is he about?"

"He did, indeed. We sent him over to Truro." Lord Louis smiled. *No one would be able to reach him.* "I expect James will keep the Overseas Security Group on their toes, what?"

The two men shook hands. Lord Louis walked him to the door, his thoughts centering in Friday's phone calls. "If we're wrong, David, they'll have your head."

It was Hamilton's first kindness of the day.

He caught the lift to the basement, and found Arnold Grimes in the middle of Emily Blackstone's call to her husband: something about not enough credit to the Rubinstein woman. Hamilton waved him off, some things were personal. The Commander questioned him for late information, and Grimes handed him the weather charts. He leafed through them. "If Commodore Blackstone calls you on the bloody carpet, play dumb," the Commander advised him, and Grimes grinned.

A cold fish, Hamilton decided, pleased.

Light rain met him at the bridge, and a lowering sky. He was still ninety miles from The Red Lion. Smythe and Longchamps—Valerie and Pierre—would be checking out, records proving they were never there. Hamilton tested the air. It was coming, all right. According to the latest, the storm should be hitting Polperro just about now.

Toward the East, he saw the wall of darkness forming. Feeling chilled, he asked the driver to turn on the blower. He leaned back. It had been a long day, and he had won. Rain, coming faster, swept before them on the dusty road, peppering the windshield.

In the skies beyond, lightning flashed.

It began to pour.

V

Click!

Practically all the Operatives, in MI.5, appeared to be somebody else. They could think what they wanted, of course, but wasn't she wasting her film? Photographs of ghost men, she had captured them as pictures of their shadows. *Was Hamilton really Hamilton?* She listened. Distant thunder was rumbling. If she was to see the town, she had best get on with it.

Sundays were not her favorite.

She remained on the veranda for a few minutes, trying to figure it, enjoying the feel of the wind. Just last night, Hamilton said, if she were left alone—! In France, he'd meant, by Pierre. Dunkirk reared in her mind: dunes of blood, salt water and screaming; Pierre, clawing through the corpses to the boats, already shot, his body bleeding...

His comrades slain.

It was the Frenchman's face now, locked in her mind, handsome and strong. She could have done worse. She rested comfortably in the thought that he would kill for her, even if Hamilton had put a tail on both of them for security reasons.

Security reasons!

Sinclair arose and stepped to the edge of the veranda. Beyond that sea, lay France. *"Valerie Marchaud,"* she said. Fist gripping the rail, dress cleaving to her legs, she stared out over the bay. Boats jerked at chains and the town waited within the cradle of its weather. On all sides, from the wild cliffs above, through the vast crater of stone, narrow and nervous streets cascaded down precipitous stairwells, leveling off onto platforms before depositing themselves, at last, at the foot of the wider avenue that ran along the seawall. Sinclair sniffed the air. The humid charm of Cornwall, thick with waves of heat, smote her senses with the lush, provocative perfume of flowers—invitation to the host of insects, gossips on wings, bearing down in angry clouds of silver from the blind and troubled sky—as if bringing messages of wickedness. She thought of the couple next door; their bed, night after night, thumping against the walls in tawdry joy. A place where men came with other men's wives, Polperro was the perfect hideaway for spies. Was that why Hamilton had selected it? Valerie, lugging her chair, walked back inside, slamming the French doors. She placed the chair in front of the mirror and sat down.

"Let's talk," she said.

A dichotomy had come between herself and Marchaud. It wasn't the child's fault. Having entered into the body of a French girl, she was having difficulty finding room for her own. She was also having difficulty in finding the girl. Sinclair did not have all day. Supporting this was an ultimate argument: it was the last day she had.

By this time tomorrow, she could be dead.

Before the mirror, Sinclair told Marchaud:

"We are going to France on the most dangerous mission of the war." She waited, to get her eye. When she had it, she said: "We are a one-girl team."

Comment?

"A one-girl team. I am Valerie Sinclair. You, my other, are Valerie Marchaud."

"Oui?"

The French girl smiled shyly, glad to know her name. Lights of chalister blue haunted their faces. Hadn't Valerie seen her before in a dream? A memory intruded, elusive... *Brittany*...but she couldn't seem to get her hands on it. The room was still where Sinclair spoke but she could not hear her own voice.

Now, beneath an orchid-colored sky, hidden from adults by the wisdom of children, *she* had come. Marchaud's pale hands were reaching out towards the mirror, her thin dress tattered. The English girl moved closer, wanting to help her. Marchaud did likewise, wanting to care...each girl passing through, exchanging catalytically with, and into, the identity of the other. *They were running*...a tunnel, shrill of a nightbird, flatlands in moonlight, the smell of the dunes.

The entrance flew towards them!

Something was calling her; someone was there...

She opened her eyes.

"—que faire de mes cheveux?" spoke her other, pointing with uncertainty. The Camera Shop, turning the CLOSED sign around, had allowed her to enter. "Oui," said Sinclair, busy. Her bobbed hair, shaved high at the neck like a bird's, shimmered blue-black in the light of the lamp. Sand clung to the clothes of the girl. Marchaud looked frightened. Behind her, spilling into the sea, Valerie could see the cliffs of the vicarage. Shrouded in fog, negatives were turning the color of blood.

She must not have taken her camera—!

Traveling on the current that lay somewhere between them, they had met in the foyer of time. They shook hands. Immediately, the woman made room for the child, who was just about her size.

"Il faut se dépêcher!"

"Of course!" Valerie was having trouble with her English. She listened. The grounds were empty, and dark with dreams. Bells were singing. Voices, more beautiful than bells themselves, echoed ringing in the yard.

Behind her, a door was opening.

Something shimmered, moving through the trees.

"Now, here's the Plan...."

Massive thunderbanks rolled out of the sky, dimming the daylight along the shore. The storm was coming, the wind racing before it. She walked to the windows, pulling the curtains. Returning, she sat on the bed.

An hour passed.

Within that time, a casual passerby would have heard two girls conversing, the younger in French. As for the passerby,

Hamilton's Security Team was making sure there weren't any. The conversation in the room continued and the tone became friendlier. Ultimately, there came sounds of agreement, then silence.

At four o'clock, Valerie gathered up her raincoat and left the hotel. Storm or no storm, it was time for her walk. In Polperro, that could have limits. She headed towards the beach, turning south, and away from the marina. She walked down the stairwell which led to the sand and stopped at the balustrade. A beam of light was shining on it.

Sitting down, she looked up:

"Get me God," she said.

Was it *him* had sent The Spy? Churchill had talked about God. Sometimes, Hitler. The Pope, too. How could he have so many partners? Until a few years ago, certainly, she would have expected him to take care of it personally. Did he have an address? God, it seemed, was in the credit business: He sent cheques. World leaders prayed to him, for loans. Afterwards, they sent him the bills. While it was not her place to speak for Higher Powers, as was obvious to any thinking person, she and Marchaud knew what *they* would do! She wondered where God was. When there was a war, he left town.

Smart chap.

Valerie prayed:

> There'll be blue-birds o-ver
> The white cliffs of Dover—!

On her cheeks, glowed the roses of hope. Her heart felt full of sunshine, her life was full of joy. Running through her prints, she saw they were snapshots of flowers; but The Spy was holding them, too, and they were the snapshots of dreams. Valerie Sinclair closed her eyes. She imagined a happy day. She concentrated. As she bent her head, she heard a sound—!

Something good?

SPLAT!

Raindrops, big as shillings, splattered on the stone.

She jumped! Thunder rolled in the distance. The sky was growing black. *Some prayer!* If he didn't want to hear it, he should have said so. Valerie hurried from the quay and turned down a side street. Following her, the storm was throwing rain. It caught up with her, dropping down, overtaking the buildings …encompassing the streets.

A giant hand had hit her on the head!

Where was her pillbox hat? She'd left it in the hotel. Valerie ducked under an awning. It had a hole in it. She turned up the collar of her raincoat, it made a funnel. Water poured into her clothes. A drenched tomcat cut in front of her, running across the street, tail straight up. Was it a message — from BEYOND? There had been so few of them, she'd best not take a chance. She ran after the cat, who turned the corner. Valerie did the same. The cat turned again and ran up onto the porch of a house.

It meowed, voice like a bell.

Valerie walked by, adjusting the hat she wasn't wearing. Blinking a couple of blinks, she took a picture of the house. It did not seem to have an address. The door opened and the tomcat walked inside. In those few seconds, from a doorway of the room within, she could see blue sparks cascading, as though from an arc welder. The cat, who had stopped, turned and looked back at her, the door closing as mysteriously as it had opened. What kind of town was this? Working, on Sunday? Valerie looked:

Ahead of her was the entrance to The Red Lion.

She was back!

About to mount the steps, she happened to glance to her right. There, two corners away, she saw a man wearing a trench coat! *The Spy!* His chauffeur was opening the door of a limousine…

It was them!

She moved around the stairwell, peeking out. The sleek silver and black juggernaut stood silently in the rain, as though waiting for ghostly passengers. Somehow, from its entrance into Hamilton's watertight security, she knew this graceful machine must be centered in laws and actions created by men who had proceeded to this small town, in this terrible raging weather, at a risk she could not imagine.

Through the windy air, through pouring rain, she observed they were preparing to leave. The Spy had entered the back seat, saying something to his driver. Sinclair looked. The limousine accelerated, moving swiftly away towards the Falmouth Road.

Valerie ran up the steps, into the hotel.

Why did she keep seeing him?

"—what?" she said, distracted: it was her own voice.

The cheerful brogue of the Porter: "It's going to be a nasty night, wi' the look of it. See now, your friends have left you to get all wet, have they? You're drenched!" His hands drummed nervously on the folded newspaper.

Valerie stared at him, trying to listen.

"—calls for a hot bath and a toddy of warm rum. A few years before *you'll* know it though"—her legal age, he meant—"strong drinks are not for the likes o' young girls like you."

"I suppose you're right," said Valerie, and she looked over her shoulder. He removed the gun from behind his newspaper, slipping it into a drawer. "Parents staying in the hotel, are they?" She waited impatiently for her key.

"...yes," she said.

Her stockings and legs were very wet. She moved, feeling a fool, up the stairs to her room. Locking the door behind her, she turned on the taps. It was her second bath of the day. It could also be her last. She undressed and got into the tub. She didn't much work at it, and toweled off quickly. She put on the pillbox hat, wishing she could take it with her. Picking up her sopping clothes, she threw them into the corner—to hell with them! She draped her raincoat over the chair. Weren't there dryer things in the closet? Opening the wardrobe, she looked in to see what they were...

Forget it!

Valerie sighed and retrieved the drenched gob from the corner, spreading it out on the floor underneath the Casablanca fan which was threatening to explode at any moment. Did they want that thing up there to fall on her head? *Where was the fan man?* She picked up her bra and underwear, clutching them in her teeth; then carried the chair, heavy with raincoat, into the middle of the room. Hanging her brassiere on one end of it, she arranged her panties on the other. She glanced at the walls, staring into the mirror. They had done an incredible job.

She would miss Madame Roc.

Wind battered at the French windows. Outside, dark voices of air were shouting. Sinclair threw back the covers, she slid into clean sheets. The Commander had not told her the time of their rendezvous in the Channel but they would be leaving England at nine. The skies had opened, rain was roaring. A few hours, as much hers as Marchaud's:

She would take them home to France.

The pulse of the storm, like a heart, was beating in the room...the child breathing.

Sinclair sleeping, Marchaud was awake:

A young girl — thin, and twelve — was looking down from a platform high on the center pole: the interior of a circus tent, somewhere in Europe, before the war and the Gestapo. Point-of-view of the *Artiste*: white-stockinged legs locked confidently to the bar, swinging high above the cheering crowd. Looking down, the great tent turning, her painted eyes aflame with dust. Kisses blown — *the buckle breaking* — and there is not a net! *The bar slips*! Fear so deep that no adult can face it, or see it, or comprehend it; for those who do, are converted into children:

Her Performance!

It was rushing up to meet her! Landing now, on the platform! *Bowing* to them...spiraling down the rope, to the ring.

The Ringmaster, booming through time:

"Merci, Mesdames et Messieurs — !"

Listening to the rain, the child closed her eyes...raindrops applauding. Safe, in the hotel, she was with her friend. The older people sleeping, her *other* had slipped into the Camera Shop, secretly setting up for some test shots. Valerie wanted the call from the British Prime Minister, approved by Hamilton, to be her greatest photograph.

Something worthy of a studio setting.

Head under the sheet, she was in the process of working out the fine points of various procedures — professional lighting and so forth — when she was interrupted by a knock at the door. "Answer it, will you?"

Marchaud rolled over, she went back to sleep.

"Oh, never mind — !" Valerie popped her head out. "Yes? Who is it?"

It was the fan man.

Sinclair got a phone call.

The Manager of the The Red Lion, ordered to release the Arab, and who had just sent his man up to fix the Casablanca fan, had included a message for the girl, who was urgently wanted in the Manager's office.

She got dressed and fled down the stairwell, leaving the man and his toolbox staring up at the ceiling. The Manager, meeting her in the lobby, led her past the front desk and into the back, where she was expecting to talk with Hamilton. If the call was coming from the Prime Minister, the Commander would certainly insist upon giving her last-minute instructions.

That wasn't it.

The first thing she noticed was that the Security people were not in the office. The Manager pointed to his desk, to where the phone was off the hook. He turned and left the room. Valerie sat at the desk and picked up the phone.

"Hello?" she said.

"*Yes. Valerie?*" He was distant. There was a crackling on the line.

"This is Valerie *Marchaud*," she said, hopefully. "To whom, sir, if I may be so bold, do I have the honor—?" It was on the Code Override.

He told her.

Speechless and wanting to thank somebody, Sinclair looked up—to where she thought God was. Would he be watching this, wearing sunglasses? For more than several minutes, she listened intensely. Finally, she spoke. As Hamilton's officers would try to explain it to him later, the nearest they could recall was that she said: "—I understand. Yes, certainly I do. But even if I did, having already done it, or will do it, or wanted to, the hotel address is still the—!"

They listened, hunched forward in their chairs on the other side of the wall.

"The name is Smythe," they heard her say. She was taking notes: rapid prints, clicked by her emergency camera. The caller appeared to be sending best wishes, for she was smiling shyly, lips slightly parted. There could be no doubt. Sinclair was impressed.

"Oh my—" she gasped.

Clear as bells, came words, ringing with AUTHORITY.

It was simple enough, the mysterious voice was asking her to remember: "—who? Yes...I think so." She remembered, "but I don't know the people there—I do? I don't—? But you—*we*

190

do? Yes, of course, if you think he won't mind—he won't? I see—he doesn't? But we should? Certainly—I do. No, I really couldn't—what? *Really?*"

Time...

"Where?"

Place...

"Yes, if I decide...yes, I understand." Sinclair hung up the phone. "Thank you," she said.

My pleasure...

It was not an order: she didn't have to. The mission was still on. When it came, as it had to, she had hoped that it might be different. Life was truth. It was like that, wasn't it? Get it all ready, and somebody had to go to the bathroom. She looked about the room. It had taken her two and a half years, but here she finally was: sitting at the Manager's desk. She started sorting through a stack of mail.

"Decisions...decisions."

The Manager opened the door and bristled quickly back into the room asking her if she had finished with her call and throwing her out of his chair. He was busy, having to attend to his guests. She was in the doorway, he looked up. " 'Smythe,' right?"

"Stick it," she said.

"*Stickett?*" Certainly, not one of the Bedford Sticketts! He'd no idea! Unfortunate oversight, these things happened. He would send complimentary champagne!

Valerie returned to her room.

Out of their telephone booths, up from their armchairs, and from behind walls, Security rushed in to fill the places they had vacated. Hamilton's Operatives were feeling privy to greatness, to that unexpected event in the affairs of men which had just included them, personally and precisely, at this moment in history. Follow-up orders were now coming in, instructing them to withdraw all surveillance the moment Sinclair headed for the marina.

There was something new under the sun. They were looking at it: it was called trust. They were a part of it! Unprecedented, this respect shown to Sinclair was viewed as a major policy change in British Intelligence.

The word had come straight from Olympus:

The girl in the pillbox hat was the envy of the Firm.

Meanwhile, up in her room, sorting it out and knowing she had to decide, Valerie Sinclair was sitting down on her chair underneath the Casablanca fan, which had been fixed by the fan man, who had also detached the electronic bug from her lamp. Arranged by Blackstone, unknown to Hamilton, it had been placed there to ensure that the Commander carried out his orders. Now, overridden by a higher authority, it had been removed. Valerie, who was noticing that the lamp was no longer sputtering, got up and turned it off.

She returned to her chair.

Uneasiness had arrived, as it had at Achnacarry, through the corridors of sleep. There, fighting for her life, instruction had entered. The Spy had helped her. But where was he now? She spun round to the mirror. Panic stared back. The peripheries of her mind had just expanded, a widening crack in the walls of containment, where light was pouring in. Through this tunnel of comprehension, she had her first glimpse of the other side, of the *other* man's side; and what she was looking at were the facts. They had told her, and had trained her to believe, that these facts did not exist. It was not just the tunnel had widened, but the war; and fear had gripped her, the way it grips a child, because of their lack of love. The Allied cause, not all of it in concert, dedicated to protect the right of free people to live, had not changed. But men of greed and vision had come, wearing masks of brightness and smiles; and they had used her, the way they would use a tool: their questions, designed for responses that had excluded her right to be. It was who *she* was that mattered, they had told her that; yet they were making sure she would be somebody else. Denied the right of choice, how could she give them what they wanted?

Especially now, that she knew.

She would have to tell them something!

She walked to the window, staring out over their world and hers. It had just been dumped in her lap. She felt humiliated because she was trembling, and her brown eyes brimmed with tears. The masters of that world were waiting for her answer:

Hamilton, in particular.

"Fuck you," she said.

Outside the skies were dark. Blue shadows shimmered about

her eyes. Lustrous as agates, they were the eyes of the living camera.

She wet her lips, tasting its current.

Recalling the conversation in the Manager's office, she remembered his voice on the phone. Having placed it, she was looking at the picture of his face:

He didn't have one.

Quelle heure est-il?

Where was she?

The girl was coming awake. Wind was blowing. It was the rain on the roof. A force shook the windows and the room was cold. She rolled over and looked at her watch: *8:15.*

She must hurry!

Her raincoat was nearly dry. Sinclair opened the wardrobe, and stared at her uniform: *was it forever,* as Hamilton had said? She took a last look round the room, then hurried down the stairs. She turned in her key.

"Checking out, Miss?

"Yes. I'm all paid up, I believe."

"Right. The bill has been settled." Buttoning her coat, Valerie caught a quick glimpse of two military types, both Royal Navy, through the partially opened door of the Manager's office. One of them was on the telephone, and his partner was lighting a cigarette. Spotting her, he walked over and closed the door.

She glanced at the clerk. His eyes, holding hard admiration, were the same eyes she had been looking at all week; now sharing victory, bigger than themselves.

They do not know...

How could they? Security was so tight not even the fog could penetrate. He saluted. "Come back and see us," he said.

Valerie looked about the lobby. It was deserted. She turned then, and moved through the doors. The girl pulled up her collar and entered the street. Leaning into the wind, she crossed. The storm had taken over. Water rushed along the curb, furrowing into culverts. Lightning shot across the sky. Raindrops ran down her cheeks. Recording them, she crossed her eyes. They were like droplets of silver light. She looked up, stopped, and stared. Arrived at the crossroads, she remembered, instructions on the phone:

House of ghostlight, bluish in the rain...
She mounted the steps, feeling welcome.

She could hear the cat. He was inside somewhere. Sinclair waited on the porch, under the dripping eaves. She had been told who to expect. Turning the corner, the limousine came into view. It pulled up to the curb and stopped. The door opened on the driver's side. He was alone. She stepped to the railing. There was no mistaking the figure—tall man, dark coat— standing just off the walk, in the downpour.

Valerie ran down the steps. She came up to him and he gripped her hand. Rain stung their faces. "Sorry you had to wait," Ryan said, "but I felt it best to avoid the sea road. Any problems at the hotel?"

"Two of Hamilton's officers spotted me on the way out." Ryan was staring up the street. "They were in the back room. One of them was on the telephone."

"Do they know who called?"

"No," she said, "I'm totally alone in this."

It was her decision.

"How do you know they were his?"

"I—" The girl looked at him helplessly. Her lips were slightly parted. She was trembling.

"Get in."

He guided her into the back seat, out of the elements. She shook the rain from her hair. It was waiting for them, this journey, the storm, a challenge they could not avoid. Fear was flapping at the glass, she let it out.

It had come, on the wings of weakness.

Rain drummed on the roof, water slamming into metal. Valerie Sinclair could hear the song of her heart. From some-where, over and above, the sound of the great motor.

They were moving...

Valerie asked him if he would be so kind as to loan her a cigarette. "For you? Sure, why not?" She looked good for it. Ryan handed her a crumpled pack of Pall Mall, three left. He had a gold lighter. It twirled on a ratchet, they had them in New York. "Light?" She leaned forward, his arm swung to the back seat.

Retractable thumb, knuckles of steel...

Dark eyes sparkled, assessing him through the flame.

* * *

A Flying Dutchman sort of night, the sea was of one mind and those who faced it another; with harbor buoys just beyond the breakwater writing lethal sonnets of sound on the plates of tremendous tides, hurling spume from the agony of their dreams into the black disgorging air. The wind was roaring; rain falling in patterns like bullets; tearing at trees and screaming high above them: voices of drowned seamen shouting demonic prayer and sweeping accusations before them along emptied streets, calling the wicked to account.

Hamilton looked up.

The report of the call to the hotel, on Code Override, had been waiting for him upon his arrival from Beaulieu; the girl having already left. While the mission was *go*, Valerie Sinclair would arrive at their Brittany rendezvous by an *alternate route*. A sudden stabbing thought intruded. Could she have been abducted? Hamilton grabbed at his mind, this was no place for fear. No, it was clear enough: unless the sending parties delivered the girl to the marina at the last minute, they were to proceed without her. The message, ciphered OPERATION TUNNEL and signed PAPA, had Blackstone's confirmation attached. Straight from the Top, this unexpected directive had caught David Hamilton flat.

His trained eyes experienced in discerning movements, the Commander peered down the street. It was approaching out of the darkness, hunched and running, often stopping, and staring up. It was formed like a werewolf, and its name was *doubt*. He got up from the bench, stepping closer to the curb. The werewolf's shadow, splintered by rain, and moving along the wall of a warehouse was down-funnelling now into the form of a man: fighting the wind, and navigating the corner. A branch crashed! Someone jumped, he raised his arm.

"Over here!"

Pierre came up, drenched.

Collar turned, he greeted the Englishman cheerfully. "*Bonsoir*! Or, should I say *bonne chance*?" Hamilton's frown welled up from the sounds of the sea.

Pierre grinned. "I hear she's not going with us." On arriving from London, he had checked it out. *It looked like Blackstone.*

"So it seems."

Messages burned in Hamilton's brain. He stepped forward,

urgency in his voice. "We mustn't keep our rendezvous waiting."
He led the Frenchman to a small launch. Unseen before now,
it bobbed uneasily in a protected shield of the quay. From the
boat, the pilot saluted them sharply.

"Filthy night, Pryor!"

"Yes, sir!"

Hamilton and the Frenchman jumped aboard, breaking out
oilskins and sou'westers. Lines were cast. Free of the marina
and the inlet, Lieutenant Pryor and the Commander compared
coordinates. The launch circled east. Polperro's harbor flattened behind them, the shores of Britain disappearing into a
black line.

Air-dropped, would she come by moon plane, or—?

"Better allow for a second sub, Pryor!"

"Right, sir!" The pilot refigured his bearing, he needed to look
at the charts.

"Me for the Con!" the Commander announced.

Taking over, he slammed the hatchway. Gripping the wheel,
Pryor forward, Hamilton thought he heard something, but at
a distance: *a vibration of some sort*, more like a ship's engine,
and driven by the shriek of the wind. There were no running
lights on the horizon; and, for that matter, no other shipping
of any kind tonight, according to Weather. No one but a mad-
man would take a boat out on a night like this! Hamilton tugged
at his hat and wondered if they were being watched, if the
enemy could possibly be aware of their purpose. He was not
a man to take chances; yet he felt reasonably certain that no
one had seen them leave. *Nothing recent on The Spy, was there?*
He had meant to call Seymour; and he glanced over his shoulder.
He listened. Whatever it was, it was not there now. The wind
slipped for a moment, and he eased forward on the throttle.
The air was black, and slippery with rain.

He had dreamt of such nights as a boy. Propped on his
elbows before the fire, intent on the book before him, he had
stood then where he stood now. The great sea novels of Her-
man Melville, Howard Pease, and Jack London had decided his
life as much as the uncompromising naval sternness of his
father. Later, studying Maritime Law at King Alfred College,
at Brighton and Hove, David Hamilton had carried a thin
volume of John Masefield in his coat the way other men carried

cigarettes. He had read all of these books by the end of his first term, dreaming at night of tramp steamers...ships with names like *Maura Queen* and *Excalibur* and *Singapore Hattie*...ships carrying Peter Lorre-looking people in white hats...slicing through Oriental waters, and furrowing through fog.

His career in the Royal Navy had been a good one.

The gale brought him out of his reverie, cold water pouring into his shoes. "Bloody bastard!" Hamilton swore, and the spoke hit him sharply on the wrist. The Commander grabbed at the helm, turned it with all his might, and brought them about. The launch plowed forward, and yawed! He couldn't hold it! The wheel was spinning!

"De Beck!"

Together, they turned it.

A bolt shot across the sky.

He could see their battered craft moving across the top of the awesome swirl. Lightning swept across yellowed oilskin, casting its unearthly pallor over de Beck, who had returned to the gunwale, his face impassive in the blinding light. Awaiting France, he was keeping a tight grip on himself. The bow shot upwards, held, and dropped, crashing back into the sea.

He had his orders...

Hamilton shouted, his voice lost in the wind. "We couldn't have picked a worse night!" Yet they both knew this was exactly why MI.5 had picked it. The launch plunged, then rose again, threatening to broach.

"Lieutenant Pryor!" shouted the Commander, "you'd better take her!" In a field of sterling qualities, Hamilton knew his limits. Pryor snapped out the light. The forward hatch burst open and he hit the deck.

The pilot grabbed the Con and spun it like a maniac, bringing them sharply about. The storm was howling downwind. They had leveled to the curve of the sea. Pryor's voice rose above the rain.

"There she is, sir, to the starboard!"

He pointed.

The sub emerged out of the Channel like a giant eel, hissing and looking about for its prey. Surfaced a hundred yards to their stern, trajectories closing, they could see the great snout streaming water and cleaving darkly through the swells. Pryor had throttled the motor, and was lining them up. Salt blew across their faces. "Easy does it," Hamilton said. He had turned.

The Frenchman was smiling.

Teeth, like piano keys, flashed in a broad white grin.

Following her conversion at Elstree, the Spy had told his bodyguard what she looked like; and Ryan, following orders, had made certain those orders had been carried through.

That Valerie was again up for grabs came as no surprise to the mysterious figure who had been tracking her movements like a shadow. Not so, however, could the same be said for the Prime Minister, unaware that Sinclair was now in motion on her own. His long weekend coming to a close, and still at Chartwell Manor where he was wrapping up War Office business, Churchill was finding that he was having to spend most of his time on the telephone—and on his private line, at that.

GOLDILOCKS, launched earlier this evening from Polperro, was as good as in the history books; but had passed up the bedtime story, and was refusing to go to sleep. It was Lord Louis Mountbatten, home for the evening at Broadlands, keeping her up. Lewis Carroll came to mind. *The Walrus* may have had a word for it, but the Prime Minister couldn't think of it.

Besides, he was on the ringer.

More than once, and again this evening, Churchill's wife Clementine had asked him about the "child spy". At fifty-nine, "Clemmy" was tall and slim; and her long grey hair was drawn behind her ears. Churchill joked about it: she did a lot of listening. Theirs was a marriage made in heaven, presuming that's where politicians went, and Clementine was very happy with Winston; but she had also become interested in Valerie Sinclair, having been the first to bring the girl to the attention of her husband. Churchill looked up. She had interrupted him.

"Oh dear," she said. "Important?"

Winston explained, he never told her all of it. Clementine returned to her room. Hand drumming on his desk, he eyed her departure over the ivory figurines; then returned to his call. As he did so, he swiveled around, so as to better observe the events of the evening.

Sunday's sun had already set.

French windows overlooked the garden, where the smell

of jasmine and summer roses permeated the air. A row of birch trees, serving as a windbreak, stood at attention on the horizon—guardsmen of a nobler time; and he saw them now as he had then: as toy soldiers, marching over the hills of a younger man's summer. But yesterday's soldiers had all gone away—their sheet-draped pianos and dusty oil paintings with them—put into storage for the duration of this brighter, and more terrible age; where round-the-clock security had surrounded, as if by walls, each personal and private aspect of his life. The Prime Minister could not envision, then, where the next few moments would take him; but he hoped they would take him to where he wanted to go. Right now, he wanted to go to bed. If he could get through this present Donnybrook with Lord Louis, at least he would be one stairwell closer. Alone in the private study, and cradled on his red telephone, he would settle for it.

This Sunday night's call from Britain's Supreme Commander, Asia, could not have come at a worse time. The briefcases were bulging. What the Prime Minister had not accomplished this weekend, he must finish up tonight. Well then, he must get to the bottom of it! With Mountbatten, that could take some doing.

"—just my own hunch, really," his Supremo had told him, but Churchill had caught his inference on the sharp edge of fury. In a word, on a tip from Alan Turing, Lord Louis had just had a look at the Bletchley files—specifically, Conrad Parker's—and what he had found there were *the codes* that did not fit.

"What codes?" asked Churchill.

"Those for *us*," responded Mountbatten, "and those for—how shall I put it—third parties?" and he proceeded to link an alternate mission; one that could tie von Schroeder to Blackstone, and von Braun to Britain. "Bankers, not all of them ours, who may be deep in Navy business."

"Stuff and nonsense!" fumed the Prime Minister. "What do you think makes the world go round?" It was as clear as crystal: the linkage was prewar. Until Germany sued for peace then, these *facts*, as Mountbatten called them, while not generally known, appeared to be out of time. If the P.M. thought about it, he might even supply a few of his own.

"There is more," Mountbatten said. He was naming names.

Like spokes on a wheel, Churchill noticed, they were all pointing to one man.

John Blackstone?

Churchill listened, not at all amused; and his hand went raking through the private files in his desk for the document that would refute it. *Dammit, where was it?* The red telephone, its receiver thrown repeatedly on the desk, was in his hand again.

"So then, Sire, this business with von Schroeder, you see? Smoke leading to fire, and so on. The very fact that John Blackstone didn't *file* it—"

"—means what? *What*—?"

"—means, in my mind at least, that there may be justification for putting a stop to it. We have turned her over to this Frenchman, Pierre de Beck—yet look who installed him." Blackstone, not Hamilton. Mountbatten had gathered as much from Seymour. "Suppose the results of the mission are being diverted? Even though GOLDILOCKS is underway, we don't know what road home she'll be taking, do we? Who's to say that Blackstone and company won't be there first? An international catch-as-catch-can, you see, with the technology up for grabs."

"Bankers, I presume," Churchill said, and he could see it now: not *theirs*? These allegations on Mountbatten's part, he knew, could not possibly arise from jealousy. That is why he was listening. The other man's dogged persistence, going on little more than a seasoned hunch, was suddenly turning this otherwise pleasant evening into something just short of bizarre.

"Well, Louis, what must I tell you? Just this, umm? There are channels that—"

"No no, sir," Lord Louis cut in, his voice strained, "it isn't about cloak-and-dagger, at all. I am not questioning his conduct, as an officer. What I *do* question is that fifteen previous agents, all female, were sent by *Bletchley*." Churchill could smell it, the abscess had opened at SOE.

Mountbatten said, "I had no direct jurisdiction at the time, if you recall. That's why—"

"No one is blaming you, sir. Your conduct throughout GOLDILOCKS has been exemplary. Still, I fail to see why you insist on pursuing this as though it were a *personal* matter. If we have a conspiracy on our hands, and you think it's Navy business, then you should have rightly placed this call to the Lord of the Admiralty."

"I did. They told me you were here."

Acknowledged by Navy men, yesterday's courtesy as it were, Churchill liked the compliment. What he wasn't liking, was the timing of this call.

Mountbatten knew that, he was thinking of the murdered women: "And Valerie Sinclair may be next."

Churchill said: "Chance we take. Get to the point."

"But the point is *loyalty!*"

"Bosh! Loyalty to whom?" Was Mountbatten calling the British Navy into question? Had black become white? Churchill sat up straight, his bottom lip was trembling. "You are speaking madness, sir! If Blackstone, in *your* view, is a bastard, at least he is a *loyal* bastard!" *Order of the British Empire, the Victoria Cross?* "A thirty-year *record* of loyalty, sir!"

Lord Louis, perhaps sitting too close to the fireplace, wiped his brow. Mountbatten put it bluntly: "I feel there is another force at work here, a force for the good of England, and the world. I hate to say this, but it's looking increasingly as though it could be that outside Operative. You remember, I'm sure. David's Report, from Weymouth?"

"Yes, of course." He had shared it with Clemmy. She had thought Edwina might appreciate it.

Mountbatten listened.

The specter of The Spy, which had haunted his days, had also advanced and deepened his dread, intruding into the most inviolable part of personal thought, where decisions were kept; so too, the ghostly footsteps, that had walked into his dreams.

"Hold it, will you?"

Reaching to make a note, an agreement to Churchill's position, the navy man had dropped his fountain pen. Bending to retrieve it, he had felt another's presence, as though the pen had been knocked from his hand. Lord Louis sat perfectly still, and yearned to be with his friends. One of them had just asked him a question.

"Yes, I think she's fine," Mountbatten said.

They were talking about Sinclair.

"I am glad to hear that," Churchill replied. Allegiance to an agent was important to him, as long as it was his.

Mountbatten assured him that she was.

They discussed Hamilton, who had launched the mission; and who was already en route to his rendezvous in the English Channel. Weather Command was reporting dangerous seas. Mountbatten felt apprehensive about the safety of the girl. Churchill nodded. The Frenchman though, he would be all right. Lord Louis got up from his desk and closed the door, leaving the phone talking: it took just a few seconds. He returned to his chair.

Churchill: "—well then! Presuming David rides it out, so will his agents." Word had it that Hamilton's Security Team, having delivered, were in high spirits at The Red Lion. "Blackstone has not yet called in—"

It was a dagger, but a sweet one.

Mountbatten listened, still not convinced. Cats *did* come out of bags; yet this one might have to be drowned at sea. If Lord Louis had to make another call, it would not be to John Blackstone.

"Calm down, Louis." The Prime Minister was on *his* side. What mattered, the central and real reason for the mission, Churchill had made clear, was to beat The First Army to the punch and to acquire the Bomb before they had to buy it. If Mountbatten had doubts, it was too late to change them; and there, effectively, rested the Prime Minister's case. For if Germany delivered it first...

They would lose.

"Come about, Louis..."

The man at Broadlands had tried harder than most to exceed. The great-grandson of Victoria, and stubborn, it was not his custom to surrender to another in matters of public opinion. If time to join the battle, the night was new. Outgunned, Lord Louis laid it on the line, the other end of which was tightly clasped in the Prime Minister's hand. "From a purely tactical view, perhaps GOLDILOCKS should not go swimming tonight."

"I am sorry, Louis," Churchill coughed, "but you are wrong about that."

Mountbatten said something.

The other said it better: *"No,"* he said. Mountbatten of Burma, who had fought him to get the mission back, had embarrassed him with Ike. Mountbatten acknowledged it, but not very much. They went into it.

It was Blackstone.

The P.M. demanded to know the charges, along with the facts — Kay Summersby? — it wouldn't wash. "Try this," Mountbatten said. Blackstone's mysterious network of connections could also be suspect; and what about the Free French — his Appointments!

De Beck, he meant.

"What about him?" This was the second time. What was the problem? The Prime Minister went on, explaining his official position: suspicions were not guilt; and sources, unnamed or withheld, were not worth a damn! Besides, who were they? Turing? *Turing didn't know.* Mountbatten couldn't say. It had come to him, that's all. His Informant did not have a name.

Just a voice...

"There! You see?" Churchill was assuring him that it was all right to be wrong. At the same time, he was revealing the nature of truth:

It was his.

"—how's that?" Lord Louis said. The German launch date for the Waterfall had come into question. The Prime Minister's *own* new sources — civilian clearance — were making clear to him that they'd been off in their assessment by over a week: *July 24th then, not August 6th.*

Three weeks.

If true, and he had no reason to think otherwise, the Prime Minister's chilling disclosure had greatly weakened Mountbatten's case. Not subject to argument, it was the Voice at the Top. Churchill had reversed the players. Of course, if Lord Louis *wanted* to share this information with John Blackstone — ? He didn't? "Well now," said Churchill, "is there something that I know that you don't know?"

Mountbatten grinned. "Bloody right!" he shot back, hoping for more. "I would certainly think that there is." All cards up, Churchill had spread the deck. It was on the table of the War Office. Blackstone's cards were not among them. Mountbatten looked: Pierre de Beck's wouldn't be there, either. Word had it that he had been rubber-stamped by Parker. Fact had it that he had been personally cleared by General LeClerc.

Winston had won.

Lord Louis acknowledged it. A leader perceived of grace and honesty, and born to it, ruthless in his own case, he threw it out. Friday's admonition had repeated itself; some Commodores never learn, and Mountbatten had again taken it on the chin. The Prime Minister assured him that he was free to call back. But later, of course, if there were still bothersome questions. In any event, GOLDILOCKS was squarely in Mountbatten's hands now, and any further decisions would be his. That settled, there were still a few odds and ends that needed to be gone over; and would Lord Louis mind not hanging up just yet? Not at all, and Mountbatten looked at his watch.

"I think I have it now," Supremo said.

"As I have already told you, you have it faster than imagined," Churchill crooned.

"Sir!"

He had put the phone down. Mountbatten was on hold.

Lord Louis had opened the drapes.

Rain blew against his window. Faces of life, of his sudden and greater duty, had arrived at his Estate unannounced. Wealth notwithstanding, it was the Estate of a man. He thought back to the First War, where like the remembered cry of a French urchin in the street, *they*—these faces of future responsibility—would be pressing themselves up against the glass. Through that mirror would come the children of the world, of all the worlds; and he knew: they would be looking back at him, through time.

"Louis—?"

There was crackling on the line.

Time is on our side...

Mountbatten glanced up. The clock on the wall was nearing midnight. He mentioned it. GOLDILOCKS would be aboard the sub in two hours. Forty-five miles away, the P.M. made a note. He spent a few moments remarking on the weather: considered essential.

Lord Louis inquired how it was.

Churchill looked.

Outside, wind was rising through the trellises, churning heat and dust against the wall of the distant storm. He asked Mount-batten to hold. "Two minutes," he said, and he turned the page.

"Governments," wrote Winston Churchill, *"were invented by people who are too lazy to work..."* True enough, he conceded. His own philosophic honesty, however publicly unadmitted, could be just the ticket here. No? He scratched through it, changing the directive, if not history itself, in the letter he had been composing to Marshal Stalin. Mountbatten was waiting. Churchill picked up the phone.

"You may well imagine what the demands are here."

Still, Sinclair had not been settled.

"So, Louis, my best advice to you is to let GOLDILOCKS have her romp. Do what you do best, dear man, but give me your word that you have laid these frightful fears to rest."

Mountbatten couldn't do that, but he agreed.

Important, from Churchill's view, his own loyalty had not been questioned. "We shall be expecting results. Good luck!"

He was wrapping it up.

"Ring you on Tuesday!" Mountbatten's voice had strengthened. James Bridley would rejoin him before dawn; they would be returning at once to Kandy. In terms of Record, Louis Mountbatten would not have been here.

"Tuesday then," the P.M. said, his voice was on the war. Mountbatten hung up.

The clock struck midnight.

Churchill smiled, his gaze spanning the room. There from behind the antique glass of the Chippendale bookcase, toy soldiers, standing guard before the Creasey collection, stormed forth upon the world. At the moment, men like he and Joseph Stalin owned it. Churchill arose from his desk and walked to the door. An Aide reached in, turned off the light, and closed it.

The Prime Minister mounted the stairs.

In the darkened study, in currents high above his desk alive with frequencies of voices past, a letter lay unsigned beside a humidor of black Havanas, next to pencils stubbed from pads of notes, with pages missing.

Upstairs, loud with voices, he entered. In the large bright maproom flashed with pointers, thick with smoke and waiting for him, the war went on that wasn't there. Calling back to them, from courage, they did not hear it:

The red telephone was ringing!

Thunder boomed beyond the windbreak.

Rains splattered across the fields. Falling away in the roar of the weather, shrill as a scream through the ghostblack night, the sound had stopped.

Valerie listened...

Giant clouds exploded ahead of them, lightning illuminating the flats of the sea. In the back seat of the speeding limousine, rich with ozone and the mysterious smell of felt, she had put down her lipstick. Ryan could hear it, too: bells and conversations, high above them, in England's stormy air. She rolled down the window, engulfed in the surge of the wind. The horizon rose distant, where hills were; and above it, the void was; and the icy bright blinking of stars.

The powerful black and silver car shot down the snake of the road! Tooling up the lanes of night, across countryside familiar, he soon had them free of the coast. Nervously, Valerie glanced over her shoulder. *Weren't they being followed?* No, not the way Ryan was driving. He said: "Why do you think he hired me?"

Valerie shook her head, she didn't know.

"For this..." the driver muttered, and he broke all laws save the laws of physics, in ascending a slippery rise. Valerie liked him, they could work together. Crashing through a roadblock, wood spun behind them. The road up ahead could be washed out any minute, because of the storm. Conquering curves, he jumped to the ALTERNATE ROUTE, tires whistling up train-dark culverts: black tracks, disappearing into rain. "—hear what I have to say," she heard him saying, "before we get there..." She had a right to know.

Valerie listened, her heart in her mouth.

Twenty years ago, before either of their times, the man destined to become The Spy had been an International Banker, secretly pledged to undermine the fascist dictator, Franco. The demands on the Spanish Dossier, represented in New York at that time by Brown Bros. Harriman, had caused him to deal heavily on the French *Bourse*. Loyal to the Bank of France, and on a tip from Rothschild, who seemed embarrassed by it, he had pursued it until it lead him to the discovery of a crooked picture: the passage of the Federal Reserve Act of 1913, effected against the interests of the people of the United States. Aware that he himself had been a party to it, though unwittingly, and at the same time enjoying enormous personal wealth, The Spy had pledged his life, his fortune, and his uncanny comprehension of The DEAL, to the redress of justice and to the protection of Individual rights...rights, if his friends, the Bankers, had their way, that were scheduled for absorption in a Treasury Series of New World Orders; where personal tax, disguised as interest; and mortgage rates, compounded over time, would absorb all profit from the produced value of work, indebting those who performed it. The self-serving convenience of invented laws by bureaucratic leaderships, particularly in the United States, would enforce the collection of money. On that day, voters voiceless, all the lemons would be squeezed dry. Thus, the Individual, correctly numbered, would serve the Bankers; and the Bank would become the State. In that same year, 1913, the Individual 1040 Tax Form slipped quietly through the American Congress, becoming the first of an arsenal of weapons by the London Financial District directed against the Constitutional protection of American citizens; and the inviolable rights of each Individual: the right to the protection of *life*, the right to the protection of *work*, and the right to the protection of *choice*. It was all figured, down to the last twenty-dollar gold piece; the actual writing, left to the Warburgs. Years would go by and the picture that was crooked, carefully concealed in those years, would begin paying off: farms would fail, the absorption of *land*. Stock markets would crash, the absorption of *gold*. And wars would follow:

The absorption of value.

Cloaked in their dark clouds, the world had narrowed, but his circle of friends had widened. One of them was the physicist Nicola Tesla. The eccentric Serb, sought by few, and master of electrical resonance, had pointed him in the right direction: quasi-organic intrusion into electronic communication, including phone lines. Later, confirming results with the renowned Dr. Steinmetz, pioneer of magnetic transformers, Ryan's employer had asked himself a question: *how safe are the secrets of time?* Advancing into chemistry, he had concluded that if they were to be safe at all, they would be safest with him. Meanwhile, the secrets of banking, and cash accumulation, along with his hard-won scientific knowledge, shared with Ryan, had put him on a parity, and in a fighting-stance position, as it were, with those whose purposes it was to pull the wool over the face of the world:

Over Eisenhower's, in particular.

From Ryan, who had driven down from Dublin, Sinclair was now hearing about Bernstein; and their impending meeting with The Spy. *Where?* That there would actually be one, coiled as it were in dark mysteries, was the news of the hour. So, for her personally then, where had it all begun? Had it started at the vicarage? When she had first known she was different? She remembered her years of struggle, to be somebody; meeting Mrs. Churchill at the Royal Hotel; the Ferry Pilots, and the months at Weymouth; Lieutenant Carrington; and David Hamilton. Suddenly, she was feeling terribly frightened: it was her son. The Allied cause was looming larger than the storm. And of England's imminent danger, her real traitors, what?

De Beck!

Ryan came out of a skid, his hands were on the wheel.

"De Beck? He's a German." He glanced at her in the rear-view mirror. "Friend of yours?"

"Blimey, *no..!*" She whacked him.

His foot hit the gas.

Valerie, fighting for the big picture, was seeing it.

There had been a dream—or was it?—the face of de Beck emerging out of it. Another's, too! Had Marchaud been there? *It was night, they had come rushing out of a tunnel...* Certainly they had! Now, as if arriving from the future, other photographs were coming into focus: falling and fluttering through the night.

Valerie grabbed at them, she was remembering:

Thursday afternoon, on their way to Polperro in the Rolls, she had noted the thickness of the Frenchman's neck, his insistence on details. His arrogance at the dance, insensitivity to her pain at Achnacarry, and flawless American accent—had not Hamilton *himself* remarked on it?—had all been pointing to the obvious, to the singular photograph of a German agent:

Teeth flashing in the sun...

The Spy had called her at The Red Lion.

Coming closer to her ideal—she was still wearing that damned Rubinstein bra! —he was also the one to whom they were going; but it was his call to her in the Manager's office, thwarting the British Override, that had forced her to decide. Trees were rushing past, eerie outposts of the dangers all around them. Valerie clung to the strap. Now, staring through the glass, catapulting through the darkness, she was witnessing the world of The Spy.

Ryan said it: She could expect him in France.

"Will there be a *mission* then?"

The driver thought that there would. Of course, it could be delayed for a few days: until General Eisenhower returned from Normandy. *Would she be going?* "That's not for me to say," Ryan said. "Why don't you just relax?" The Spy was leaving England, they would protect her son.

"Got it."

Ryan had heard something, he was watching the heavens. Valerie leaned forward, she looked through the windshield: *Ursa Major* stood before them.

It was upside down.

With polarized light for the central girders, otherwise known as *stars*, their floor of work had become the *other* part of the physical tunnel of time...reaching all the way into France. Slowed to twenty-nine miles per hour, Ryan held them steady.

Valerie started blinking...

Ursa Major turned right side up.

Click!

Ryan shifted gears, the Camera Shop was open.

Night closed over the Channel, strong winds running north. Prints of the *Alternate Route*, taken as living pictures, they were developing on the submarine:

The Captain appeared.

The whole place smelled of carbide!

Sounds and great, deep rumblings...

The submarine was ascending.

She could feel it in the change of pressure and in the quiet sway of bulkheads, along passageways devoid of men. It was Blackstone's voice, addressing the ship:

A woman on a man-o-war!

Step by step, Hamilton was hurting. His refraction of this basic law, necessitated by the undisciplined nature of men, had led him to the isle of the leper. With a will of iron, he was leading her, the untouchable, by the hand.

Step lively now, he could hear himself saying, *come along this way, child, this way*, they were at a ladder, *careful now—*

The submarine surfaced.

Hamilton and de Beck climbed through the conning tower and down the rungs onto the deck. The Captain and several of his crew, working forward, were preparing to launch a small rubber raft.

It was the Carley float.

Hamilton moved forward to the bow. His eyes searched the skies, as if looking for the approach of her plane. The rains had stopped. Waves sloshed gently against the hull.

De Beck studied the shoreline, where fog was forming. It was not a clear sea, but that would be in his favor. Binoculars swept the beach. "Seems clear," the Skipper said, his face shadowed. "Yes, Sparks, what is it?" The radioman had approached, he stood at the Captain's side. The men were proceeding with the raft. Silently, Pierre joined them. Hamilton was observing.

"Commander Hamilton?"

Hamilton turned. The Captain handed him the radiogram, it was deciphered. From Commodore Lord Louis Mountbatten; Mountbatten of Burma:

Beaulieu...

Hamilton read it, he glanced at the sky. Dieppe came to mind. He remembered her, the way she had looked. *Strapped into a parachute, she had just had her teeth cleaned. He had bought her a drink, at Leed's...Mary Gladstone, Number Fifteen.* The radiogram had released him from his chains, defining Number Sixteen, Sinclair's, question: *If neither she nor de Beck made it, what would happen to England?*

Hamilton pocketed the paper. He motioned the Captain aside, away from de Beck; and they had a quiet conversation. The Captain nodded, he said something to his men: the Carley float was being pulled back aboard. Pierre had seen it:

Something wasn't right!

Hamilton was looking at him. The Commander's eyes were hard, like stars. De Beck wheeled, he was staring at the beach; his mind punctured, as though by injections of ether...

What has happened to GOLDILOCKS?

She is smiling shyly. Softly, she was singing: a lullaby in French, her child's voice melding with the mourning of the owls.

She was there! Ahead of him! In his future!

Behind that tree—and *there*—from the black draconian tunnel, emerging out of blue light into Brittany, two girls had hurried to be ready. Through the physical tunnel of time, one of them is carried home to England. *The other* remains, waiting to welcome him. She stands, in reception, shadowless in the white heat of the moon. Behind her, swastikas, bobbing in torchlight, and the final dreams of children. Her arm reached out, she was waving to him! Pierre was wild, they had pulled him to the deck.

Valerie! Nous le tenons!

Hands, bearing handcuffs, had taken hold of him; he was beyond help. God was singing. Her song was Justice. Holding high a torch, she was coming for him: for what he had done, for who he was; for the unspeakable thing he had become:

Le Partenaire, n'est ce pas?

De Beck was screaming.

Back ablaze by moonlight, he was seeing it before: glancing over his shoulder, in darkness, on last night's rutted road. Sweet as the sting of a black, black rose with its single thorn of death... calling his name from the shores of France:

Stood the girl he had left behind!

Sinclair sorted through the photographs.

The prints of her friend, standing on the beach in France, would become her favorite. Valerie tapped Ryan on the shoulder. He turned. She handed him his lighter. He had wondered where it was. The limousine was accelerating. She looked out the window: the stars were blue. Having geared herself for raindrops, here they were, speeding through surprises.

Was it because of the weather?

Along the windy reaches of the road, and spinning behind them, projections of her past had become mirror images. Faces on prints, emerged out of time, they were the pictures of *the people of the secrets.* Sent by an English shopgirl who had photographed their motives, and who wasn't as dumb as she looked, Valerie had forwarded the proofs.

They had been delivered to the secret place of The Spy, along deserted corners of counterespionage, somewhere up ahead. There, balancing a flashlight, he would be looking at them:

Hamilton, loyal Welshman, yet in the dark following Blackstone's orders; taking Pierre to France without her; his grey eyes searching the skies for a plane.

De Beck, teeth flashing in the sun, spying for—

The black glove turned another...

—*von Schroeder*, Commandant of *Abwehr*: a position allowing the Nazi banker to steal the Bomb from his own people. Summer days in snapshots: Berlin. London. Marley Square, home of *Abwehr*; home of bankers, of apple strudel and cinnamon; and handcuffs and black chains, and years of trust:

Mary Gladstone.

Mountbatten, studio pose, who in ordering the arrest of de Beck had blocked von Schroeder's transfer of atomic secrets; preventing the completion by the Gestapo of the murder of Valerie Marchaud...

The flip side.

Saving Sinclair.

In Blackstone's reverse shot, a *montage*, Mountbatten is perceived as having become irresponsible to the real purposes of GOLDILOCKS. Parker takes credit. Full control of the mission, reverted to Blackstone, would ensure the successful return of the German data by de Beck.

Black glove, finger missing, turned the prints...

Churchill, a glossy, shown later in his published works, will leave the Waterfall, carrier for the first nuclear bomb, unnamed; an oversight that will prompt MI.5, on the first anniversary of the fire at the Hotel Ritz, to burn their card catalogues. What will *not* burn, passionately protected and held in *Egalité* by General LeClerc of the Free French, will be the biological transcripts of the two Valeries, Sinclair and Marchaud:

Who were separate, if equal; and often on the run.

Meanwhile, The Spy, entering once again into the life of Valerie Sinclair, and in a personal way, had fitted his movements to hers, like a hand to a glove. Having made the arrangements with Ryan to escort the British photographer to her mysterious rendezvous, hadn't he overlooked something?

Valerie fished through her prints.

The London Financial District!

Protected by Bletchley Park, yet dealing from the Top to steal nuclear technology for his partners, Blackstone's Blackmail List had come back to haunt him—leaving Mountbatten a hero, stuck with Bull Durham; and with Sinclair in the Middle:

Which is no place for a Lady to be.

Mouse in a hole and plugged by the Override Code; seemingly, with no way of escape, The Spy had appeared and belled the cat for Valerie Sinclair, freeing her from the grip of the British Lion.

The snout of the car was gulping at the fog.

It was the mist, curling across the blinded fields pierced by the chilling lamps of the car. Valerie snuggled deeper into her coat. The motor throbbed, devouring the miles. "What are your hobbies?" She was asking Ryan.

He thought about it. "Welding, maybe."

"Was it *you* then, in Polperro, at the tomcat's house!"

Ryan wouldn't say that it wasn't. He was talking.

He spun them over a bridge. It led to Bernstein. Hearing from the Boffin, James Bridley, that his best bet to get to the girl would probably be The Spy, Bernstein had immediately forced Bridley into a corner. Returning his call, and being low on chips, James Bridley had cashed his last one, lifted from Parker; and *dealt the Override to Bernstein.* Armed with the Code, whose parts were now in order, thanks to Bridley, in debt to Alan Turing; the lawyer had cut a deal with the Boffin for Ryan's unlisted telephone number, courtesy of the El Flamingo. After various negotiations, the lawyer buying the drinks, Ryan had put him in touch with his employer. Receiving *the Override* from Bernstein, The Spy had used it to call Sinclair; by-passing Hamilton, while duping his Security Team into thinking it from Churchill.

Seems Bridley and The Spy had once worked together on the same motion picture; Bridley, on behalf of the Baker Street Irregulars, having used the occasion to get the goods on actor Herbert Marshall—politically suspect at the time—background information he hoped to peddle to the War Office. Tossing a few after work at their favorite bar—farewell drinks prior to Bridley's departure to join Mountbatten—The Spy had suggested that Bridley try wiring the urinal downstairs, since Marshal was in the habit of talking to himself while using it, a consequence of faulty zippers in the flys of his suits, picked up dirt cheap from that British assistant of Madame Roc's. Unquestionably upset by it, Marshall had been drinking more than he ought; an unfortunate fact which had furthered his problem, in the El Flamingo, around the corner from Harrod's and just up the street from the back room of Bobby Blake's.

Well sir!

Never one to let a zipper stand in his way, Bridley *would* have wired that urinal too, had it not been for the intervention of that Irishman, Ryan, waiting to spirit The Spy up to Scotland. Ryan, the first to check the call from Bernstein, had also been the first to read the letter from Ike: carried in the lawyers' briefcase, from Southwick. Checking the signature, he had transferred it immediately to The Spy; who was glad to hear that Bridley was still alive.

Agreeing that the girl held the key to the bankers' acquisition of the Bomb, and seeing the bases loaded, the lawyer and The Spy had proceeded to clear them. Lest Lord Louis succeed in cutting Ike off at home plate, they had to move quickly. Bridley, who had called the play, had been thrown out. As for de Beck's long throw to Blackstone, via von Schroeder, Mountbatten was certain to hear it from *somebody*!

Could that somebody be The Spy?

Captain Bernstein, in a later brief circulated among the Bletchley barristers, expressed it about as well as anyone in a cryptic statement that could have come straight from the bench of the First Judicial District of New York: "So! What did you think, Tex? Dwight Eisenhower is a *Putz*?"

With De Gaulle emerging at the Top—looking good in that blazing green Rolls—the Brits, who had been caught red-handed, finding themselves at the Bottom, were trying to get back to the Middle:

A place they had vacated, now occupied by the girl.

Employing the Authority which had overridden the codes, her pursuer had become THE MAN WITHOUT A FACE. But he himself was being pursued, was he not? And if not, why not? Without knowing why, yet knowing she would, Sinclair had begun to suspect that she might have to protect him. As was obvious to any thinking person:

The Spy was on the lam.

In reconstituting *Marchaud,* England's Ultimate Female Weapon will prove an unqualified success. Within days, GOLDI-LOCKS will be rejoined; and the new mission pushed forward. With the German launch date just three weeks away, the Water-fall, its shadow falling across England, would have to be im-mediately located and destroyed. As for Valerie's position, it would be decided. She could be in serious trouble. Snapping at her heels were men without smiles; and powerful forces were converging on her life. Instructed to put the guilt on somebody else, the girl from Newton Swyre had put it where it belonged. Hidden in darkness, measuring her motives, The Spy had followed her progress. Satisfied that international bankers were using her for their own purposes, yet seeing a real future for her in the Free World, once she owned up to it, The Spy had called her, presenting her with the facts, while at the same time giving her an opportunity to do something about them. Safe in the speeding limo, Valerie Sinclair, who was putting on her lipstick, was busy mulling this over while observing the world of night:

At the moment, it was where her life was.

In that other world, the New World Order, where the mega-phonic money was printed—magic act of the Tattooer's Art—arms of the Indian Snakemen, rippling in the Blackpool sun, had reached out to her, preventing her from falling. In running from them, she had brought the negative with her, a picture that could not be erased. Photographed in the secret streets and alleyways of Cockney confidence, hung on clothespins in the lawful interfaces between the Top and the Bottom; it was The Official Portrait of the Seventeen Merchant Bankers, who were the owners of the American Federal Reserve. Clipping coupons, selling occasional arms, and giving each other discounts, they were looking through the lens; holding out their hands in trust and understanding to the producers of the world, to a great and tired people, who had accepted their beneficence like the sun.

Yet Valerie wasn't fooled.

In her honest heart, she knew the picture was just a print; and that it had been retouched, long before the Camera came. Owned by Bankers, it had belonged to the man whose name was #4. Before the negative could be exposed, he had turned it over in the rain one night, at the funeral of a great man—who had betrayed his country. Loyal to banks, afflicted with vanity and self-pride, the deceased had been split down the middle.

Did you ever...? Valerie commented, shocked.

The scrim, or backdrop of the shot, Washington D.C., was strange to her; the film having been developed before the age of recorded sound. A note, in russet India ink, on the back and in one of the corners used for mounting, had been initialed by the Photographer. Setting the timer, had he hurried to join the group? But where was he? Where was the Photographer?

Valerie looked, he wasn't there.

Elusive as the wine of Castile, and trading heavily in Spanish Futures; something new, with camera, had entered into banking. Shy, secretive, and with shadowy countenance; by 1924, he was making his mark. Sponsored by Brown Bros. Harriman, he had been elected to the Jekyll Island Club. They had given him a ring, secret to their members; and he couldn't get it off his finger. Sharing brass rails and wicker chairs, in Georgia, with Mellon, Vanderbilt, and Loeb, his name was #2.

File missing, from Blackstone's desk.

It was winter and the voiceless streets were draped with black. Limbs of the cherry trees glazed with ice; faces were blue. Two men stood. From glove of Spanish leather to brown-pocked glove of camel, a small round box had slipped to greatcoat pocket trimmed with velvet. Inside were six tablets, shimmering like jewels: pale blue, like the light found in space. Something had passed, beneath the umbrellas, and into the hands of #4. Receiving what he valued more, for what he valued most, the other had forced him to wait: the extended handshake, unacceptable.

IN GOD WE TRUST, was on the money; but a nation had been stolen; and the trusted god was gone. The extended hand of the German had not moved: *the fait accompli*. Beneath Spanish glove, a part of his finger, the other could feel their ring: a brand he would carry for life. How would he get it off? Well, there were ways. Now, crackling with fury, the dark sidereal rays of sounds, the antique warning...the voice, in the German head, hissing an ice-song along the glide of an alien wall. Appendage of betrayal, the hand of Warburg had trembled and dropped. Something had been thrown at his feet! Tinged with gold, glistening on frozen spikes of grass, a club card lay. It had been the privilege, of #2.

"Nein!"

The Spy looked up.

Tears had fallen then, like rain: numb, oppressive tears that had blotted out the sunshine of their days. In the world without witnesses, retribution would come quietly. For the one, a wide-brimmed hat, destruction of his past, and exile. Costing him dearly, he would need tools. Science would come naturally to him, and truth would be his friend. He would enter discovery, and from that day on, the night would own him. He looked at Warburg, at his memories: trapped, in the small round box of the future. Forgiven, #4 had turned away: from eyes that followed him until he'd joined the funeral throng, a sea of derbies bobbing in the grey; and there, above the stairs, beyond the icy stone, he'd paused, and thought he'd seen a man without a face.

Ghostly in lamplight, Lincoln looked out into the night.

The Receipt was in the hands of The Spy.

"Rain's over," Ryan said. The storms had stopped. She had packed away the photographs—camera too!—and was sitting up straight in her seat. Stars were blinking, windows dark.

Sunday—! she'd heard him say.

Valerie looked. They were in some new place. Having been left out, she could feel it. Was it love? Was it in the air? Was it *him* then, had set her heart to racing? Something good was coming her way:

It was a golf ball.

Shot by a slow pro, it had landed in her lap one rainy Sunday afternoon on her way back to Blackstone's hotel. It was outside the door of the darkroom where tomcats foraged; and where she had lifted the lid, photographing its contents. There, where The Spy had left it, still stood the trash can that contained the box, that had contained the film:

That was on its way to Southwick.

Valerie, having left Hamilton's money on the dresser, and endeavouring to remember what was best about him, could see it: her photogravure of *the Secret Agent*: his hooded eyes, measuring the dark waters: tramp steamers, come from other places, black with barnacles and smelling of orange paint; their high decks, far above her and late at night, where hawsers, tin cones protecting against rats, trailed away into fog. Footsteps echoed there, under street lights; men without histories, hat brims pulled against the rain; glancing over their shoulders, and pausing sometimes, to look up at you, with eyes of steel illumed in the sudden flare of a match.

Sinclair had photographed it, the portable model of British Intelligence, from the poster of Orson Welles. Holding a cigar, and obligingly nailing her with the look of God, he had seemed to be nodding his approval. A curious position, in view of the fact that he had refused to work for them; some flap or other about Rockefeller having pulled *Citizen Kane* from its World Premier at Radio City Music Hall on a complaint by Hearst that the popular film portrayed an interlocutory relative of Dwight Eisenhower's personal lawyer. She remembered it now because Lieutenant Seymour had once confided to her, having got it from Bridley, that Orson Welles sometimes looked a little cross-eyed, as she did—a consequence of having been secretly zapped by Martians. Checking it out, photographing his motives as it were, she had come up with two prints. The first was of Seymour, who had hoped to take her to bed. The second, that of Welles himself, who'd had to settle for the El Flamingo; since the Germans, in Paris, had taken over Harry's Bar.

Unfortunately for Martin Seymour, who liked whiskey, he wouldn't be able to go there. Following his promotion, he would be too busy running the Southampton Office; when Hamilton— his Requisition for sea-duty rubber-stamped by a thoroughly blackmailed Blackstone—would join his ship, after a few days in Brighton, taking John Carrington with him:

Leaving Loot, in Manchester.

In Berlin, within months, flames would race through bunkers; bringing an end to the New World Order. Hitler, ignoring his phone bill; gobbling chocolates and unable to locate Albert Speer, would lose his credit with Schroeder; who would get a *disconnect notice,* from a man whose name was *#9,* from an office in the London Financial District:

Where something had entered...

Bells were ringing; they were ringing in the fields of England. It would be years yet, but Valerie could already hear them. They were ringing for the Allies. If GOLDILOCKS was good enough for The Supreme Allied Commander, that was good enough for her! The stars were approaching midnight. The limousine was slowing. They were somewhere in Kent.

"Here's the airstrip," Ryan said.

Cutting his lights, he pulled right, passing through gates that others didn't know about. Mist curled along the runway. She could see the plane, silhouetted against the lighter dark; and he drove out to it. He parked, opened the door for her, and she got out.

There were two men. They were part of the night.

The first, a Captain Bernstein, stepped forward and introduced himself. In dress jacket and tan slacks, sharp crease, Ike's lawyer sized her up. Technically, the Brits could press for a charge of defection, but he doubted it. The Royal Navy was in no position to take on Bull Durham again. She stood in front of him, and he seemed to be looking at a child. He had never seen anyone like her; and he was aware of her eyes: large, liquid, and overwrought with light. "Is that what they gave you to wear?" She nodded. "Turn around," he said. She spun on her heel. Bernstein grinned, he was looking at a music box.

"Valerie, right?"

"Yes, sir."

"Call me Morris," he advised her.

"Yes, sir, Morris."

"And, of course, this is—" But she knew who he was and she felt that the breeze might have started to blow. At the end of the runway, leaves rustling overhead, the man without a face turned around. His features hidden by the wide brim of his hat, she was looking at shadow. High above them, clouds were moving, closing ranks against the stars. It was as though the world had suddenly shifted, to protect him.

Remember me?

From a window of a train, the Conservatory, lights blinking in the night: "—remember me?"

"Yes," Valerie said. It was him. "So nice to...*see* you again," she managed. In the doorway: *he had raised his hand.* Now, he was offering it, and she accepted it, remembering the way it was: strewn about through the canvas and the familiar shelves of the Camera Shop, looking upwards at the giant tripods, and peering outwards through the night: the beaches of blood in Brittany; the flight through the rock; the photograph of Mary

Gladstone; von Schroeder and Pierre; the long stretches of voices that wouldn't help her, screaming through corridors of sleep devoured by distance, and spilling out onto the rutted road, the girl at her side.

The Spy, seeing she was back and with no hard feelings, thought he might appreciate her better and he liked her grip. Having observed in her the makings of a true professional, something that he looked for in a woman, and in the same voice he'd used on the telephone, he told her the following:

"I trust my driver, Ryan, whom you have met. I trust myself—Captain Bernstein here, of course—and this same trust is extended to you. The purpose of your mission—without the knowledge of the Allies—was to obtain the secret of a new weapon. The men who trained you, were in turn trained by these men. Among these men were those who would have used it to enslave the world, and your life would have been forfeit." He looked at her. "It is called the *Atom Bomb*."

She had wondered what they were going to call it.

"In fleeing Germany," The Spy explained, "Albert Einstein had to leave certain parts of it behind."

She could understand that.

"For security reasons, sir?"

"Mum is the word, Sinclair?"

"Yes, sir. I couldn't have said it better myself, sir."

"Excuse me—?" It was Bernstein, he had a question. The man in the trench coat listened.

"Get to work," he said.

The Spy was considering his next move.

"We'll take care of the Royal Navy for you," he resumed. Bernstein made a note, figuring punitive damages. "For now, I wouldn't expect them to be sending you any bills. Once they sort it out, they will probably give you a medal. Indeed, the entire Free World owes you a vote of thanks!"

"It is you, sir," she countered, "whom they will thank. If you hadn't of called me—"

A frog croaked.

"But my dear Sinclair," intoned The Spy, "that was to my best interest."

She had wondered who he worked for.

Valerie looked up, the stars hung like diamonds. She still

hadn't seen his face. It was not as if she *couldn't* see it—others had, hadn't they?—just that she had not been able to photograph it. A Traveler, circumspect about British Agents who wanted to take his picture, The Spy had kept her memory at bay—and a good thing, too! If she remembered what he looked like, so could others, who might try to put him in a file, marked KEEP or DESTROY. While there was little doubt that Valerie Sinclair had photographed his *motives;* what she had *not* been able to photograph, was his conscience:

Not having had one herself, until now.

Some minor fault of the lens, a blind spot as it were, she would need to polish it up. "A moment," said The Spy. He was talking to Bernstein. The lawyer would meet her at the plane. Looking towards Ryan, The Spy nodded that they must leave.

As for the race for the Waterfall, Ryan had said she could expect The Spy in France. There could yet be a mission. In that event, he would be looking in on her. Having turned his back, Ryan's employer was reading the heavens. *Next week?* The scimitar of his wide-brimmed hat filled the sky, black moon rising.

Sunday, he decided.

Would she be on it?

The pilot had started the engines.

Leaves were blowing across the field.

"Here's to the road," The Spy said. It was a toast. They could both use a shot. Caught in the wind from the props, they were bending together. "Remember," The Spy said to her, "when it comes to *work*, no one can duplicate that which they dare not experience." He snapped the brim of his hat, throwing his face— if that is the word she wanted—into deeper shadow yet. So then, where was it? Victory, denied to those who could not stay, was available to those who escaped:

It was time to go.

"Don't worry, sir," Valerie said. "Your secret is safe with me." She stared at the black glove. Was it missing a finger?

Adios, Valerie...

They shook hands.

Bernstein was motioning. Valerie ran to the plane. He pull- ed her in. The door slammed! A lever fell. The motors roared, and the twin-engine swung forward. Shaking cabin sealed, clamped tight to bumping hardpack, side-gravitized and wind-socked, they roared down the secret runway. Gathering speed, battling the earth, trees at the far end were rushing to meet them.

At the last second, they lifted!

"—you all right?" Since Captain Morris Bernstein cared about her rights, he had a right to ask her.

"Who? Me?"

The American handed her a smoke. He lit it for her, and she took it like a lady. One who is nervous. The world was falling away beneath them. The way she saw it, she had left England.

The pilot grinned: it was her first aeroplane ride.

"Take a look," the Captain offered, he was sitting by the window. They exchanged places. She could feel the plane. The pilot turned off the lights. Sinclair pulled the curtain, she leaned forward, peering into the night. Staring quietly, she imagined the face of The Spy: another assignment, another success. She thought of his phone call, through the storm far ahead of her. The future. Was *that* why she hadn't seen his face? Would that explain Marchaud? Had Marchaud seen his face? No? Had anyone? Survivor of Necropolis, who he worked for no longer mattered to her—he worked for the good of his soul. In doing so, the harder job, he worked for the good of the world. Did she love him? She couldn't say. Would she meet him again? *Yes...*

She stared at the flaps. Beyond the horizon, needle of light across England's vastness, were the cliffs where she was brought up; the vicarage, a blur of blackened woods and stone. This time of night, the *Inhabitants* would be standing there between the trees, silvery in starlight, tears in their eyes. Far below, white-caps would be crashing soundlessly against the iron lock of the sea. Valerie brushed at her cheeks.

The plane banked, leveling for Southwick.

Marchaud, the child of the trapeze, had stayed in France. Sinclair, her other, was on her way to Eisenhower. Bernstein filled her in. The General was out of town. He was in a big fight in Normandy: something about British Army movements. Kicking butts, as it were, he would be back on Tuesday. Mrs. Summersby would meet them.

She was the general's girlfriend.

Valerie was glad that somebody was.

Hanging above the highway, flying low to avoid radar, Valerie felt like a bird. She looked, and did a double-take! The silver and black limousine was traveling the road just beneath them: so close, she could see the back window down!

Bernstein threw it a glance. "How about that?"

The Spy was there, he was looking up. Blinking like a code, blue rays shone about his face...glittering like agates. Valerie could taste it: *a vibration*...something had entered her thinking:

His photograph!

Had she not taken it yet! From her bedroom, she had been called to the telephone. Having scheduled a studio appointment for Winston Churchill on Hamilton's say so and on her day off, the surprise call from The Spy had pulled her out of the dark-room. Sinclair looked down. *Was there still time?* There was? Or would be? There was! She waved. Well then! If the pilot would hold the customer, she would get right on it. An introductory offer:

She was lining it up...

CLICK!

A tremendous LIGHT, like a *flashbulb*, shook the air outside the plane, echoing ahead of them and booming through the heavens!

"Son of a *bitch!*" Bernstein said. "Did you see that?"

Cross-eyed, Valerie shook her head.

Speeding away, The Spy rolled up his window...his eyes flashing with facts, like Holmes. "—looks like a clean hit!" he remarked to the driver, there being no other witnesses and of-fering congratulations all the way around. Overhead, the plane roared—dipping its wings.

Ryan looked up.

The Spy laughed.

A long shot, he had caught her on the fast shutter.